Truth or Dare You

Truth or Dare You

THE LOVE GAME: BOOK TWO

ELIZABETH HAYLEY

WATERHOUSE PRESS

ISBN: 978-1-64263-252-1

To Pop Culture, you were almost edited away from us,
but we'll never let you go. "As if!"

Chapter One

SOPHIA

I ran my brush through my hair again and took one last look in the mirror before applying a little pink lip gloss and heading downstairs.

I'd been home for weeks, and I'd only seen Taylor once. She'd traveled a bit to visit family and had other holiday obligations, but now that Christmas had passed, it was time to celebrate properly with my best friend. And what better way to do that than to go to some dive bar where we used to use our fake IDs when we were in high school?

Taylor texted that she was outside, so as I raced by the family room, I shouted my goodbyes to my parents.

"I'm going out. See you later."

"When will you be home?" my mom called.

From the end of the hall, I could see her look up from the book she'd been reading on the couch. My dad was in his leather recliner with the hockey game on while he simultaneously clicked around on his phone.

"Next year," I yelled back.

"Don't be smart," my dad replied dryly without bothering to look up from his screen.

I flashed him a smile he of course couldn't see. "How dare you ask me to sacrifice my intelligence?" I tried to keep my tone light as I joked, but the words tasted bitter, stale.

"Watch it," said my dad, who was otherwise preoccupied.

I nearly asked what he wanted me to watch but managed to bite my tongue.

"Seriously, Soph," my mom said. "New Year's Eve scares me. Let me know where you end up. Don't drink and drive—"

"We have an Uber," I promised her.

"Don't talk to any strange men."

"How would you define 'strange'?"

"Sophia, please! I already have one child who's seeking refuge from this family in another country. I don't need another disappearing."

"I'll text you when I'm on my way home." I grabbed my coat and headed out the door.

Once again, I was torn between feeling happy she cared so much about me and wondering why I always had to live up to standards that my fuckup brother, Brody, didn't.

After they'd discovered Brody had hired someone to impersonate him so he didn't have to go back to school, they'd accepted his refusal to return home because, well, that was just Brody.

Long ago, he'd painted the dog's fur with glitter glue, then he'd tried to grow marijuana in our backyard, he'd flunked out of college more than once, and finally he'd moved to Europe without telling anyone.

I was their only hope of raising a successful child.

Until I'd gone and fallen in love with the guy Brody had

hired to pretend to be him. Strange when I thought about it like that—falling for someone I had to call Brody all semester—but Drew was sweet and cute and funny and all the things female fantasies were made of.

That my dad clearly couldn't stand him only made Drew more appealing. That is, if he hadn't left right after our charade was up. I still wasn't sure what my dad had said to him while I'd been at my sorority meeting, but whatever it was had Drew running like Forrest fucking Gump.

He'd packed his shit, left, and I hadn't heard from him since. Maybe he was better at being Brody than I'd given him credit for.

Not that I'd expected him to call from the ICU.

I opened the back door of the white SUV and gave Taylor a quick hug.

"What's up, biotch?" she asked.

"Well, my parents are acting like I'm a spoiled toddler, Brody may never come home, and Drew's still in the hospital. So nothing, really."

She put her arm around me as much as her seat belt would allow and pulled me closer. "You need a Taylor hug."

"I really don't."

"Nonsense. Let TayTay take care of you." She rocked me against her.

"Don't ever call yourself that again."

Continuing to sway back and forth, I found myself resting my head on her shoulder.

"TayTay can't make any promises."

"I can't stand you," I told her.

"You love me."

"Maybe a little."

"You ladies are a cute couple," a male voice interrupted.

It took me a moment to remember a third person was in the car, and once I did, I realized what type of men my mom had been trying to warn me about.

In the rearview mirror, I could make out the Uber driver's eyebrows—lifted above wide eyes that suggested he'd been thinking we were more than just cute.

X_0

Two hours later, we were both successfully drunk, surrounded by people who were about three times our age. When we'd arrived, there had been a younger crowd, but at some point between my first Jolly Rancher and—I looked down at the glass I was holding—well, whatever I was currently drinking, the patrons had transitioned from kids like us to people like . . . our parents?

"Why are there all these old people here?" I yelled over a cover of Bon Jovi's "It's My Life."

Taylor looked up from where she'd been picking a seed out of her lemon. She squinted as she panned the room from her high seat against the wall, appearing confused.

"Don't know," she slurred before returning to her lemon.

I tried to decide if it'd be worth it to call another Uber and go to another bar, but I wasn't in the mood to run into anyone from high school, which would be exactly what would happen if we headed over to Timothy's or Dino's.

Taylor and I would have more fun hanging here with each other, drinking shots of well tequila and dancing poorly to eighties rock. And as I pulled her out onto the clear space that served as a dance floor near the tiny stage and we began dancing like children whose parents let them stay up to see the ball drop, I knew I'd made the right decision: this was exactly where I was supposed to be and who I was supposed to be with.

Eventually, we decided it would be a good idea to get some food and water, so we headed up to the bar to ask for menus. We ordered some wings, and once they arrived we dug in. I was sure we were covered in wing sauce and blue cheese. There was truly nothing more satisfying than fried food while drinking.

We drank a few glasses of water each, rehydrating ourselves from what the sauce and the alcohol had done to our bodies, and headed to the bathroom to clean ourselves up.

"What time is it?" Taylor asked after we washed our lips off and touched up our makeup a bit.

I dried my hands the best I could with an old white air dryer before conceding defeat and wiping them on my jeans.

I knew it hadn't struck midnight yet, but it could've been nine or eleven forty-five. I had no idea, so I pulled my phone out to check.

"It's almost eleven," I said, swiping open a text from Carter and staring at it a little too long.

"What?" asked Taylor. "What's wrong?"

I couldn't respond. I had to read everything Carter had written first.

Happy almost New Year!! Hope ur having fun at home. Just wanted to let you know that Drew finally got out of the ICU yesterday. Went to see him earlier. Seems like the worst is behind him. Just needs a lot of PT and rehab, and he should be good.

I tried not to think about the night Drew had been in that accident or how Carter and I had rushed to the hospital but were refused entry because we weren't immediate family. How scared we'd been. How scared I still was.

Though Drew had left abruptly, everything leading up to that had been anything but impulsive. We'd pushed our feelings for each other deep down until the pressure inside us was too much to contain. And when we finally exploded like volcanoes of raw emotion and desire, we'd both wondered why we'd tried to resist it for so long.

Yup, I'd do better not to think about any of that.

But Carter had gone to see Drew a few times and had been texting me updates since I'd left for break, and he'd filled me in on Drew's injuries: a broken leg, arm, and a few ribs as well as some superficial cuts and bruises.

I couldn't decide if knowing how Drew was doing was healthy for my getting past our breakup, but I'd decided a few weeks ago that it didn't matter. Even if I never saw him again, I needed to know how he was. I needed to know he would be okay.

But apparently I wasn't the only one who needed to know the other was okay.

He's asking about you, Carter had passed along before suggesting I at least *consider* visiting Drew since he'd probably be in the hospital for another week or so.

I held out the phone for Taylor to see.

She took a moment to read through the texts. "That's great!" She sounded much more enthusiastic than I felt.

"What part?"

"All of it."

She pulled open the bathroom door so we could exit, but

we stayed tucked away in the dimly lit hallway since it was easier to hear.

"That he's out of intensive care and seems like he'll be okay." She hesitated. "And I think it's good he's asking for you."

"He's not asking *for* me. Just *about* me. It's completely different."

"Is it?"

Narrowing my eyes at her, I said, "You shouldn't try to be cryptic when you're drunk. You just sound confused."

She rolled her eyes at me. "And you shouldn't try to avoid reality."

"I'm not avoiding reality. I'm avoiding Drew. If you remember, that's what he wants anyway."

She leaned her head against the chipped wooden wall and folded her arms. I really hoped she wasn't going to give me some sort of best-friend pep talk that she thought was going to get me to run to Drew's side. Not when he'd run *away* from me. I wasn't desperate, and I certainly wasn't stupid.

"What?" I asked after she hadn't said anything.

She shrugged. "Maybe he doesn't want that anymore."

"Doesn't want what?"

Running dark-red nails through waves of her blond hair, she let out a sigh. "Why are you so dense? Aren't you supposed to be the smart one between the two of us?" Her question was clearly rhetorical because she continued as if she hadn't asked one. "I bet he doesn't want to run anymore. His brush with death probably made him realize he's only gonna live once. He woke up from whatever coma he was—"

"He wasn't in a coma."

Taylor gestured with her hand like she was shooing me away. "Whatever. He's probably been eating ice chips and peeing in a bottle for the better part of December. That's basically the same thing."

"It's not at all," I argued. "And it's a good thing you're not going into the medical field. You have the bedside manner of Nurse Ratched."

"I'll pretend I get that reference and that it's a compliment."

At least that had me laughing. What had begun as a carefree girls' night and a fun way to ring in the new year had quickly shifted to something more serious. And I didn't want serious. I'd have to go back to school in a couple of weeks, integrate myself back into the sorority house, begin a new semester, and pretend much of the last one hadn't happened.

Until then, I wanted light and airy, not heavy and suffocating. But unfortunately, pretty much everything that had to do with Drew Nolan felt oppressive, from his accident to the mysterious way he'd fled the apartment we'd shared.

I began to sober up. Well, maybe *sober up* was an exaggeration. It was probably more like *began to speak without slurring* or something of the sort. I was definitely still drunk and would be for a while, but somehow my thoughts became clearer than they'd been in weeks.

Drew had left without so much as a goodbye, and he hadn't given me a valid reason for his sudden change of heart. My gut told me Dad had scared him shitless, but it just didn't seem like Drew to give up so easily on something he wanted.

Which left me with only one explanation. He didn't want me.

Chapter Two

SOPHIA

Despite it taking a while to decide that I wanted—or maybe *needed*—to see Drew, it took me no time at all to hustle my ass to the hospital once I'd made up my mind.

I borrowed my mom's Lexus under the guise of having to check in at the sorority house—something I would actually do once I saw that Drew was in one piece so I could put him behind me for good.

Maybe there'd be some fun drama floating around that I could lose myself in for a while—as long as it didn't involve me. I'd had enough to last a lifetime. Or at least a semester.

I pulled into the underground garage and descended quite a ways into its bowels before finally finding an empty spot. After thrusting the car into park, I returned my hand to the steering wheel and sat for a second.

The hour-and-a-half drive here had given me time to run through scenarios in my head of how this might go. Every instance I'd brought to mind was awkward as hell and consisted of me seeing he was fine and then counting down the seconds until I could leave without seeming like a heartless bitch.

But as I sat in my mom's SUV, staring at the spray-painted *Compact* in front of me, another possibility came to mind: What if I didn't want to leave? What if I saw him lying in a hospital bed, and begging and pleading words tumbled out of me unchecked? Things like, "Please keep me," and "I love you. Why don't you love me?"

How absolutely fucking horrifying.

Mild panic started to fill me. I gripped the steering wheel tightly, closed my eyes, and took a few deep breaths. This man had left me. With hardly any explanation, he'd razed everything we'd built between us as soon as the real world came calling. And while I still missed him with an ache that kept time with the staccato rhythm of my heart, he didn't need to know that.

He didn't *deserve* to know it. Just because I wasn't as callous as he was and cared whether he lived or died did *not* mean that I owed him anything. I was here for me, for peace of mind so that I could move forward without having to waste another second of mental energy on him.

Right. Good. This was good.

I pulled the visor down and checked my makeup. It couldn't hurt to remind him of what he'd given up. A girl had a right to be a little superficial in times like this.

Satisfied with what I saw, I flipped the visor closed, grabbed my purse, and exited the vehicle. The double beep of the lock mechanism echoed in the cavernous garage, as did the click of my heels against the pavement as I approached the elevator. The doors slid open, and I stepped inside.

When the doors opened again, I was in a bustling lobby. It took me a second to get my bearings and locate the main desk. Even though I'd come here the night of Drew's accident, that entire night was a blur.

Carter had told me Drew's room number, but the hospital was massive, and the last thing I wanted was to get lost in here. I was sure there were at least five horror movies that involved some hapless co-ed making a wrong turn, ending up in the morgue, and getting murdered by a psycho masquerading as a surgeon. No thanks.

When it was my turn, I approached the woman working the desk. She looked like she had absolutely zero fucks to give.

"Hi, um, hello. I'm, uh, looking for the way to room 407."

She looked at me like she'd discovered a particularly stupid species of humanoid. Rolling her eyes, she gestured behind me.

"Take the elevator to the fourth floor, and then follow the signs for the room you're looking for."

I glanced over my shoulder at where she'd pointed and then back to her. Surely it couldn't be that easy. Weren't hospitals known for being labyrinths?

She raised her eyebrows as if daring me to ask another question before saying, "Next."

All righty, then.

I moved toward the bank of elevators. There were other people waiting, so I stood in solidarity with them as we watched the numbers tick down from the other floors as if we were glued to breaking news.

Finally one arrived, and we moved as a horde toward it, bumping shoulders and crushing spirits as it became clear only the strong would board. A man dressed in scrubs crashed into an older man wearing an American flag headband, and while they argued over who was at fault for the collision—it was the one in scrubs—I slipped past them both just before the doors slid closed.

The button for the fourth floor had already been pressed, so I clasped my hands in front of me and tried to keep my breathing even. Other than moving aside to let people off the elevator, I remained still and composed. On the outside, that is. On the inside, I was squirrels at a rave.

When we reached the fourth floor, I stepped off and moved toward the signs the delightful woman downstairs had told me to find. Rooms 400-435 were to the right, so to the right I went, albeit slowly. I approached room 407 as one might approach a viper.

The door was slightly ajar, and I could hear voices from within.

Hesitating, I listened to see if I could discern who was in there. Maybe it was a doctor discussing something that was none of my business. Or a nurse giving him a sponge bath. Should I wait a bit and see if someone came out? Should I knock? Should I run away screaming? What was the correct protocol for barging in on the guy who'd broken my heart and then almost died? Why was everything involving Drew so damn difficult?

My existential crisis was interrupted by a girl, maybe five to ten years older than me—it was difficult to tell with all the makeup shellacked on her face—ripping the door of his room open.

"Oh," she said. "Can I help you?"

Her tone made it clear she had no desire to actually help me with anything. It was nasally and snide and oddly helped me relax. Catty bitches I could handle.

But then my gaze drifted beyond her and settled on the bed, in which lay a thinner and paler but no less devastatingly attractive Drew. A noise left me of its own volition—some kind of cross between a gasp and a sob—and it got Drew's attention.

He swiveled his head toward me, his eyes grew wide, and his mouth dropped open.

"Sophia."

My name left his lips in a near whisper, his voice sounding hoarse, like he hadn't used it much recently.

Everyone in the room looked at me, and while I noticed their attention, I only had eyes for the man in the bed. The man who'd left me yet still looked happy to see me. I'd imagined this moment, but I'd never once considered what the hell I'd say when I first saw him again.

Though there weren't *too* many options.

"Hi, Drew."

DREW

She was here. The one person I'd wanted to see the most but had no right to ask to come was here. And she looked... beautiful. The best sight I'd seen in a while, that was for sure.

"Andrew? Are you going to introduce us, honey?"

I'd been staring at Sophia, but my mom's voice broke the spell I'd been caught in.

"Yeah," I croaked. Christ, how long was my throat going to feel so raw? "Sorry. Mom, this is my... friend... Sophia." How big of a cop-out was that? *Friend?* She was simultaneously so much more and, sadly, so much less than that. "Sophia, this is my mom and sisters."

They'd have to introduce themselves. My voice struggled even when I *wasn't* in shock.

"Hi. I'm Pam Nolan. These are my daughters—Amber,

Courtney, and Heather."

My sisters murmured hellos and issued small waves with their acrylic talons.

I needed to get them out of here. They'd been suffocating me ever since I'd woken up, and while I'm sure they thought their presence was comforting, the truth was I couldn't relax around any of them.

We weren't close in the best of times, and their pantomime of a doting family wasn't convincing. I'd actually wondered a few times if this entire experience was turning them into Munchausen syndrome by proxy perpetrators.

Sophia took a few steps into the room but then stopped. "It's nice to meet you. I heard Drew was out of the ICU, and I wanted to see how he was doing. But I don't want to intrude, so—"

"You're not," I quickly interjected, sure I would have yelled it had I been capable of such a thing. "It . . . it's good to see you."

She looked at me for a long moment. "You too." She sounded conflicted about whether she meant it or not.

"Mom, could you give us a couple minutes?" I asked without taking my eyes off Sophia.

Sophia adjusted her grip on her purse, which she was clutching in front of her with both hands. She turned her head to look out the window to the left of my bed, but she didn't verbally object to my request for privacy.

"Oh, um, sure. I guess. Come along, girls. We'll go down to the cafeteria for a bite to eat. Want anything?" she asked me.

"No, thanks."

"Okay, then. It was nice meeting you, Sophia."

"You too," Sophia responded as my mom and sisters filed

past her and left the room.

We stared at each other awkwardly for a few seconds before I broke the silence.

"Thanks for coming. It's great to see you."

"Yeah, of course. And it's good to see you too. You're looking good."

I huffed a laugh that sounded harsher than I intended it to. "I look like shit, but thanks for saying otherwise."

"Nah. Alive is a good look on you."

"Can't argue with that."

We lapsed into silence again, and I hated it. Not even the first day we'd met had things been this stilted between us. And while I knew I was the one who'd made it this way, I wasn't sure how to repair it. Or if I even *should* repair it.

When I'd told her she could do better, I wasn't lying. But I would've given anything to have been worthy of her. To have been able to beg her to give me another chance to get it right.

My throat began to tickle, and I fought to clear it before a coughing fit came on. I stretched to get the water that was on the table by my bed, but it was just out of my reach.

Just as I was readjusting myself so I could get my hands on it, Sophia was there, grabbing the pitcher and filling a cup for me.

"Thank you," I said, though it came out more as a grunt. When my throat wasn't feeling so Sahara-like, I set the cup down and looked up at her. "Sorry. My throat's still sore. They had to, uh, intubate me when I first came in, and it stayed in for a while when I was in the ICU. It's better than it was, but I'm still pretty rough sounding."

She opened her mouth to reply, but instead of saying anything, she blew out a breath and turned slightly away from me for a second. When she looked at me again, her eyes were watery.

"That's ... Don't apologize ... I ... Shit, I'm sorry. That you went through all that. That's ... " Her voice trailed off, and a tear slipped out the corner of her eye and slid down her cheek until she swiped a hand at it.

Not knowing what else to do, I reached out and grasped her fingers. She startled at the contact but didn't pull away. She lifted her head so her eyes could meet mine.

I smiled. "You did warn me about the bike."

She sniffled and gave my fingers a squeeze. "Well, I am always right, so ... "

I laughed and she smiled, and I thought that maybe this could be enough. Maybe this small moment where we got to be the people we'd been two months ago could be the closure we'd both need to move on without the other.

"Thanks for coming," I said again. "Really."

She seemed to search my face for something, and I had no idea if she found it or not, but she offered me another small smile.

"You're welcome."

She sat down on the edge of my bed, and we chatted for a bit about unimportant things—like how hospital food was surprisingly good and how I'd been binge-watching *Law and Order*—both of us obviously making it a point to stay away from anything personal, even though I was desperate to hear everything she'd been up to since I'd last seen her. Eventually, I couldn't resist trying to delve a shred deeper.

"What's going on with Brody?"

Her face shuttered instantly, and I internally cursed myself for ruining our easy conversation. I should've known better than to ask about her family of all things.

"I have no idea," she finally said. "We haven't heard from him since Christmas, when he made it clear he had no plans to come home anytime soon. He's dead in a hostel somewhere for all we know."

Her words were harsh, but I saw the hurt beneath them. It was one thing for Brody to go AWOL on her parents, but for him to cut off contact with her too was rough. Especially considering they'd spent the entire fall semester having each other's backs.

"My phone broke in the accident," I said, "so I don't know if he's reached out to me or not. I asked my family to get me a replacement, but you'd have thought I was asking them for a kidney."

She chuckled, but I could tell it was more out of politeness than anything else. She rose, and I knew her stay was over. It was probably for the best anyway. We'd been able to have a good conversation, even if it had been about as deep as a puddle. This was good. We'd be able to leave things on a better note than I'd left them in November.

She slung her purse strap over her shoulder and looked down at me. "I should get going."

"Yeah, yeah, it's probably getting late."

"Little bit. Just . . . take care of yourself, okay?"

"I will. I promise."

She smiled. "Good. Bye, Drew."

"Bye, Sophia."

We stared at each other, suspended in time, until she blinked and freed herself from the trance. She made her way toward the door with none of the trepidation she'd had when she came in.

She was fleeing, and a good man—a better man—would've

let her get away cleanly. But I just wasn't that guy.

"Sophia," I called out as best I could as she reached the door.

Her shoulders bunched up at my voice, but she turned around and looked at me expectantly.

"If you ever felt like stopping by again—and I'd understand if you didn't want to—but if you ever felt like it, I'd . . . I'd really enjoy it."

I could see the struggle on her face, and I hated myself for putting her in that position, but not enough to take my words back. It's a wonder what she ever saw in me. I was such a selfish asshole.

Finally, she spoke. "Maybe, okay? The best I can do is maybe."

"Maybe is more than I deserve, so I'll take it."

She didn't disagree—not that she should've. She didn't reply at all. The door opened and then she was gone, and I was left watching the space she'd just filled, hoping like hell I'd see her again.

Chapter Three

DREW

It had been a week since I'd seen Sophia, and I hadn't heard from her—not that I really expected to. But for some reason, I was upset by the lack of contact, even though I knew I had absolutely no right to be.

I tried to focus on other things, but those other things consisted mostly of my aching ribs and lack of mobility. And thinking about how much recovery time I had ahead of me wasn't a good way to improve my mood.

As I lay there feeling sorry for myself, a knock sounded on my door, and a foolish part of me hoped it was Sophia. But when the door opened and I saw the bespectacled face of my doctor instead of the radiant one of Sophia, my mood turned sour again.

Thankfully, he got right to the point.

"With all the progress you've made, I'd say you are ready to go home," said Dr. Kline. "Not today, but we can probably discharge you tomorrow." The tall, lean doctor smiled down at me as my mom fluffed my pillow for the fifth time since he'd arrived.

She always turned into Carol Brady whenever a doctor came into the room, and that shit was getting old fast.

My sanity had come to a screeching halt today when my mom had been informed that I might be released. She then ordered our whole family to the hospital, and they'd descended like locusts. Well, everyone except Cody, who was in school.

"A nurse will come in to review the paperwork with you," Dr. Kline continued, "but there will be a number of restrictions. Your leg still can't bear weight, and you're going to need assistance with a lot of the ordinary day-to-day activities while your other injuries continue to heal. It's also imperative that you go to all of your follow-up appointments so we can continue to monitor your recovery." He gave a quick look around at my family before looking back at me. "Do you have someone who can help you manage?"

Despite Florence Nightingale by my ear, the doctor looked dubious.

I shared his feelings. While I knew my parents had managed to keep me alive during my formative years, I didn't want to have to depend on them to do it again. I had no doubt they'd help me out, but that support would become an annoyance for them after two days. They'd be ignoring me and leaving my meals by the door like I was an inmate in no time.

Not to mention the fact that nothing with them was free. Anytime they wanted something from me, they'd remind me of the time they so selflessly nursed me back to health.

No thanks.

I'd already found a place to stay, and while it wasn't ideal, at least it wasn't with my parents. I opened my mouth to respond, but my mom cut me off.

"We'll take care of him, won't we?"

My dad grunted in response. He'd been sitting in a chair staring up at my little TV for the past hour. He didn't seem to care what was on—he was currently watching *Days of Our Lives* or some shit like that—as long as it prevented him from interacting with the rest of us. I couldn't really blame him.

I'd actually had a reprieve from all of them for the past week. The drama of me being in the ICU had appealed to them, but once I'd been downgraded to a normal patient, they'd all lost interest. I hadn't seen my sisters since the day Sophia had stopped by, and my mom had only blustered in once or twice.

This was the first time I was seeing my dad without needing to be high on sedatives to prevent me from yanking the tube out of my throat.

Cody was the only one who'd come around fairly regularly, stopping by almost every other night, but he typically tried to avoid the times everyone else was here. He was a man after my own heart.

Dr. Kline gave me a few more instructions before excusing himself from the room. I had to fight down the urge to beg him to take me with him.

"These doctors keep getting younger and younger, I swear," my mom said as she sat in the chair beside my bed and pulled out her phone.

"He's forty at least," I said.

She raised an eyebrow at me. "And that's old?"

"It's not young."

"It is to me."

"You're ten years older than him max."

She waved her hand at me dismissively and continued pecking around on her phone.

"Can we go?" my oldest sister, Amber, asked. "If he's not

getting out today, we don't need to be here, right?"

"I can't come tomorrow," Courtney added. "I have a shift at the salon at three."

"What if he gets out in the morning?" my mom asked.

Courtney scoffed at that. "I can't get up *early*. Alejandro said if I show up to work tired one more time, he's firing me."

I'd bet my life he'd told her not to show up hungover, but at least she seemed to care about keeping her job.

"What about you two?" Mom asked my other sisters.

"I told Hazel I'd come to her school for Career Day," Amber said. Hazel was her boyfriend's eight-year-old daughter, and from what I could tell, the young girl hated my sister with a passion that rivaled the Romans' hatred of Jesus. I highly doubted Hazel had willingly invited my sister to her school.

"Aren't you supposed to have a career to speak at one of those?" I asked, unable to stop myself.

Her answering glare told me my comment wasn't appreciated. "I'll have you know that I am a certified teaching assistant."

"Who's never taught or assisted anyone a day in her life."

"At least I can go to the bathroom by myself," she retorted smugly.

"Well, you didn't almost die and shatter your femur to pieces either, so . . . "

"Okay, enough!" My mom ran a hand through her frizzy blond hair. "I swear, you're as bad as you were when you were kids. What about you, Heather?"

"I guess I can be here," she said, her voice lacking any emotion whatsoever.

"I can save everyone a lot of time," I said. "I already have a place to stay lined up, and I can get myself over there."

"What are you talking about?" my mom asked. "You're coming home so we can take care of you."

"No, really, it's fine. A friend of mine can help me out."

"That's ridiculous. Drew, tell Andrew he's being ridiculous," she said to my dad.

"Stop being ridiculous, Andrew."

I rolled my eyes at my dad's forced concern. I'd never exactly liked being a junior, mainly because it meant I needed to share a name with a person who mostly moonlighted as a parrot.

"No random person is going to take proper care of you," my mom added.

I wanted to argue that *she* wouldn't take proper care of me either, but insulting her wasn't going to get me anywhere.

"It's not a 'random person.' It's a good friend of mine. And I'm not completely useless. I'll be fine."

"But why would you go there instead of staying with your family who loves you? It doesn't make any sense."

It actually made perfect sense. When I'd moved back into my parents' house after leaving Sophia, I'd lasted two days before I'd felt the mental breakdown coming on. I'd worked as many hours as Rafferty's would give me, and I'd just picked up another job so I could earn enough money to get out of there ASAP.

If I went back there to recover, I'd be stuck in the house twenty-four hours a day. We'd be a *True Crimes* documentary within a week because I'd murder them with my crutches.

"I'm a grown man," I said wearily. "I can make my own decisions about where I'm going to go."

"If you had somewhere else to go, why did you move home in the first place?" she asked.

"Because they didn't have space for me then."

"And they do now?"

Not really. "Yes."

My mom crossed her arms over her chest. "Andrew, this has gone far enough. You're not staying in some run-down hovel with a bunch of rowdy guys. You'll never get better there."

"That's not how it is," I argued weakly because that was exactly how it was.

I knew I was being a little stubborn and probably a lot stupid, but I genuinely believed that, even under those kinds of circumstances, I'd still have an easier recovery than if I moved home. There was something to be said for my mental health too, wasn't there?

"Fine," my mom said. "Then tell this Good Samaritan I'll drop you off over there after you're discharged."

"What?"

"You heard me. I'll drive you to wherever your new place is, scope it out, and if it seems fit for you to be there, I'll drop you off and disappear from your life like you so obviously want."

Wow, that guilt trip was as subtle as a two-by-four.

"I don't need you to go to all that trouble. You could have Cody drop some of my stuff off here later, and then I'll call you when I get settled."

"No, I'm not budging on this. I at least get to *meet* the person. And as God as my witness, if some meathead shows up here, I'm getting one of those caseworkers involved."

Well…fuck. That was exactly who would show up, and there was no way I could get any kind of caseworker involved since the place I was staying wasn't somewhere I was strictly allowed to be. Why was she choosing right now to give a shit? I'd been out on my own since I was eighteen. Granted, I hadn't been recuperating from a motorcycle accident then, but still.

My brain was scrambled as I tried to think of who I could get to show up and take me where I needed to go.

"Um, excuse me. Is this a bad time?"

My head whipped toward the door, and I beheld my savior.

"There she is, Mom. That's who I'm staying with. You remember Sophia, right?"

SOPHIA

I'd never understood the expression *You could've knocked me over with a feather*.

I mean, how could a feather ever knock anyone over? But after hearing Drew's words, I finally understood. I felt my brow crinkle as my eyes narrowed.

"What now?"

Drew's eyes grew comically wide, as if he were trying to telepathically make me understand what the hell was going on.

"You have perfect timing," he said.

I doubted that. It seemed like horrible timing.

"My mom was just asking to meet the person I was going to stay with," he continued, enunciating each word and boring his eyes into mine, "while I recuperate. So I don't have to burden them. Because I'll be with you. At your apartment. That you live in."

"With me?"

He nodded slowly.

I looked around at all the expectant eyes on me—

everyone's except those belonging to the old guy in the chair who was just staring at the TV.

Drew must not want to go home with these people, and he needed me to play along. *Because I owe it to him to do that.*

Swallowing my inner catty bitch, I straightened my shoulders. "Right. Yeah. With me. Awesome."

My droll delivery might have needed a bit of work, but beggars couldn't be choosers. I'd only stopped down here because I'd moved back into the sorority house that morning and had the afternoon free. Well, that and Drew's last request before I'd left him the last time had been weighing on me.

He'd asked to see me again, and for no other reason than I was an apparent glutton for punishment, I'd wanted to see him again too. Fuck me and my good deeds.

"Oh, well . . ." Drew's mom dropped her arms to her sides and looked back and forth between Drew and me. "How well do you two even know each other? I've never heard you mention her before we met the other week, Andrew."

There was no use lying about it—that one stung a bit. Not that I'd expected him to tell his parents, but still . . . ouch.

"Oh, we've known one another for a while. Right, Soph?"

So it's "Soph" now, is it?

"Yup," I said, popping the *p*.

"Are you two dating? Because this is a lot to ask of a new girlfriend. It'll put a lot of strain on the relationship, and I just don't think—"

"She's my fiancée," Drew interrupted, the words booming out of him like he was yelling through a megaphone. The loud sound startled me so much, it took a second for his words to sink in. His eyes rounded and his mouth dropped open as if even he couldn't believe the words that had just spilled out of his mouth.

His sisters all gasped before everyone started speaking at once.

"Wait. I said wait!" his mother yelled. "Andrew, what are you talking about? When you introduced her the other day, you said she was your friend. Now she's your fiancée? What in the hell is going on? Drew, are you hearing this?"

A muttered, "Yeah, yeah," filtered across the room.

"Start talking," Pam told her son.

"We, uh, we didn't want to tell you . . . like this. I, um, I proposed last week. When she came to see me."

"You proposed to her in a hospital?" one of his sisters asked. "Gross."

"Yeah, I, um, I . . . " He cut his eyes over to me, and part of me wanted to let him drown in his own lie.

But we'd been in so many situations during our short time together that mirrored this one. It was almost instinct for me to step in.

"We'd fought before the accident. Broken up. I didn't know what had happened to him until a friend let me know, and that's when I came to see him. Knowing I'd almost lost him, it, uh . . . " I cleared my throat. "Almost losing him made me realize how much I loved him."

My throat burned after the words left it. I was giving too much of myself away. Sure, I could make the case that I was just saying things that would sound good to his mom. But Drew *knew* me. He'd hear the truth I'd desperately wanted to keep buried.

There was a collective "Aw" from his sisters, and even his mom was smiling softly.

"Well, I obviously want to hear all about you and this engagement," she said, "but for now I guess I just need to make sure you're up for taking care of him. I'm sure we'll have plenty of time to get to know one another once he's healed."

I let out a deep sigh before saying, "I'm up for it," even though I really wasn't even sure what was going on.

After a bit more get-to-know-you small talk and a promise by his mom that she'd stop by and see us soon, Drew's family left.

When the door was closed behind them, he sagged into the bed. "Christ, I thought they'd never leave."

I lowered myself into the chair beside his bed and stared at him.

"What?" he asked.

"Are you fucking kidding me right now?"

He had the good sense to at least look abashed. "I'm sorry. I panicked."

"Seriously, though, what the fuck? I can't take you back to the sorority house. Where are you going to go?"

"I already have that all worked out, but my mom was never going to let it happen, so I needed to adjust my story on the fly."

"You have it worked out? So where are you staying?"

"At Carter's."

"At Carter's! You can't go there. You'll catch an infection the second you step over the threshold. Not to mention the fact he lives with four other guys in a house that wouldn't even be inhabitable by *Animal House* standards."

"It'll be fine. Besides, I don't have much choice. I *cannot* be stuck in my parents' house while I can barely walk. My mom acts like she's dependable, but she isn't. After a couple days, they'll leave me to fend for myself. And if that's what's going to happen anyway, I may as well at least be in a place that isn't a fucking circus."

"Drew, you're going to be living with five football players. If that's not a circus, I don't know what is."

"Yeah, but it's different." He groaned, clearly getting frustrated. "My sisters are always at the house, and they're always arguing. Everyone's mad at everyone else, they're manipulating each other, manipulating me... I just... I can't, okay? Even if it's insane at Carter's, at least I'll know they probably aren't stealing money out of my wallet while I'm sleeping or taking off with my stuff."

That brought me up short. For as insane as my family could be, we weren't *steal your shit after your near-death experience* crazy. An idea popped into my mind, and I tried to tell myself to quash it. This was a headache I didn't need or want. After all the bullshit last semester, I just wanted a low-key spring to lick my wounds and get back to my old self. Except...

"I'll take you to Brody's." There was no mistaking the defeat in my voice, even though I'd only beaten my better sense. "My dad signed a year-long lease, and it's still sitting empty. We can stay there until you're better."

"I can't ask you to do that." His tone told me he meant the words, but there was no hiding the bloom of hope in his eyes. And no matter what my brain said, my heart couldn't extinguish it.

"You didn't ask. I'll get the nurse, and we'll see about getting you out of here."

Chapter Four

SOPHIA

"Dude, you're heavier than you look," Carter said, his arm wrapped around Drew's body as he helped him out of his car. Thank God for Carter. After team workouts, he'd helped me bring down Drew's things from his hospital room, driven us to Brody's, and volunteered the rest of his Saturday to help me get Drew settled in and unpacked.

Drew hopped up on the sidewalk and took the crutches I had waiting for him. "I'm not sure if that's a compliment or an insult."

Carter thought for a moment. "I'm not sure either."

"Thanks for your help, man. I mean it," Drew told him. "And for checking in on me so much."

Even though I knew Drew's comment had been directed at Carter and had only been made out of appreciation, I couldn't help but feel guilty that I hadn't gone to visit him since the night of the accident.

Though I truly cared about Drew's well-being, I'd cared more about saving face and not acting overly concerned for a person who'd left me without any explanation.

And since Carter had been going to the hospital and getting updates from the nurses by phone, I could make sure Drew was making progress without ever having to inquire about him myself.

"You don't need to thank me. I was happy to do it."

"Well, I just want you to know it means a lot. Being in the hospital for a month can get pretty lonely, especially without a working phone."

As I listened to this bromance developing on the street, it became abundantly clear how selfish my choice to avoid Drew had been. And though I had every right to be selfish after how Drew had acted, the situation had become bigger than my feelings. Because even though Drew might not have wanted *me*, he needed me in a way I wasn't aware of until I'd finally gone to see him.

And even that had been Carter's suggestion. He'd even offered to let Drew stay at his house with him and the other guys. Granted, that place was a maggot-infested dump, but still. There was definitely a special place in heaven for Carter.

"Oh yeah, the no-phone thing must've been rough. Having to jerk off without porn is a hardship I hope I never have to face," Carter said, his tone grave. "You're truly a survivor."

Drew laughed, causing Carter to break into a smile. He didn't disagree or say anything at all to Carter, and I wished that during the silence I could think of anything other than Drew's penis. Goddamn Carter.

I grabbed two of Drew's bags out of Carter's SUV, and he shut the trunk before taking the larger of the two bags from me and rushing over to Drew's side. He pulled open the door and helped Drew up the small step toward the stairway that led to Brody's apartment.

When I'd thought of using it as a place for Drew to stay, it had been a stroke of genius on my part. The place was empty except for furniture and some of Brody's stuff he'd left there months ago.

The fact that our parents hadn't tried to get out of the lease early just showed how much blind hope they had. Brody didn't even want to live in this country, let alone go back to college. Luckily, their misplaced faith in him meant that Drew had a quiet place to relax while he rehabbed. It'd taken a little convincing on my part to get him there, but we both knew his options were limited.

We ascended the stairs slowly, Drew repeatedly wincing in pain and looking a little pale but never complaining. Once we reached the landing, I fished my keys out of my bag, simultaneously glad my dad had never asked for my key back and hoping the reason he hadn't wasn't because he'd had the locks changed over winter break.

When the key slid in easily and the lock clicked over, I breathed a sigh of relief because as good as this plan had been, it had been my only one. Carter and I could get Drew situated with some food, a new phone, and a comfortable place to sleep where no one—mainly his mom and sisters—could bother him.

Or we'd be doing something else entirely... Because there, on the couch, covered in Dorito crumbs and self-pity, was Brody.

The fuck?

DREW

"Brody?" both Sophia and I said, as if we weren't sure if

the creature in front of us was real or some sort of illusion—like a Tupac hologram minus the talent or drive.

He brought the can of Coke away from where he'd just had it at his lips. "What the hell are you doing here?"

Sophia's eyes opened so wide I thought they might actually fall out of her head. "I think we should be the ones asking *you* that!"

Careful not to bump into me, she pushed past Carter and headed for her brother. He didn't look nearly as frightened as he should've been at Sophia's approach. Once she was close enough to reach him, she grabbed the bag of chips off his lap and tossed them aside before smacking him on the arm.

Brody rubbed at his bicep, looking confused. "Ouch. What was that for?"

"You've gotta be kidding me." Sophia turned to Carter and me. "Is he fucking kidding right now? He better be fucking kidding."

I wasn't sure I'd ever heard Sophia curse that much in such a short period of time, and I found it oddly appealing.

"I'd tell her you were kidding," Carter advised him as he helped me into a chair. Then he put down my bag and walked over to the couch, extending a hand. "Hey, man. I'm Carter Blaine. It's good to finally meet you. The *real* you." He glanced at me for a moment before turning back to Brody. "You guys do look pretty similar, though."

Brody put the soda on the table and shook Carter's hand. "Brody. And don't believe any of what you heard if it came from my sister."

"Jesus Christ! This isn't the time to make new friends," Sophia said, grabbing the remote and shutting off the TV.

"What the fuck?" Brody said, snatching it back. "I

was watching that. Jon Snow was just about to find out his girlfriend's his aunt."

"Oh, I'm sorry," Sophia replied. Even Brody couldn't miss the sarcasm in her voice. "I'm home handing Mom tissues on Christmas Eve because she thinks you can't even stand to be in the same country as us, and you're forty miles away the whole time, binging junk food and *Game of Thrones* reruns?"

Other than the crunch of the chip Brody had just placed in his mouth, the apartment was silent.

"How long have you been here?" She looked around the apartment like it might provide some clues. Though I had no idea what any of them might be.

Brody looked to Carter and me, his eyes begging for help neither of us was going to give him. "I feel like there isn't a good answer to that."

Sophia spun on her heels and grabbed the purse she'd dropped to the floor minutes earlier. "That's it. I'm not covering for your stupid ass anymore. If I have to deal with Mom and Dad, so do you." She pulled out her phone, but Carter's voice stopped her from actually calling them.

"Wait, wait, wait," he said. "You can't tell them Brody's here. How are you gonna let Drew stay here if your parents know Brody's home? They'll be up his ass immediately."

Thank God for Carter.

The long sigh Sophia released told me she knew Carter had a point. And truthfully, Sophia's comment had probably been more of an impulsive threat than it had been an actual intention. In the time I'd known her, she'd never once thought of diming Brody out, even if he'd deserved it.

"Wait, why's Drew staying here? He doesn't need to pretend to be me anymore." He set his eyes on me curiously.

"What the hell happened to you anyway? You look like shit."

"He wrecked his bike," Carter explained. "He's been in the hospital for the last month. Sophia figured he could stay here till he's fully recovered."

"Maybe you would've known that if you'd bothered to contact the guy who pretended to be you for an entire semester," Sophia added, making me smile internally. Other than offering to help me out by letting me stay at Brody's, it was the first bit of concern for me she'd shown since I'd left. I hoped it wouldn't be the last.

"Oh. Sorry to hear that, man," Brody said, standing to brush the crumbs off his sweatpants. "I actually did try texting you a few weeks ago, you know to say Merry Christmas and whatnot, but I didn't hear back."

"My phone broke in the crash," I explained.

Brody's eyes widened. "Dude, that blows."

"Yup, pretty much everything about the past month blows. I'm hoping the beginning of the new year will be better than the end of the last." I raised an eyebrow at him hopefully. "So . . . is it cool if I stay here?"

"Oh, yeah, sure. Sorry. Totally should've said that earlier. Though I'm not sure my style of living will be conducive to healing."

Laughing, I said, "Well, I don't have many other good options. After I left your apartment, I was working on getting a place of my own, but the accident happened before I could find anything. I could still stay with my parents, though, if—"

"No! No friend of mine is going to stay with his mom and dad," Brody said, as if the idea were akin to suggesting I board at a dog kennel. "You're more than welcome to stay here. I'll . . ."

He looked around at the disaster surrounding him—clothing, dirty dishes, and so many pillows and couch cushions in strange places, it looked like he'd been trying to build a fort to entertain himself. I actually wouldn't have been surprised to hear he'd done that at some point. "I'll clean the place up and put some sheets on the bed for you."

"Thanks, Bro." I had no idea Brody considered me a friend, but I wasn't exactly in a position to disagree. If he was okay with sharing his apartment with me, I certainly wasn't going to stop him. "But I can take the couch."

Sophia looked at me. "But where am I gonna sleep? Not with Brody."

"Fire escape? Bathtub? Coffin?" Brody chimed in. "Who cares? Why would you even stay here? Didn't you just spend all last semester talking your way back into the sorority house?"

"You know I did."

"And what better way to prove your devotion to that ho train than to desert them again? They're so lucky to have you."

Sophia looked like she was trying to compose herself before she jumped on him and clawed his eyes out like a cat on PCP.

"Drew needs someone to help take care of him," she finally said, "and I don't think someone who looks like he hasn't bathed since Thanksgiving is up for the task."

Brody looked more confused than insulted. "You say that like I was volunteering to give him his sponge baths or something."

Brody and Sophia were firing shots at each other so quickly, I felt like I was watching a Ping-Pong match. Who was going to get smashed in the face with the ball first? Carter appeared thoroughly entertained. And though it *was* technically entertaining, it also made me feel like complete shit. Which was really saying something, considering the fact I spent the better part of the last month downing hospital food and painkillers.

If it weren't for me, Sophia wouldn't even have known Brody was here. She could've gone on with her sorority life, and Brody could've gone on with...whatever the fuck he'd been doing.

"So you were just volunteering to let him waste away on the couch?" she asked.

"I never said I'd let him *waste away*. There definitely isn't a shortage of food here. And *he* was the one who said he'd take the couch. I offered to give him the bed."

"Oh, my mistake. Let me notify the Vatican so they can canonize you."

"You have to be dead for that, Dumbo," Brody replied.

She glared harshly at him for a moment. "Give me ten minutes."

It was like they had reverted back to what they'd probably been like as kids.

Brody's arms had been crossed, but he dropped them with a deep breath. I took it as a show of surrender, but I couldn't be sure. I'd only met the guy the handful of times he'd come into the bar.

"Fine. You can stay, too," he told her. "You did me a solid last semester, even if it didn't work out exactly as I planned."

Sophia rolled her eyes, but I could tell it was more for show than an actual representation of her true feelings.

"Maybe that's because you never actually *plan* anything," she said, but the spunk she'd had a few moments ago had evaporated with Brody's offer.

Brody smiled at the halfhearted jab before tossing one of his own out. "And you can? I'm guessing your crystal ball didn't tell you you'd get kicked out of a club you had to pay to be a part of in the first place."

"As soon as I can go back to work, I'll be outta here," I promised, hoping that my comment would divert their attention away from each other for a bit.

"You still working at Rafferty's?" Brody asked.

"Yeah." Which reminded me that I still needed to update my boss at the bar on my plans to return. "Or I will be eventually." Sean was a good guy and I'd known him for years, so he'd assured me there would be a job for me whenever I was ready to come back. "Unfortunately, the same probably can't be said for the warehouse I started working at right before my accident."

They hadn't exactly fired me—most likely because firing someone who'd almost died would've looked extra shitty—but there was no way they would hold that job for me when I couldn't even walk without assistance. "I'm sure once they find out I'm not in any danger of dying, they won't feel guilty about letting me go."

Brody's head jerked back like that surprised him. "Seriously? That's so fucked up."

I shrugged. "It is what it is. It's a physical job. I can't blame them for wanting someone who can actually lift things."

Brody was already throwing random trash into a garbage bag he'd grabbed from the kitchen. I had a feeling it was the most he'd moved since he'd gotten back from Italy.

"I'll do it," he said.

"Do what?"

"Fill in for you until you can go back. You think they'd let me?"

"I doubt it. I'm sure they already hired someone to fill my shift. They're probably just holding off on actually telling me."

Sophia was quick to interject. "I wouldn't let Brody take over for you anyway. He's never worked a day in his life."

"And you have?" Brody said, looking genuinely insulted.

"I have a work *ethic*, at least. You avoid anything that requires brain cells or physical exertion."

Brody crossed his arms, and Sophia mirrored him, her eyes narrowing to a harsh glare. But since he really couldn't disagree, the two remained in some sort of silent standoff until eventually Sophia seemed to get irritated enough that she gave up and turned away from him.

"Yes!" Brody said, thrusting his arms into the air in victory. "I win that every time."

Living with these two is going to be a fucking blast . . .

. . . said no one ever.

Chapter Five

DREW

Unsurprisingly, Brody went back to the couch as Carter and Sophia unpacked some of my things and tried to make them easily accessible from Brody's bed, where I'd probably be most of the time.

I tried to do what I could, but the outcome wasn't quite representative of my effort.

"You need anything else before I take off?" Carter asked, stretching his arms over his head.

I couldn't wait until I started seeing significant progress from my rehab. I still had to go to physical therapy once a week and had my own exercises I was supposed to do at home, but it would be a while before I got back to the shape I'd been in before the crash. Seeing Carter made me feel even worse about my current physical condition.

"Nah, I'm good. Thanks for everything, man."

"Of course." Carter reached a hand out to me but then seemed to rethink it and leaned in to give me a hug instead. Which would've been fine if it hadn't turned into an awkward fumbling of hands around my neck like we were at a junior high dance trying to find a position that didn't make us both crawl out of our skin.

After he gave me a hard pat on my back—most likely to make his embrace seem manlier—he pulled away quickly.

"That was . . . weird. Next time I'll just wave, I guess."

Laughing, I said, "That's probably best. Though we did kiss in the middle of campus, so this isn't even close to the most awkward encounter I've had with you."

All of us laughed, including Sophia, which was nice to see.

"Dude," Brody yelled from the couch. "No wonder my parents thought I was gay. Why the hell were you kissing random guys in public?"

We didn't even know he'd heard us.

"Who you calling random?" Carter yelled back in defense.

We laughed even harder, and I pressed a hand against my ribs to keep them from moving too much. Until I'd cracked a few of them, I'd never realized how important ribs and the muscles surrounding them were to everyday movements. I also realized I hadn't laughed this hard in a really long time. I'd missed it.

Even if I was far from being back to my old self again, it felt good to have some of my old life back. And a large part of that life included Sophia.

Carter said bye to Brody and Sophia, and then it was just the two of us in Brody's room. It occurred to me that the last time we'd been in here alone had been the day I'd left, and I suddenly wanted to wrap her up in my arms and tell her that all of it had been a mistake. But there was so much she didn't know about what had happened.

Or maybe she did. I didn't actually know what she knew

and what she didn't, and I wasn't sure I wanted to ask.

I doubted it mattered anyway. The hows and the whys were unimportant. All that mattered was that I'd left. Left *her*. And the memory of it had me feeling sorrier for myself than I'd felt in a long time, which was really saying something, considering I'd spent the holidays in intensive care.

"I'm okay," I told her. "Don't feel like you have to stay."

She looked me over like the idea of leaving was about as responsible as leaving a toddler unattended.

"I swear, I'm fine. I'm just gonna rest. Cody's supposed to be coming over as soon as he gets off work." I looked at the watch on my wrist that wasn't covered by a cast. "He should be here soon actually. He asked to leave early."

"Oh, that's good. Then I guess I'll head over to the sorority house and grab the rest of my things. I also need to tell Aamee and the girls that I won't be around as much."

"Good luck with that," I said.

She picked up a pair of balled-up socks and chucked them at me. "Thanks a lot."

"Hey, you shouldn't assault someone who's already wounded."

"I don't think tossing socks at someone counts as assault." She smiled as she threw another pair at me before heading for the doorway. "I'll be back in a little while."

"I'll be here," I replied cheerily. Where else *would* I be?

And I was looking forward to it.

SOPHIA

I'm not sure what possessed Brody to offer to help me pack

up what I had at the sorority house, but when he suggested it, I couldn't turn him down. Especially since he had a car, which meant I didn't need to call an Uber or ask one of the girls to help.

Once I finished helping Drew get settled, Brody was already showered, shaved, and dressed. Maybe he was trying to prove he wasn't a worthless bum.

"So how many girls live here?" he asked as we approached the house.

Or maybe Brody was just being Brody and he was trying to get laid.

"Not enough that you have a chance with any of them."

He shoved his hands into the pockets of his jeans, looking casual as we walked up the five steps to the porch.

"You really have such little faith in me."

"Obviously."

He reached out to open the door, but I stuck my arm out to stop him from entering the house, his solid body almost breaking my arm when they came into contact. How the guy still maintained his physique despite doing nothing but snacking and relaxing for the past month, I had no idea. Once guys gained muscle, it seemed to stick to them easily. Even Drew had managed to not look emaciated—just leaner than he'd been.

"Seriously, though, I don't need you trying to bang any of these girls. Just come in, help me, and leave without speaking. You spent time in another country, so why don't you just pretend you don't speak English?"

"You realize I don't need English to get laid, right?"

"I hate you," I said as I smacked his hand from the doorknob so I could be the first one inside. "Just don't embarrass me."

"No problem. You can do that easily enough yourself."

Glaring at him in a way that I hoped sufficiently warned him I was serious, I pointed up the stairs. I could hear voices coming from the kitchen, but I figured I'd head down there once Brody was in my room packing things up.

As we crept—well, *I* crept because Brody had the stealth of a rhino on acid—the floors creaked beneath our feet. Once we made it to the top, I led him to the room I shared with Gina. I knew she was at work, and since I'd already told her I planned to stay at Brody's for a bit to help a friend recover, I could get the rest of my things without bothering her.

"What stuff are we taking?" Brody asked as he eyed the small room.

Two twin beds sat close together, with various old furniture surrounding them, including two dressers that didn't even begin to hold Gina's and my clothes. The rest of our things were stuffed in Rubbermaid containers and shoved under our beds.

I slid one out toward Brody's feet.

"There's one more of these under there," I said, "and then I guess I'll take my bedding and pillows and stuff."

"Yeah, you'll need that since you'll be on the floor."

"Um, I'm *not* going to be sleeping on the floor."

"Well, then, where are you planning to sleep? With Drew?" He laughed. "I mean, I know you guys were… whatever you were, but Mom said that was done, so I didn't think you'd wanna share a bed with the guy."

"When did you talk to Mom?" I asked, choosing not to address the idea of sleeping with Drew.

Brody shrugged as he pulled my sheets off and began balling them up instead of folding them. "I don't know. I didn't mark the date on my calendar. Like a couple of weeks ago, I guess. Near Christmas."

"Wait, does she know you're home?"

"No! And you better not tell her, or I'll tell her you're helping *Drew!*"

"I already promised I wouldn't tell her," I said defensively. "And you don't need to mess with Drew just to get back at me."

Not that I fully understood why I was even threatened by his statement. It wasn't like helping a friend was a punishable offense. Though I knew with the way Drew had spent a semester impersonating Brody while he flitted around Europe, which involved him sharing an apartment with me that my parents were paying for, Drew wasn't high up on their list of people they'd want to help. But I couldn't help feeling irritated by it anyway.

It wasn't like it was Drew's fault that Brody found it impossible to maintain any type of responsibility. Brody would've done that shit regardless of who was filling in for him. And Drew hadn't done anything to *me* that should make my parents dislike him.

I was saved from having to think more about it by the sound of the door to my room being shoved open. Even in the colder weather, it still seemed to stick enough that we had to really put some muscle into it. I looked over to see Aamee making an entrance that made me wonder if she was auditioning for the part of Kramer in a *Seinfeld* remake or something.

"Oh, hey," I said, hoping she picked up on my lack of excitement.

"Hey. Were you going to say hi or just sneak up to your room and hide out all day?"

"I'm actually leaving for a couple weeks. I'll be in and out, but I won't be sleeping here. So don't worry, I'll be out of your bleached hair soon."

"Perfect," she replied with a fake smile. Then she nodded toward Brody. "Planning to have a guy stay the night so you're kicking yourself out this time. How noble of you."

"Ew, no. He's not spending the night."

Aamee moved closer, her short skirt riding up a bit as she approached my brother.

"That's a shame," she said.

The way her eyes moved over him, taking him in one inch at a time, made her look like she was sizing him up like some sort of a dessert she was contemplating eating for a bedtime snack.

And Brody looked like he couldn't wait for Aamee to put her mouth on him.

The whole thing was gross.

Eventually she must've decided that the caloric intake wasn't worth it, so she extended her hand to him. "I'm Aamee, sorority president," she said with a seductive smile as Brody took her hand. She really had no shame.

Brody smiled back. And because he was an impulsive asshole who thought with his dick, he said, "I'm Brody, Sophia's brother."

Aamee's head panned to me, her lips pressing together in what looked to be satisfaction, before she focused her attention back on Brody. "You certainly are."

Chapter Six

SOPHIA

"Oh, you've gotta be kidding me," I said, holding back the vomit that threatened to make its way up my esophagus at the sight of the two of them. If eyes could fuck, theirs would need a room.

"Um, I think *you're* the one who was kidding all of us for the last few months," Aamee pointed out.

And though I couldn't disagree, I rolled my eyes anyway.

Brody took his eyes off my nemesis long enough to look at me and ask, "She knows about Drew?"

I didn't exactly know what he was asking because it could've been a number of things. Did she know the person she thought was Brody was really Drew? Did she know Drew left me? Did she know Drew was in an accident? Or that I was planning on nursing him back to health instead of living in the sorority house I'd fought so hard to get back into?

"What about him?" I finally asked.

"Ahh, so is Drew the name of your fuck buddy from last semester?" Aamee asked me, though her eyes remained on Brody.

"He wasn't a 'fuck buddy.'"

She plopped down on my bed like she was welcome there. "Relax. At least I didn't think you were fucking your actual brother like the rest of the campus."

Brody's eyes widened, and his head swung toward me. "You didn't tell me people thought we were…" He let his sentence remain unfinished, probably feeling as disgusted as I was at the thought.

"Why would I tell you that? We barely speak, and you were in Europe."

Aamee looked absolutely thrilled as she watched us bicker like she'd paid for admission and gotten front-row seats.

Brody laughed harshly and then said, "You could've warned me that most of my school thinks I'm puttin' it in my sister. I didn't know anyone knew about the two of you."

"First of all, it's not your school. You dropped out. Again. Remember? Second of all, you were in Italy." I emphasized the country in case Brody forgot that he was half a world away when all of this was happening. And the last thing I was concerned with was how it would affect my self-centered brother.

Aamee's smile spread so high on her face, she looked like Arthur Fleck after he'd perfected his Joker persona. She was probably also almost as crazy.

"See? Now this is how siblings interact," she said. "I knew from the beginning that Brody…or Drew," she corrected herself, "wasn't your brother. You two were too sweet to each other." Scooting back as she shoved my pillows onto the floor so she could rest her back against the wall, she said, "How is Drew anyway? That boy *is* gorgeous."

"He's also recovering from a motorcycle accident that put him in intensive care for the past month," I told her.

Her eyes narrowed like she wasn't sure if I was just messing with her. "Seriously?" She looked to Brody when I didn't answer.

Brody nodded, his face softening because even Brody wasn't that much of a dick. He wasn't going to make a joke out of something that wasn't. And he seemed to know how much I cared for Drew.

"Sorry to hear that," Aamee said, her tone caught somewhere between apathy and real concern. It was a broad spectrum, and I had no idea how she could seem both indifferent and sorry at the same time. She was truly a paradox.

"Thanks," I told her, deciding to think that she actually cared about Drew. I knew better than to think that her condolences were for me. "He's fine now. Well, not fine yet, but he will be. He's recovering at Brody's."

"That's nice of you," Aamee said to Brody. "To help him."

Brody sat down on my bed near Aamee. "It's the least I could do. I've never nursed someone back to health before. Well, other than a baby bird our childhood cat brought in one time, but—"

The sound of my hand hitting him on the back of his head interrupted his story.

"Stop it," I scolded before refocusing on Aamee. "I'm the one who's going to be taking care of Drew. And I was the one who helped with the bird too." I turned back to Brody. "You wanted to have it for dinner with mashed potatoes."

"I was joking when I said that. We couldn't have even made one chicken finger out of that bird." Turning back to Aamee, he said, "I'm here to help Sophia pack up because she's staying with us until Drew's a little more self-sufficient. I'm generous like that."

"You're pathetic is what you are. He's trying to get in your pants, Aamee. As much as it pains me to say it, even *you* can do better."

I walked over to the closet to grab a duffel bag and began tossing some clothes into it. Thankfully, most of my shoes were still in the trash bag I'd brought them back over in, so I slid those out into the main part of the room. When I turned around, Aamee had the stupidest smile on her face.

"That might be the nicest thing you've ever said to me."

"It's *definitely* the nicest thing I've ever said to you."

"Does anyone care that it was at my expense?" Brody asked.

"No," Aamee and I said in unison.

I almost smiled. And for a moment, there was a connection between the two of us that it seemed neither of us wanted to acknowledge. Our eyes darted to one another and then awkwardly away again.

Aamee stood suddenly, looking around at the things I'd pulled out from my dresser and various corners of the room. "So you're really leaving again?"

"Yup." I thought I heard a hint of disappointment in her voice, but I'd never call her out on it. Besides, it was probably only contempt masquerading as something more palatable because she didn't want Brody to realize what a bitch she was. "Don't miss me too much."

"You don't have to worry about that," she said. "Having you gone's like coming into a house after an exterminator's gotten rid of the rats."

I bit my upper lip to keep from smirking as I headed to the bathroom down the hall to grab my toiletries.

"Do you have enough suitcases, or do you need another

garbage bag for the rest of your trash?" she called after me.

"Garbage bag would be great," I yelled back. "Thanks."

And as she walked past the bathroom toward the stairs, she muttered, "You know where they are."

That time I couldn't help but smile. *Asshole.*

DREW

I hadn't seen Cody in at least two weeks, and I was happy he was coming over. He'd visited often while I was in the hospital, but his shifts had changed at work, so he hadn't been able to come to the apartment to see me yet, which seemed to be a running theme with my family.

Not that I was exactly begging for someone to be with me constantly. It was great that people cared, but most of the time I preferred to be alone. Just me, my self-destructive thoughts, and I.

Before the accident, I'd promised my mom I'd help plan Cody's eighteenth birthday party because, well, because I'd been the one to suggest throwing one for him. I hadn't been surprised to learn that after the accident they'd done little more than get him an ice cream cake, and I felt guiltier than I probably should've.

It hadn't been my fault that Cody never got his party, but I felt he deserved one all the same, even if it would have to be a month or two late. December babies always got screwed one way or another.

Cody told me he'd be over in the afternoon, but I wasn't surprised his boss made him stay even though he'd promised Cody he'd let him leave early. People were always calling out, and Cody'd been there longer than any of the other kids who worked there, so he got paid more.

Unfortunately, that also meant he often got more responsibility, whether he wanted it or not. In addition to being in school all day, he worked over thirty hours per week making gourmet doughnuts at a local family-owned shop. He'd changed his clothes before coming over, though he still smelled sweet and doughy, even from across the living room.

As I motioned toward the pizza box on the coffee table, Cody leaned over and passed me another slice. He'd only been here for fifteen minutes, and we'd almost finished an entire pie.

"You need anything else?" he asked, wiping his hands on a paper towel as he headed to the kitchen.

"Nah, I'm good for right now. Thanks."

I heard the fridge open, and when I looked over, Cody was opening up one of Brody's beers.

"What are you doing?"

"Getting a drink," he answered. "Did your vision get fucked up in the accident too?"

"You're eighteen, and you're driving. You realize I almost died in a car accident, right?"

"Technically, there was no car involved. It was just you, your Razor Scooter, and some snow."

Leave it to Cody not to treat me like a fragile baby. I couldn't help but appreciate him for it.

"It's not a Razor Scooter." I tried, and most likely failed, to put some sternness into my voice. Fucking Cody.

He moved over to me and crouched down to put an arm around my shoulder and gave it a squeeze, but it was lighter than it probably would've been if I hadn't been injured.

"You love me," he said.

"Yeah. But you really make it difficult sometimes."

Cody laughed at that and looked at his beer. "I won't have any more after this one." He probably knew I wasn't so sure because he added, "Promise."

Cody finished his beer, we both finished the pizza, and Cody was cleaning up when I heard the door open and saw Brody and Sophia come in with their hands full. Sophia dropped a suitcase and a trash bag on the ground and helped Brody set down the two boxes he was balancing. I wondered how he even made it up the stairs with them in front of his face.

"Oh, hey, man, you must be Drew's brother."

Cody was already heading over, and Brody met him halfway. "Cody."

"Good to finally meet ya. I'm Brody."

They shook hands before Cody turned his attention to Sophia and raised an eyebrow. "And you must be the fiancée."

Sophia looked momentarily stunned as she probably wondered if she'd have to spend another chunk of time pretending we were something we weren't. She shook his hand but remained silent, her mouth open enough that it looked like words should be coming out.

When it was clear she didn't know how to respond, I said, "He's kidding. Cody knows we're not engaged."

Sophia's shoulders fell, and she let out a quiet sigh.

"Either way," Cody said, "thanks for taking care of my brother."

"Of course," she replied. "I'm happy to."

I wondered if the second part was true or if it was just something she'd said to be polite. Just because she'd offered to help me didn't mean she was *happy* to do it.

"Smells like pizza," Brody said, sniffing the air and

walking around the apartment like a bloodhound searching for a missing person.

"Oh, um, we just finished one," Cody said, sounding apologetic.

"Marco's?" Brody asked.

"Of course," I answered.

"Drew practically survived off that pizza last semester," Sophia told the guys. Then she grabbed a pillow from the chair and put it under my casted arm so I had somewhere to rest it.

"I miss the wings at Rafferty's," Brody said. "Now I can go back again. I didn't want you to know I was home, but now that that plan's shot to shit, it doesn't matter. Wish I would've known you weren't even working. I've been missing out on their wings for weeks."

I just shook my head at him.

Brody grabbed a beer out of the fridge, and when he saw Cody's empty on the table, he asked if he wanted another.

"He's done for the night," I told him, but my eyes went to Cody.

"Yeah, I'm good. Thanks, though."

"You want one, Drew?"

"I do, but I don't think that's a good idea with the painkillers."

"Oh, right." Brody settled into one of the chairs and put a foot on the edge of the coffee table.

"I'm fine too," Sophia said slowly so Brody wouldn't miss the sarcasm. "Thanks for asking."

And as if it truly hadn't occurred to him to offer a beer to his sister, he said, "Oh, my bad. Did you want one?" He pointed a thumb toward the fridge but made no move to get up.

"No wonder you had to go to a non-English-speaking

country to find a female who'd go anywhere near you."

I laughed, but Brody didn't seem to think Sophia's comment was funny. Or he was at least pretending not to. He just took another sip of his beer and eyed her disdainfully.

"So how was everything at the sorority?" I asked, hoping to change the subject.

"All right," Sophia said.

"Did anyone give you a hard time about leaving?"

By "anyone," I'd meant Aamee because I didn't think any of the other girls would. Not that they didn't care about Sophia or want her to spend time in the house but because they were more understanding. I had no idea what Sophia's relationship with Aamee was like at this point, but I couldn't imagine it was suddenly a good one.

"Not really. I didn't see that many of the girls. I guess you could say Aamee helped me pack."

"She told her where the trash bags were," Brody clarified as he gave a nod toward the bags she'd brought in.

"Who's Aamee?" Cody asked.

Sophia and I filled him in on what had transpired last semester: Sophia getting kicked out of the house because of Carter and then eventually using a loophole I'd discovered that allowed her to run for sorority president against Aamee, who'd held the position at that time. Cody nodded along as if it all made perfect sense until I'd told him Sophia had won only to let Aamee keep the position anyway.

Cody's head snapped to where Sophia was sitting. "What? Why?"

"'Cause Aamee's hot," Brody provided.

Sophia rolled her eyes. "It was definitely *not* because she's hot." Then she looked at me. "Do *you* think she's hot?"

What was an appropriate answer? I couldn't say no too quickly because it would look like I was just avoiding complimenting another female in Sophia's presence, and since we weren't together, there was no reason I should do that. And I didn't want to agree with Brody necessarily.

So I went with "I could see how some guys might think she's attractive, but once you get to know her, it's a different story."

"Huh," Brody said, his voice rich with intrigue like the statement had been a challenge instead of a warning. "I'm gonna order another pizza. Anyone want anything?"

"Nah, I think I've had enough," I told him. "I should probably start trying to save money now that I'm not eating free hospital food anymore. Though, actually, I don't know that I should consider it free with the amount of medical bills I have coming my way."

"That bad?" Cody asked. "Didn't you get some sort of insurance at some point?"

"Yeah, but it's not anything that would cover the amount of shit I had done. It'll be nice when I can go back to the bar and maybe even pick up a second job. I have *some* money, but I'm sure it's not enough to cover it."

Brody seemed to be taking in everything I was saying, his lips in a tight line and his eyebrows pressed together like he was thinking hard about something. Finally, he said, "I can help out. Let me know when you start getting bills."

"I appreciate it, but I can't take your money." His offer truly surprised me. It was generous and unexpected, and even though he seemed absolutely sincere, I couldn't accept it.

"That's what you said last semester, but I owe you. Seriously. If it weren't for you, I would've been stuck at Lazarus trying to act like I gave a shit about my classes and grades."

I tried not to let his comment bother me because it was just Brody being Brody and he was trying to be nice. But I would've loved to have been given the opportunities he'd been given in his life, and he was just pissing it away every chance he got. It was infuriating to watch.

"Plus," Brody went on, "it's my parents' money anyway. They haven't cut me off yet."

"I definitely can't take your parents' money."

Sophia looked almost murderous. "For real? Why are they still giving you money?"

Brody shrugged casually. "Beats me. Maybe since they still think I'm in Europe, they don't want to worry that I won't have a place to stay or food to eat. Just because I disobeyed them doesn't mean they want me to end up begging tourists for change."

Sophia stared blankly at him for a few moments before saying, "God forbid you get a job."

Brody still had his phone in his hand, ready to order his food, but hadn't actually called yet. "Dude, enough with the job shit already. You act like I'm incapable of working."

"No, *you* act like you're incapable of working."

As Brody walked toward where his sister was standing in the kitchen after getting a water bottle, I adjusted my position on the couch so I could watch the interaction. I wasn't sure if one of their sibling squabbles might eventually turn into some sort of wrestling match, but I was glad Cody was here to break it up if it did.

I was by no means a stranger to disagreements involving siblings, but I rarely experienced the level of bickering with my sisters and brother that these two had become accustomed to.

At least since we'd become adults.

Brody scratched at the back of his head, messing up his dark hair that he had styled before he'd gone to the sorority house. "I have an idea," he said to Sophia before turning toward me. "Since Drew can't work right now, I'll get a job. It'll prove to *you*"—he looked at Sophia again—"that I can work for a living, and it'll let me help Drew out with his bills." He looked back to me. "I can deposit my checks right into your account. Make me feel like I'm paying you back a little. Plus, I'll be out of your hair while you're trying to recover."

I considered it for a minute. "You'd really do that?"

"I *want* to do that."

I couldn't explain why his doing this felt different from not wanting to take the money his parents gave him. Maybe because taking their money was a sensitive topic for me. Or maybe it was because it wasn't like I was taking any of his inheritance from him. Regardless of what it was, I was touched instead of repelled by the offer.

Despite Sophia's opinion of her brother, I couldn't help but think he was a pretty good guy.

Chapter Seven

SOPHIA

I trudged up the stairs to Brody's apartment, hoping that my brother would be out somewhere. Interacting with him was getting a little draining.

I wondered how Drew had made out for the few hours I was gone, though I knew asking him was futile. Whenever I asked him if he needed anything or if he was feeling okay, he always said he was fine.

We'd only been in the apartment for a week, but in that time, Drew had hardly let me help him with anything, clearly not wanting to be a bother. Why didn't he see that—for reasons I'd prefer not to admit out loud—I *wanted* to help him?

His insistence that he was okay made me feel like he didn't need me, and that wasn't a feeling I enjoyed experiencing again. It made me wonder if I should even be at the apartment, but the thought of leaving him with only Brody to help him gave me hives.

Arriving at the apartment door, I pulled out my key and let myself inside. The main living area was empty, and all was quiet. Maybe they'd both gone out? I shuddered at the thought.

Brody had no business taking someone in Drew's condition anywhere. Honestly, he had no business taking an *able-bodied* person anywhere. I stepped farther into the apartment and listened carefully. Was that . . . mumbling?

I started down the hall and saw light emanating from under the closed bathroom door. When I reached it, I put my ear up and listened for a second.

"Okay, Drew, you got this. Make this bathtub your bitch."

A snort of laughter escaped before I could stop it. I slapped a hand over my mouth as the muttering continued from within.

"How hard can it be? People in way worse shape than me bathe themselves every day."

Was this fool really trying to give himself a bath with a cast that came up to his hip as well as one on his forearm? Irritation stamped out the humor as my knuckles rapped harshly on the wooden door.

"Jesus Christ!" Drew yelped. "Brody?"

"No, it's me. What the hell is going on in there?"

The door suddenly flew open, and the words I'd been about to spit out at him evaporated as I let my eyes rove over him. He was naked save for a pair of navy-blue boxer briefs and his casts.

This.

This was exactly why I shouldn't have offered that he could stay here.

How was I supposed to keep a clear head when he looked like that? Granted, he was skinnier than when I'd last mapped his abs with my tongue, and his skin was still a bit mottled in places from his healing injuries, but there was no denying what a fine piece of man he was. Fuck every part of my life.

"Sophia, what are you doing here?"

"Why are you naked? I mean—" I closed my eyes in a grimace before rephrasing. "Are you seriously trying to give yourself a bath? Are you sure you don't have any lasting brain damage from your accident?"

He leaned against the doorjamb and crossed his arms over his chest. "Nice to see you too," he said dryly.

"You're not supposed to get your casts wet."

"I'm aware."

"How were you planning on accomplishing that?"

"Carefully."

"Why didn't you just text and ask me when I would be home so I could help?" God, this man was so irritating. He could tell his entire family we were engaged, but he couldn't pick up a goddamn phone?

He rolled his eyes, which only increased my homicidal ideations.

"I'm capable of bathing myself," he said.

"Really? Because I distinctly remember the nurse saying differently before you were discharged."

"That was almost a week ago. She couldn't have meant for me to wipe myself down with wet wipes for the rest of my life. I'm fine."

You're not fine. You almost died.

Just thinking the words made my breath stutter and my sinuses burn. I closed my eyes and pinched the bridge of my nose so I could give myself a second without letting on how emotionally devastating all of this was. It was better to have him think I was annoyed by his existence than to have him realize how much I cared about having him in the world.

"Drew, she was very clear. Not only do you have the casts,

but you have incisions that can't be soaked in water."

"I wasn't going to soak. I was just going to stand under the shower for a couple minutes."

"You? Were going to *stand*? In a slippery bathtub. On one leg." I punctuated each phrase in the hopes that it would get through his thick skull.

"No, as a matter of fact, I wasn't."

"Then what were you going to do? Lie down while the water rained all over you and got everywhere? And how were you planning to get back out?"

Hadn't he thought of *any* of these things? I felt like he used to have better ideas, but then I remembered that he'd been convinced by my dumbass brother to take over his shitstorm of a life for a semester, and suddenly Drew's idiocy made more sense.

How had I forgotten I was dealing with a moron?

"Wrong again, Yoda. I had it all figured out. So if you'll just see yourself out, I'll get back to my business." He attempted to close the door in my face, which nearly made me forget how sad I'd been that he'd almost died. I was getting ready to kill him myself.

I put my foot against the door to halt its progress. "I'm so sorry, *fiancé*, but your business *is* my business now. You put us in this situation, so you can just simmer your ass down and let me help you."

"I don't need your help, Sophia. I can do this myself."

The last sentence was spoken through gritted teeth, and I suddenly understood that this was about more than a shower. Drew had been relying on himself for a long time, and all of that was stripped away in a flash. Granted, that flash had been his own goddamn fault, because *seriously*, who rode a motorcycle in a snowstorm? But still, maybe he deserved a little more compassion.

I took a deep breath and looked up at him. "Show me how you were going to go about it, and if I'm reasonably sure you won't break your neck attempting it, I'll leave you alone."

He looked at me for a moment before releasing an audible sigh and hopped back a bit—sounding like the sudden movement cost him dearly as he sharply inhaled—so I could push the door open and he could lean against the sink.

"I dragged that in here so I could sit on it. I have it all planned out. It'll be fine."

After I took a couple steps into the bathroom, I saw what he was referring to. He'd brought one of the plastic chairs from Brody's small kitchen table into the bathroom and somehow managed to get it into the tub. I had no idea how he'd managed to accomplish such a feat and didn't feel up to asking.

It actually wasn't the worst idea I'd seen him have, and I felt frustrated with myself for not thinking of getting him one of those shower chairs earlier. My grandmom had needed one after she'd had her hip replaced.

I moved closer to the tub to better assess the situation. The chair wasn't a perfect fit. The legs didn't sit on the bottom of the tub but rested along the side, which probably wasn't very stable. Not to mention the added issue of him getting into the tub in the first place. He'd have to basically throw himself into the chair in order to clear the lip of the tub, and then he'd have to hope the chair held him.

It was precarious at best.

"I'm really not in the mood for an ER trip today. Just let me help you."

He groaned, but it sounded more from frustration than

anger at me. "I don't want someone to wipe me down. I want to enjoy a hot shower like a normal human being."

"So dramatic. I wasn't planning on 'wiping you down,' as you so appealingly put it. Just let me help you into the tub, and then I'll hold on to the chair to make sure it doesn't fall."

His brow furrowed in a way that I absolutely did *not* find adorable. "Wait...how are you going to do that?" His eyes widened. "Are you going to get in the shower with me?"

"No. Jesus. I'll get you settled and then try my best to reach around the shower curtain and hold on to it. You just need to keep your boxers on."

A smirk started to spread across his lips. "It's not like you haven't—"

"Nope. Stop right there. Boxers stay on, or you can forget this whole thing."

"Okay, okay, whatever you say," he placated. "So, how do you want me?"

If there was ever a loaded question, it was that one.

DREW

Sophia did this cute thing with her lips, almost like she was giving someone a crooked kiss, as she took in her surroundings and tried to figure out the best way to give me what I asked for.

I truly did appreciate that she hadn't totally shut me down. I knew I was maybe coming across as a baby, but living this way was wearing on me. While I knew my situation would be so much worse without people who gave a shit about me, it wasn't easy being stuck in an apartment and unable to do basic things for myself. I needed this shower in a way that didn't even make a whole lot of sense to *me*, let alone Sophia. But it was what it was.

"Okay, so if you shuffle close to the tub and put your arm around me, I can sort of hip-toss you over the side. But gently."

"So...your grand plan is to lift me into the tub?" I didn't mean to shit all over her plan, but seriously. I probably outweighed her by at least sixty pounds. And that was a conservative estimate.

Her narrowed eyes told me I should've just gone along with her, certain death be damned.

"You have a better idea?"

"Yeah, you leave, forget you ever saw me in here, and we'll let the cards fall where they may."

She sighed like I was the most annoying person on earth. "It's *you* falling that worries me. Though I'm not sure why. It'd serve you right for being such a pain in the ass."

She took a couple steps closer to the tub, but I shot my hand out and gently took hold of her bicep.

"I'm sorry. The last thing I wanted was to make your life harder."

It was why I'd left in the first place. Being with me would never give as much as it would cost her. Yet here I was, taking from her anyway. But right now, I was too selfish to do anything differently. Apologies were all I had to offer, even though they'd never be enough.

Sophia stared at me for a second before giving her head a small shake and pulling her arm from my grasp.

"It's fine." Though the sound of her voice told me it was anything but. She grabbed a towel hanging on the back of the door and slung it over the shower curtain rod. "Okay, put your bad arm around my shoulder, and grab on to the towel with your good arm. Between the two things, we should be able to get you into the tub."

As much as I hated to shoot down another one of her ideas, I had to.

"There's no way that bar will hold me. I don't want to break shit we'd have to call a landlord in to fix."

Putting her hands on her hips, she stared down at the tub like it had personally offended her.

"What about this?" I began. "You can help me lower down so I'm sitting on the edge. Then I'll use my good arm to scoot back onto the chair, and you can help me swing around. Then we'll just drape the curtain over my leg cast to keep it dry. I have wraps for the one on my arm, but I can also probably keep it elevated out of the spray as long as we position the showerhead the right way."

She thought for a second before saying, "Yeah, okay, that could work."

A smile lit up my face. "Great." I stood up, putting all my weight on my good leg. But I must've risen too fast, because momentum pitched me too far forward.

Sophia registered what was happening quickly and stepped toward me so she could catch me. I felt her arms wrap around me, and though she was strong for a girl of her size, gravity was on my side.

It felt like slow motion: the way she shuffled back like someone who's carrying a load too heavy for them, the way she bent her knees to try to grab me around my core, the way I silently prayed that I didn't smash this beautiful girl—probably the love of my life—like she was a gnat beneath me.

Soon, we were nearly horizontal, both of us falling like

giant oaks in the forest. I extended my good arm to try to keep my weight from crashing down on her. I heard her grunt as she hit the floor, her arms still wrapped around me, her body weight pulling mine down hard on top of her.

Pain ricocheted up my body as my injuries screamed from the jarring contact. But instead of moving off Sophia, I looked down at her frantically.

"Holy shit, are you okay?"

She opened her mouth to reply, but her words were cut off by a familiar voice. I looked up to see Brody standing in the doorway, eyeing us curiously.

"Did I just walk in on some kinky shit?" he asked. "Because I can come back later."

Sophia groaned beneath me while I glared at Brody.

"Help us up, you asshole."

"You guys are a mess," he said as he came over and hoisted me up. "How did you ever survive without me?"

It showed how fucked up my life truly was that I didn't have a good answer.

Chapter Eight

SOPHIA

"I don't need a babysitter."

Drew sat on the couch, arms crossed over his chest, looking as indignant and pouty as a toddler who'd missed his nap.

It'd been two days since Bathgate, and Drew and I had silently decided to never mention it again. I was also striving to never *think* about it again. But it was slightly difficult to forget a mostly naked Drew on top of me, even if the circumstances hadn't been particularly sexy. The way my mind kept trying to replay the event *was* sexy, in a warped, desperate way that made me ashamed to be alive.

"You kinda do," I replied. "That's why we're in this whole mess."

"No, we're in this whole mess because Mother Nature is a frozen whore."

Okay . . .

"Maybe so, but that doesn't change the fact that things are how they are. You need to go to the doctor, and you can't go alone, so someone has to take you. And seeing as how you proposed to me in a hospital room—" The power of his glare momentarily interrupted me, but I managed to forge on. "I'm the logical choice to take you. So, chop."

He was in a worn pair of sweats and a threadbare T-shirt. Personally, I liked the look on him, but the doctor—and the January temperatures—would likely be unimpressed.

"You have class."

I sighed dramatically. "The things I sacrifice for my fiancé."

"Will you stop with that?" he grumbled. "I said it in a moment of temporary insanity."

"Hmm, your insanity seems pretty permanent to me."

"Has she always been like this?" Drew yelled around me to Brody, who was sitting at the table eating a bowl of Froot Loops.

"Since the womb."

I scowled at my brother. Looking at his cereal, I said, "You do realize it's almost one, don't you?"

"Toucan Sam can't tell time," he quipped.

"What the hell does that even mean?"

"Figure it out, Dean's List."

"I could if it made sense, America's Least Wanted List."

Brody's lip twisted on one side as he squinted. "Much too long to be an effective insult. Maybe you do need to go to class. Your brain is clearly degrading."

"Must be the company I keep."

He nodded. "That was better." He rose from the table and put his bowl in the sink.

"Put your bowl in the dishwasher. There's no maid coming to clean up after you."

"Obviously. Why would a maid come when you're here?"

I was going to kill him. It'd be worth the jail time to no longer have to share the world's oxygen with him.

"If you two are finished, can you both leave so I can take a nap?" Drew asked as he began the arduous task of lying down.

"No way. Get up. We're going."

"*We're* not going anywhere. *I'll* call an Uber and get myself to the appointment. I'm just going to rest my eyes for a second."

He started his descent again, so I was forced to close the distance between us and grab on to his shirt. As I tugged in the opposite direction gravity was pulling him, he squawked like an affronted seagull.

"What the hell are you doing? This is abuse," he yelled as he tried to resist my pull, which wouldn't have been hard had he not been injured.

Maybe manhandling him wasn't the best plan of action. I abruptly let go, afraid of hurting him. But that was an even worse idea because it caused him to flop down inelegantly.

"Oh shit," I said before covering my mouth with my hands. "Are you okay?"

"Why is it every time you try to help me, I end up falling over?"

I smiled meekly. "At least this time it was a soft landing."

"Tell that to my ribs," he grumbled.

He wasn't wrong, but his tone irritated me. Couldn't he see I was trying to help him?

"I said I was sorry."

"Yeah, so did Chris Brown."

"You did not just compare me to a batterer!"

Drew opened his mouth to retort but was interrupted

by a shrill whistle. We both turned to look at Brody, who was leaning on the low wall that separated the kitchen from the living room.

"As fun as this has been, can we all call a truce for a minute? Sophia, go to class. I'll take Drew to his appointment."

"I think a responsible adult should take him," I replied coolly.

"Like one who just dropped him on a couch? Or maybe the one who threw him onto the bathroom floor?"

"I didn't *throw* him," I muttered.

"For once, do the thing that makes sense instead of arguing about it forever just because it wasn't your idea."

"I don't do that." I totally did, but I'd be damned if I'd ever admit it to these jackholes. When I turned to look at Drew, he was smirking at me. "I don't."

Deny, deny, deny.

"Of course not. Have fun in class."

"You're both really annoying," I complained as I made my way toward the bedroom to get ready. I closed the door on their laughing.

Bastards.

DREW

I knew that waiting interminably for the doctor to see me was fairly standard medical procedure, but this had to be bordering on malpractice.

I'd already had to see a whole slew of doctors before I could leave the godforsaken hospital after I'd fucked up almost my entire body in the accident. One mishap had turned me into someone who had *specialists*. I was too young for this shit.

Had I been alone here, it might not have been so horrible, but waiting with Brody was awful. He had the patience of a gremlin and absolutely no chill. I'd seen people on speed sit stiller than him. His leg was bouncing so hard, his seat was shaking.

He hunched forward a bit before throwing himself back against the chair, making the thing bang against the wall.

"Dude, you want to wait outside or something?" I asked him. "I can text you when I'm done."

"Nah, I'm fine. Plus, Sophia would kill me if I left you here alone."

I scoffed. "She's not my keeper. You don't have to answer to her."

He gave me a look that called bullshit, and I felt myself grow indignant as I crossed my arms over my chest—a move that was less smooth with the cast on my arm.

"What? She's not."

He smirked as he reached forward to riffle through the magazines on the table.

"Whatever you say, dude."

He reclined back, holding a *Highlights* magazine, which made me realize how futile it was to argue with a man-child. After thumbing through it, he let out a guffaw. "Man, that Goofus and Gallant . . . classic. Do you have a pen?"

"No, and I'm pretty sure they don't want you writing in their magazines."

Brody shrugged and continued looking through the magazine. Seriously, how the fuck had he and Sophia come from the same gene pool?

The magazine kept him occupied for about another minute and a half, and then he tossed it onto the table, causing the glass top to clatter. Everyone in the room turned to look at us—a fact only I noticed because while I was busy apologizing to everyone with my eyes, Brody's focus was on me.

"So what's going on between you and my sister?" he asked.

"Nothing."

That single word came out of my mouth so defensively, I couldn't even be mad at the raised eyebrow he shot me in response.

"Seriously, we're just friends." Though I honestly wasn't even sure we were that. There was no name for a woman a guy had a shit ton of feelings for but had to pretend that he didn't while still depending on her for survival and as a faux-fiancée. Complicated didn't even begin to describe the shitshow that was my relationship with Sophia.

"Come on, man. I caught you two basically humping in the bathroom, which is really inconsiderate seeing as how I have to use it too."

"Dude, I *fell* on her. We weren't...humping." I said the last word on a whisper, a courtesy he hadn't afforded me when he declared it to the room seconds before.

"I think she was into it."

"What..." I shook my head, trying to extinguish the flicker of hope that maybe she *had* liked it. I was as fucked up as the dumbass talking to me. "She wasn't into it. Neither of us was. It was an unfortunate accident that I pray is never repeated, and I would appreciate it if we never spoke of it again."

"Why can't we speak of it? Are you embarrassed to

be with my little sister? You think you're better than her or something?"

My jaw nearly fell into my lap as I stuttered through a variety of sounds in an attempt to formulate a response, but before I was able to string anything together in a way that made sense, Brody smiled.

"I'm just fucking with you. On that last part at least. I do think there's something between you and Sophia, and I think my parents ruined it somehow, which isn't all that surprising considering they ruin everything that even slightly resembles a good time, but I digress. I just . . ."

He hesitated, looking unsure, which was a weird vibe for Brody since the guy oozed confidence, even when he had no right to it.

"I'm a pretty shitty brother, but that doesn't mean I don't care about her. And while my dad would love nothing more than for her to marry some investment broker who works sixty hours a week and drinks Johnnie Walker Blue Label, that guy will also hit his mid-forties and play a losing game of Russian Roulette with his life savings and a stripper named Chastity, and Sophia doesn't need the hassle. Not to mention that's not her type. She doesn't want a partner in a firm somewhere; she wants a partner in *life*. And the way you two look at each other sometimes, not to mention the fact that she's willing to play nursemaid to you when she would've told me to fuck all the way off if I asked her to get me a Band-Aid, makes me think that you could maybe fill that role."

He paused, looking down at his lap where his fingers were doing some kind of interpretive dance, before sighing heavily and looking back to me.

"What I'm trying to say is if you want that role, you

should fucking take it before she starts auditioning a bunch of fucking losers and you lose your chance. And if you don't want that role...then maybe you should hurry up and heal so you can get the hell out of her life. For good this time." He ended his speech with a definitive nod, as if to punctuate his feelings.

I sank back into my chair, staring straight ahead but not truly looking at anything. My brain replayed Brody's speech, and I tried to sort out how I felt about it.

For one, I wished I'd filmed it because no way would Sophia ever believe Brody had given me a protective older brother speech. Her world would be rocked, but I knew I'd never tell her about it. Not only would that be a betrayal to Brody, who'd let himself be vulnerable for a minute as he broadcasted the fact that he was actually an incredibly decent human being, but I also didn't want to have to discuss all the things he'd brought up.

Because he was right—at least partly. I wasn't sure that Sophia looked at me any special kind of way, but I had no doubt that I stared at her like she hung the fucking moon when I thought no one was looking.

I didn't try to delude myself—I could absolutely see sharing a life with her. And when I imagined it, it was perfect in its imperfection. We'd fight and argue and then have amazing make-up sex and then laugh about how stupid and stubborn we both were. It'd be fantastic.

If only I deserved to have it with her.

I knew there was going to be a time when she started dating someone else, and there was no way I was going to be able to handle that. So while I wished I could be option number one in Brody's scenario, that just wasn't going to be the case.

I needed to get some good news from this doctor and get back on my feet, literally and figuratively, so I could finally walk out of Sophia's life and let the poor girl start finding her happily ever after.

Chapter Nine

SOPHIA

"Where are your crutches?"

Drew's whole body jerked as he tightened his hold on the refrigerator door to keep himself standing.

"Jesus Christ, you nearly gave me a heart attack. And with my laundry list of other medical problems, I don't feel we need to add that to the list."

I guess my voice had been a little shriller than I'd intended.

He closed the door and leaned sideways until his hand came into contact with the counter, which he then used to pull the rest of his body toward it.

"The doctor told you not to walk without the crutches yet. Where are they?"

He shuffled a bit more to the right, glaring at me the entire time, until he could reach the crutches he'd left against the wall that was a solid ten feet from where he'd just been.

"I'd sarcastically refer to you as my mother, but she wouldn't be nearly as irritating as you."

I bit back my retort that that was the reason he was here in the first place, because being a petty bitch of that caliber wasn't a good look on anyone.

"Your leg is going to be messed up forever if you don't do what the doctor told you to do."

He rolled his eyes as he made his way past me—on crutches this time. He plodded over to the couch and plopped down.

"I never should've told you about the appointment."

"Yes, you should've. I can't help you if I don't know what's going on."

Though honestly, I kind of wished he hadn't told me about it. We'd both been high-strung since he'd come home, but for different reasons.

While Drew seemed to be angry that his injuries weren't healing as quickly as he hoped they would, I was a nervous wreck that he was going to have permanent injuries from the accident.

The doctor had been happy to report that there wasn't any lingering brain swelling or damage, and his lungs were also in good shape, despite his being on the ventilator. But while the plates and screws in his leg were holding fast, his orthopedist had very serious concerns about lasting nerve damage.

He'd said that Drew was healed enough to begin outpatient physical therapy—which he hadn't been to since leaving the hospital—and they'd hope that the issue resolved itself as he got stronger. Still, the doctor told him to prepare for a long road ahead.

His fractured arm and broken ribs were all healing as well as could be expected, which were positives I wished he'd been able to focus on more. Not that I could blame him for having a surly, depressed attitude. It couldn't have been easy hearing that he might never walk normally again.

"I'm tired of needing help," he muttered, his voice cracking a bit at the end.

I swear, if that man hadn't already broken my heart, those words would've done it. Not so much what he'd said but how he'd said it. He sounded so . . . lost. And so unbelievably sad.

Drew wasn't this person. At least not the Drew I'd gotten to know. That Drew was funny and upbeat and happy. It made me feel useless that I couldn't help him regain some of that.

Or maybe I could.

"I need to make a phone call," I said as I hustled to the bedroom.

"Good talk," I heard him mumble sarcastically.

I sent up a silent prayer that my idea worked, because the miserable jackass squatting on my brother's couch was getting on my nerves.

DREW

I'd been flicking through channels ever since Sophia escaped to her room to "make a phone call." Not that I could blame her for running away from me. I knew I was being a moody jerk, but I didn't know how to stop.

I'd been taking care of myself for a long time, and having to depend on people was wearing on me. I hated being a burden, especially on Sophia, who really didn't owe me anything. So hearing that I was still a long way from being able to get back on my feet—literally—was a tough pill to swallow.

Add in the fact that I was going stir-crazy in Brody's apartment, and it was a recipe that had turned me into a miserable fuck. I knew if I asked, they'd take me out so I could get some fresh air, but then I would be even more of a needy puppy. Everything just … sucked.

My pity party was interrupted by a knock on the door. Maybe Sophia had called one of her friends to come over.

"Soph? Someone's at the door."

I heard her coming down the hallway before I saw her. She barely looked at me as she hurried over.

"I would've answered it, but I was worried you'd castrate me for getting up."

She paused in unlocking the door to shoot me a withering look that made me internally cringe. It was like I couldn't help but be an asshole at this point.

She turned the deadbolt and pulled the door open, gesturing at her guests to enter with a flourish of her hand.

"Please do something about him," she said.

My eyes widened as I saw who she was ushering into the apartment.

Aniyah!

"Wow. Sophia said you looked like shit, but I wasn't expecting you to be *this* bad."

Despite Aniyah's harsh words, I couldn't stop the smile from spreading over my face. "Well, I almost died. What's your excuse?"

"Ooh, Imposter Boy's got jokes."

"He ain't wrong, though," Xander said as he stepped around Aniyah and came over to me, sticking out his hand for me to clasp as he leaned down for a bro-hug. Toby followed close behind, a broad smile on his face that I couldn't help but return.

Aniyah walked over to a chair and sat down. "You look like

you smell, so I'm not hugging you."

I opened my arms toward her. "Come on. You know you wanna."

"I know no such thing."

Raising my eyebrows and widening my smile at her with my arms still outstretched caused her to shoot her eyes toward heaven, but she stepped forward and leaned down to embrace me.

Her arms wrapped around me much tighter than I'd expected, but it was exactly what I'd needed: a firm hug from someone who wasn't afraid I would break.

"Don't ever pull some stupid white boy shit like this again," she whispered fiercely in my ear.

"I won't. I promise."

She gave me one final squeeze before pulling free and subtly swiping at her eyes, a move all of us pretended not to notice. When she turned back to her chair, Xander was sitting in it, smirking.

She stared at him for a moment.

He didn't move.

"Have I ever mentioned that my great-aunt in New Orleans makes voodoo dolls of annoying dickheads from the skin of slaughtered swine?"

Her not-so-thinly-veiled threat only made Xander waggle his eyebrows at her.

She huffed before muttering something under her breath and sitting on the opposite end of the couch from me.

I looked around at my former project-mates who'd become close friends of mine last semester. Friends I'd dropped when I'd run from Sophia. I was glad they'd all been willing and able to come see me. I'd missed them more than I'd allowed myself to think about.

Toby, who was sitting between us, leaned toward Aniyah.

"Does your aunt really do that?"

She looked at him blandly. "What do you think?"

He looked at her for a second before righting himself and averting his gaze. Poor Toby—such a simple soul.

"So what are you guys doing here?" I asked, excitement slipping into my voice for the first time in months. I was happy as fuck to see them.

"Sophia called us and said you were being a pain in the ass," Aniyah explained. "Which didn't sound like you at all. Though I guess that makes sense since, as it turns out, we don't actually know you. So, *Drew*, why don't you tell us a bit about yourself?"

I swung my gaze to Sophia, who was leaning against the wall with a dry look on her face.

My mind flitted back to when Aniyah had called me Imposter Boy when she'd come in. I hadn't thought much about it at the time, but it became clear that Sophia had told them at least some of the truth. Though she didn't seem keen on helping me explain any further.

"Yeah, uh, well . . . this is awk—"

Another knock interrupted my attempt to figure out where the hell to start. Sophia answered it, and a disheveled Carter bustled through the doorway.

"What are you doing here?" Sophia asked as she closed the door.

"T-Man texted and said he was coming over here to see Brody/Drew, and there was no way I was missing this explanation."

"Who's T-Man?" Sophia asked.

That question was answered when Carter walked over to Toby, who stood so they could perform some sort of intricate handshake that looked like it should grant them entrance to an underground Boy Scout lair.

Carter then grabbed a chair from the kitchen, dragged it into the living room, and parked himself in it, staring at all of us as if he expected us to perform some sort of song and dance number.

"As you were," he said.

I stared at him for a second, trying to figure out how I'd become such good friends with such an odd person. When I gave up on that, I looked at the others.

"How much do you guys know?"

"Sophia gave me a brief overview when she called," Aniyah said. "And I relayed all that to the boys. Basically that her brother Brody paid you to be him for a semester and that when you'd finished your job as his doppelganger, you'd decided to assume the identity of Evel Knievel and almost got yourself killed."

"That's . . . about accurate." I turned my attention to Carter. "You never told Toby about any of this?" They'd clearly grown close, if their Hogwarts handshake was anything to judge by, so I was surprised that Carter hadn't shared anything with him.

Carter shrugged. "Wasn't my story to tell."

Funnily enough, it didn't really feel like mine to tell either. It was mostly Brody's, but I supposed part of it belonged to the guy who'd lived his life for him—a guy who seemed so different from the one who could barely get his busted ass off the couch.

I cleared my throat before beginning. "Yeah, so I pretended to be Brody last semester. I didn't mean to lie to you, but it was kind of part and parcel with the whole thing. So while I'm sorry I wasn't honest, I also wouldn't do anything differently."

I couldn't help but let my eyes stray to Sophia when I said that last part. No matter how things had ended, I'd never regret getting to know her.

"But then Sophia's parents figured out what was going on, and that was it. My life as Brody was over, so I went back to being Drew Nolan."

"And Drew Nolan thought it was a good idea to ghost the friends he'd made?" Aniyah asked, her tone stern and almost reprimanding. "Carter and Sophia both said you'd left but didn't say more than that. You just left us . . . hanging."

"No," I said softly, shaking my head. "I just didn't know what else to do. I guess I felt like I didn't deserve you. Any of you." I flicked my eyes in Sophia's direction long enough to see her fidget.

"Hmm, and here I thought you were smart," Toby said, sounding like he was truly baffled by my idiocy.

I huffed a laugh. "I guess I really played the part well, then."

"Brody is *not* smart. The fact that anyone believed he was just shows how much you sucked at being him." Sophia's words were laced with humor, but her face was solemn for reasons I couldn't figure out.

"You stayed in touch with Carter," Aniyah pointed out, distracting me from staring at Sophia's annoyingly gorgeous face.

"No, he didn't," Carter answered. "I stayed in touch with him." He smiled at me. "I'm hard to get rid of."

"Well, so are we, now that we know where to find you." Aniyah managed to make a promise of friendship sound menacing, and I felt something loosen inside of me and settle into place at how fiercely she seemed to want to be my friend.

"I'm good with that," I replied, my voice rough.

She nodded once, and that was that.

"Can we come back to the part where you impersonated a student for a semester and almost no one knew?" Xander said. "Because that may just beat my library story."

Carter visibly shuddered. "Why you gotta ruin a perfectly good time by mentioning the library?"

"Nothing will ever beat the story of you burning down the school's library," Aniyah scolded. "Stop trying to lessen your survivor's guilt with false comparisons."

"The only guilt I have is that that librarian didn't throw herself on the stacks in sacrifice to the reference gods."

"So many books lost," Toby lamented sadly.

As I looked around at this pack of misfits I'd only met because of a lie, I realized it had been a long time since anything had felt this real.

Chapter Ten

DREW

"I'd like to let all of you know that I did it."

Pausing my arm as I lifted the spoonful of Raisin Bran to my mouth, I looked up to see Brody grinning ear to ear, his arms high and wide in the air like he was officiating a football game and had just decided a field goal was good.

I looked around the apartment I knew was empty except for me and now Brody.

"Who's all of you, and what did you do?"

Brody lowered his arms and looked down the hall. "Sophia, get out here!"

"She's in class."

I'm not sure why, but he seemed surprised by her whereabouts.

"Hmm," he said, seeming to contemplate something. "I guess I'll have to tell her later, then."

I lifted my eyebrows as I waited for whatever news he was so excited to share.

"I got a job," he said so slowly that I knew I was supposed

to seem more impressed than I actually was.

Still, he'd gotten a job to help *me*, which was pretty freakin' awesome.

"Congratulations, man! That didn't take long."

"Thanks." He took a seat across from me at the small table. "I can't wait to tell Soph. She'll never believe it."

"I think she just likes bustin' your balls. I'm sure she doesn't actually think you're incapable of getting a job."

"I'm not," he confirmed with a proud smile.

"So where is it?"

"Marco's. You're lookin' at their new delivery boy. I start tonight."

"Nice." I finished my cereal and hopped over to the sink to rinse my bowl before putting it in the dishwasher. "That'll give you a little freedom since you won't be stuck in the same place when you're working. After being hospitalized for a month and now basically confined to a one-bedroom apartment—no offense—I definitely know what it feels like to go stir-crazy when you're in one place for too long."

"That's what I figured. Plus, I'm hoping we get some free food out of the deal."

"For sure. I didn't really plan on eating cereal for lunch, but it's one of the only things I can make easily on crutches. I thought there was some lasagna left over from what Sophia made yesterday, but I didn't see any."

I opened the door to the fridge again to double-check.

"Oh, um, I ate that this morning. Sorry."

Shutting the door, I turned around and worked my way across the small kitchen, using the countertops for support because it was easier than using crutches if I was only going a few feet.

"You ate lasagna for breakfast? Who are you? Garfield?"

Brody laughed. "I guess that'd make you Odie, then." Before I could say anything, he added, "Or maybe Sophia's Odie, because she's the idiot."

"You guys are horrible to each other," I said on a laugh. "Have you ever gotten along?"

Brody seemed to think hard about his answer as he headed into the kitchen. He pulled out the peanut butter, jelly, and bread. I thought I saw him open his mouth a few times like he was about to tell me about a time he remembered, but he never actually shared anything.

"Not really" was his only answer.

Though I suspected much of his interaction with Sophia that I'd witnessed hadn't had much malice on either side.

"So you wanna come with me tonight?" Brody asked through a bite of his sandwich.

"Come where?" I wasn't exactly in any shape to be doing anything. I couldn't even bathe myself.

"My first delivery shift. They told me I could come in for two hours tonight just to get a feel for things."

His eyes lit up like he was inviting me to go on a ride-along in an undercover police car and not asking me if I wanted to sit shotgun while he brought wings to college kids.

How could I say no?

"Sure. I guess. It'll be fun," I told him. Which wasn't exactly a lie since I hadn't done much of anything except drown in my own self-pity for the better part of the last two months.

My answer made Brody look even more excited. "Sweet. We'll leave a few minutes before five."

"When's your shift start?"

"Five," he said, like the question was a ridiculous one.

"I'll take some time to get down the stairs and into your car. I don't wanna make you late for your first day. Figured you'd wanna get there a little early to make a good impression."

"Oh, yeah. Good point. Ten of, then?"

I tried to suppress my amusement. I couldn't help but think that the impossible feat wasn't Brody getting a job. It was *keeping* it.

SOPHIA

My day had been filled with classes. Even though they were interesting to me because they were part of my marketing major curriculum, they were practically back to back, which left me with no break for lunch.

I'd eaten a small box of raisins for breakfast when I'd walked across campus to my ten o'clock class, but I hadn't had anything since.

By the time I got to the sorority house, I was starving. I grabbed a bag of thin pretzels to munch on while we waited for the food we'd ordered.

It was the first time since winter break that most of the girls were in the house at the same time, and even though this month's meeting had been more of a formality or tradition than it had been a necessity, I was thankful for it. It felt good to relax, listen to some of the girls' stories about their boyfriends, and just talk about meaningless gossip.

"I think Xavier's gonna propose soon," Gina said, though she sounded more frightened than excited.

The room was filled with *Reallys?* and *Seriouslys?* as we all were no doubt trying to wrap our brains around the frat boy proposing. He was nice enough, from what I knew of him, but he didn't exactly scream commitment.

"What makes you think that?" Aamee asked.

"I was going through his things before break," she said, like that was totally normal and acceptable, "and I saw a small box from a nice jewelry store. I didn't open it because I wanted my gifts to be a surprise—"

Emma's eyes softened, most likely in sympathy for Xavier's breach of privacy. "So why were you snooping, then?"

"I wasn't sure what he'd gotten me or even if he'd gotten me anything. We've only been together since September. I wanted to know what I should get him."

"And that decision was based on what he got you?" Emma asked.

"Exactly. But then when he gave me my gifts, none of them were jewelry. Just some shirts and leggings. I mean, I like them, but I bought him an Apple Watch. Not exactly the same price point."

"Asshole," Aamee said, causing Gina's head to snap back like she'd been hit. "Not you, him," she clarified.

"He's an asshole because he's gonna propose?" Gina asked, pulling both legs onto the couch so she could curl up at the end.

"No. He's an asshole because the jewelry wasn't for you." Aamee'd said it like the statement was an obvious one, even though she seemed to be the only one who'd thought of it. "He probably has some girl back home he's stringing along so he has a steady piece when he's home on breaks."

"Or maybe it was for his mom or something," I offered quickly.

"Yeah, maybe." Gina didn't sound too convinced. She

looked around at the rest of us, which caused all of us to look around at each other in response. The room was eerily quiet until Gina finally spoke again. "Which one of you can I trust to be my shovel buddy?"

"What are you talking about?"

"God, are you gonna make me say it out loud? What if Siri's listening?"

"Huh?" I was getting even more confused, and by the looks of the rest of the group, so was everyone else.

Gina practically groaned before whispering, "Like someone who can help me bury his body if something were to happen to it."

"I'm in," Aamee said without hesitation.

Looking at her phone, Emma raised her hand until finally Gina realized she wasn't going to speak until she was called on.

"Yes, Emma?"

"That's not what a shovel buddy is. According to Urban Dictionary, a shovel buddy is 'A close friend who, in the event of your death, will remove any and all embarrassing personal items from your home you do not wish family to see, i.e. pornography, sex toys, or drug paraphernalia.' It also says you should alert us with a loud horn." Emma looked up from her phone to see everyone's eyes fixed on her. "Some guy named Steve Morrison from a radio show called Preston & Steve wrote it, so I'm not sure how accurate it is."

"Well," Gina said casually, "I may need one of those too."

The group erupted in laughter, and when we finally calmed down a bit, Gina said, "Seriously though. I can't let my dad see what's in my nightstand."

The doorbell interrupted our second bout of laughter, and I rose first because I was still starving. "I'll get it," I said, grabbing the cash from the table near the door.

I was so focused on the pizzas in the delivery boy's hand, it took me until I handed him the money to notice Brody was the one I'd handed it to.

"What are *you* doing here?"

"Uh, delivering pizzas."

"I mean why?"

The smile he'd had already broadened. "I got a job. You proud of me?"

"We'll see if you keep it."

"I will," he said. "Oh, and thanks for the tip."

As he walked down our front steps and toward his car, I thought about chasing him down and yanking the tip from his hands. But then I remembered the reason he'd gotten the job to begin with.

And that reason was currently reclined back in the passenger's seat with a hand covering his gorgeous face.

Aamee grabbed two of the pizzas from me and set them down on the coffee table. I closed the door and leaned against it before setting the other two on top of the pizzas Aamee had just put down.

"Who was that?" Bethany asked. "He was cute."

"The delivery guy. I'll grab some plates and napkins," I said, wanting to get away from the girls and any further questions.

"Do you know him?" someone else asked.

"Yeah, it definitely seemed like you knew him," another voice said.

"I don't. Not really." I set the napkins and plates down next to the pizzas when I returned to the living room.

"Yes, you do," Aamee practically sang.

Speaking of shovels, I wished I had one so I could hit her over the head with it. Instead, I just glared at her, my eyes hopefully warning her to keep her mouth shut.

"She has a class with him." Aamee smiled sweetly at me.

"Right. Yeah, but I don't really know much about him."

"What's his name?" Bethany asked.

"Br…Brian." I'd known not to say Brody, but for some reason, my mind couldn't think of a name that began with any other sound.

"With an *i* or a *y*?"

"Does it matter?"

"Of course," some of the other girls agreed.

"A *y* is way hotter," Emma added.

"I'm pretty sure it's an *i*. Sorry," I said with a shrug.

Some disappointed *Ohs* carried through the room, but the general consensus seemed to be that the spelling didn't make him any less hot. It just didn't make him hot*er* than he already was. The entire conversation would've made me lose my appetite if I hadn't been so famished.

The irony wasn't lost on me that people thought my pretend brother was hot last semester and then those same people, along with much of the campus, thought I was sleeping with him. And now they were discussing at length the things they wanted to do to my real brother all while thinking he was someone I barely knew.

I almost spit out my water when Bethany asked me if I had any intention of "pursuing" him. It made me feel awkward in a new way. And I was familiar with awkward.

"No. Definitely not," I assured her. "Go for it."

I didn't think Bethany was Brody's type—not that I knew if he even had a type—but I figured if she wanted to go out with him, I wasn't going to stop her. Brody could definitely do worse than Bethany.

"Actually," Aamee said, "I think Brian and I kind of connected the first time we met. But I'll let you know if it doesn't work out." She smiled at Bethany, but the gesture was more of a warning than a comfort.

Fucking Aamee.

Chapter Eleven

SOPHIA

"How do you think you did on the test?"

It took me longer than it should have to realize the voice was directed at me. It wasn't until I looked up from putting my laptop and notebook in my bag that I noticed a guy two seats down staring at me expectantly. His eyes were almost a turquoise, and it made me wonder if they changed color depending on the environment like some sort of genetic mood ring.

There was a bit of scruff around his jaw, and he rubbed a hand over it. It wasn't enough that I thought it was there intentionally—more like he just hadn't bothered to shave in the last twenty-four hours or so. I wasn't sure exactly why I was analyzing his hygiene habits, but I was. His dark hair was shaved close on the sides and styled neatly to the side with a hard part.

I couldn't deny he was good-looking. Very, actually. He was handsome in a traditional sense—strong jaw, broad chest, and muscular with just enough meat on his bones to make me think his physique was more due to natural selection and an active lifestyle than hours spent at the gym.

When he smiled at me, looking amused, I noticed a small gap between two of his teeth—the first hint of a flaw that somehow only made him more adorable.

Under normal circumstances I would've noticed him before now, especially because he'd most likely been sitting near me since the beginning of the semester. But my mind had been preoccupied with all things Drew...

Will he be okay? What more can I do to help him? Will we ever be even close to what we were before my world came crashing in?

It seemed extreme to think of it that way, but I couldn't help it. One minute, Drew and I were...something, and the next we were nothing at all.

And the more I thought about the past few weeks, the more I realized that his health struggle had been a distraction—probably to both of us. It allowed us to have a purpose that included the other without having to actually focus on what had happened between us.

"The test?" the cute guy said with a small laugh.

"Oh, yeah, sorry. I don't know." I pushed some hair away from my face. "I studied, but I feel like econ isn't really in my wheelhouse."

He adjusted his bag on his shoulder. "That's how I feel about most subjects." He let out a self-deprecating laugh. "I'm Justin, by the way. I think we've had a few classes together the last year or so."

"Oh yeah, I think you're right," I told him, though I had no idea if that was true.

Justin kind of stood there, seeming unsure of what to say.

I was surprised at how shy he seemed, but I wasn't sure why I would assume that a good-looking guy wouldn't be reserved. Maybe I'd become used to Drew's confidence and his casual attitude under pressure. He was so easygoing but had ambition and passion for things that mattered.

Except for me.

"So I guess I'll see you Wednesday?" I tried to sound upbeat, but Justin seemed to take it for what it was: a dismissal disguised as a polite *see you later.*

I was unfocused for the rest of the day, and by the time I'd gone through my last class of the day and walked back to Brody's apartment, my mind was a tornado of questions and emotions.

Talking to Justin hadn't made me realize my feelings for Drew. They'd always been there and would most likely be there for the foreseeable future. But Justin had caused me to examine my current living arrangement.

I was rooming with my brother, who I despised half the time, and my ex-whatever-he-was because I told myself he needed me when the truth was he most likely didn't.

The longer I "helped" Drew, the longer it would take me to get over him. So while my living with him probably made his life easier, the ugly truth was that it would make mine harder. And if there was one person I had to look out for, it was myself.

I opened the door to the apartment with such urgency that I woke Drew up. He'd been asleep on the couch and sat up abruptly—well, as much as he was able to with a cast on his arm and leg.

"What? What's wrong?" he asked, still groggy. He rubbed at his eyes and yawned widely. His hair was tousled in a way that made him look more rugged than he typically did, and the

T-shirt he wore was torn around the collar. Why did he have to look so damn good when he should've looked so damn bad?

Part of me wanted to go to him, kiss him, and tell him I'd missed him even though he'd been right here with me the past few weeks. But the stronger, more rational part of me thankfully won out.

"Everything."

I let out a sigh that helped to release some of the tension I'd been holding and moved slowly over to the chair near the couch. I couldn't risk sitting on the same piece of furniture as Drew because I didn't trust my body to control itself when I was within reach of him.

Placing my bag down gently at my feet, I took in his expression. Concern? Curiosity maybe?

"Everything's wrong. Or I don't know. Maybe it isn't."

"I'm confused."

"*You're* confused? You left without so much as an explanation."

His shoulders fell at my words, and he seemed to deflate. I was sure out of all the things I could've said, that was one he didn't expect. He was quiet, his head hanging down as he focused on the floor. There was a long silence, but I refused to fill it. He's the one who needed to talk.

Finally he seemed to realize that I wasn't going to let him off the hook.

He looked up and said, "I explained it that day."

"That's bullshit, and you know it." My voice was too calm for my words, and I knew with near certainty that he could hear the sadness in it. "Suddenly telling me I'm too good for you and packing up your stuff isn't an explanation. It's a coward's way out."

"So you're calling me a coward?" He didn't sound mad, just offended.

"Yeah. I guess I am. I was scared to visit you in the hospital because I had no idea if you really wanted me there, and I don't want to have this conversation right now because I'm afraid to hear the truth. But I'm here anyway. I've spent the better part of the last few weeks helping you however I knew how, and now I'm asking you for a simple explanation and you can't even give me one."

Leaning back against the couch, he rubbed a hand over his face and dropped his head back so he was staring at the ceiling. "I told you you're too good for me because you are."

Shaking my head, I let out a soft laugh to let Drew know how ridiculous I thought his comment was.

"No, you're wrong." I waited until his eyes locked with mine because I needed him to know that what I was about to say was the truth. "I'm not too good for you. We're good *together*."

He ran his tongue over his bottom lip before biting down on it as he seemed to be letting the weight of my words sink in. Maybe he really did think he wasn't worthy of me, but he was so fucking wrong. If anyone wasn't worthy, it was me. He was gorgeous and sweet and . . . sitting too far away from me. I needed to be closer.

As I approached him, he reached out to grab my hand and guide me down to sit beside him, our fingers intertwined in a way they hadn't been since before the crash. He used to hold my hand like this when we'd lie in bed. He'd look at my fingers, softly tracing the paths where they linked to his. This felt so comfortable, so right, and I wondered if it felt the same for Drew.

"I know," he finally said. "Of all the things I've done in my life, leaving you was one of the hardest." He let go of my hand and brought his slowly up my arm until he reached the back of my neck. Fisting my hair in his hand gently, he let his head drop against mine so our foreheads were touching. "We were good together."

"Then why aren't we?" I whispered. "Together, I mean."

"Because I'm a fucking idiot," he answered softly before his lips touched mine.

DREW

From the time Sophia had entered my hospital room that day, I'd wanted to kiss her. Who was I kidding? I'd wanted to kiss her from the second she'd entered my life.

And somehow I'd been convinced that being with her was a mistake—one that would ruin her future and maybe her life. Her father had been concerned about my presence in Brody's life too, but I couldn't find it in myself to care about him.

I'd left because if Mr. Mason was right, there was no way I could live with the guilt of knowing I'd brought Sophia down when she deserved to have someone who'd lift her up.

How does that saying go? If you love someone, let them go?

But now that I had her, literally in my arms, my mouth doing things to hers I'd only fantasized about since I'd lost her, I wondered how I could've ever willingly given this up. Mr. Mason thought I was a dumbass, and apparently he hadn't been wrong.

Though as I slid my hand over her and under her shirt and

began to slowly inch it higher as I rediscovered the feel of her skin against mine, I also knew this wasn't how it should be.

I swore my heart actually hurt when I pulled away, but I was used to pain, both physical and emotional, especially lately. As soon as our lips separated, I wanted to bring them back together until every part of our bodies connected.

She was so fucking sexy, so fucking perfect. And I was so fucking naïve if I thought we could pick up where we left off.

We needed to restart. And restarting our relationship when I was trying to restart my life was asking for failure.

"Can we wait?" I asked, breathless after only three words.

Looking like she was unsure of how she wanted to respond, Sophia just swallowed before tucking her hair behind one ear and wrapping it over her other shoulder. She straightened her shirt, attempting to pull herself together like we hadn't both been turned on, and stiffened her posture.

"Sure. Yeah, of course. Are you in pain or . . . We can wait until you're feeling better. I shouldn't have—"

"No, um, nothing hurts. It's just that . . . God, this is so hard." I inhaled deeply and let the air settle into my chest before speaking again. "I already fucked up once, and I can't let that happen again. You're right. We're good together. But we're not gonna be good together when I'm like this." I looked down at my body, casts, scars, and faded bruises. "I can't concentrate on getting us to a good place when I need to get myself to one."

"It's not your responsibility to get us to a good place."

"Yes, it is. I need to fix what's broken. What *I* broke," I added. I knew I sounded like a martyr, but I meant it. The garden needed more than just the seeds to grow.

"Okay," she said, probably knowing it was an argument she wasn't going to win. "I'll be here whenever you're ready, then." Rubbing her hands over her thighs, she began to stand, but I grabbed her hand before she could go anywhere.

"I'd understand if you wanna move on. You shouldn't have to wait for me." But I sure as shit hoped she would.

She smiled a little smile that only showed on one corner of her mouth.

"Maybe not. But I'll let my offer stand anyway."

I really *didn't* deserve her.

Chapter Twelve

DREW

"Why do you keep unbuckling your seat belt?"

I looked over at Brody in annoyance. "Because I keep having to shift around to get comfortable, and your stupid seat belt keeps locking up and crushing my arm."

"Well, get fucking over it. My car keeps beeping at me because you won't keep the stupid thing buckled."

Sucking in an audible breath, I slid the belt into the socket. "If you stopped making me buckle it in, it would stop beeping eventually."

Brody put the next address in his GPS and pulled away from the curb. "You'd think someone who'd been in a near-fatal accident would take more safety precautions."

"What can I say? I like to live on the wild side."

"Yeah, well, you go through the windshield, and you'll be living on the dead side."

I felt my face scrunch up in confusion. "That makes no sense."

Brody sighed. "Dude, I'm delivering pizzas because I'm

not qualified to do anything better. Expect smart shit from someone else."

There was really no way to respond to that, so I sat back and enjoyed the ride. I'd gone out on deliveries with Brody a few times, and it demonstrated how pathetic my life was that I enjoyed it.

"Oh man, I think the next place is a frat. Someone better be conscious enough to pay for these pizzas."

I watched the houses whirl by as he drove past, the Greek letters affixed to them soundly. Part of me wondered what it was like to belong to something like that while another part thought it was strange how content these people all seemed to be with sharing an identity—like a cult with nonlethal Kool-Aid.

Sophia seemed to both love it and hate it simultaneously. Though she also seemed to feel that way about me, so maybe that was just who she was as a person.

"This is it," Brody said as he stopped in front of a large stone house that appeared to have every light on inside.

There weren't people spilling out the front door and I didn't hear music pumping from the house, so maybe Brody wouldn't have a hard time getting someone to pay the tab.

"Be right back." He exited, only to pull open the back door and extract eight boxes. "I'll have to come back for the others."

"Others? How many did they order?"

"Twenty."

"Jesus Christ," I muttered as Brody kicked the door closed and ambled to the front door, thumping on it with his foot since his hands were full.

I watched as the door flew open and three guys filled the entrance, gesturing wildly and laughing. One took the pizzas and disappeared. Brody gestured over his shoulder, probably telling the guys that he had the rest of their order in his car.

Another guy, who was wearing cargo shorts and a striped collared shirt, seemed to wave him off and yelled into the house. Within seconds, three other guys appeared. Collared-shirt guy gestured toward the car, and the three men started toward me. When they opened the back door, I turned as much as I could to see them.

"Hey, dude, thanks for the pizzas," one of them said.

"No problem," I replied, because what was I supposed to say? It wasn't like I'd made them or was even supposed to be in the car while Brody delivered them, but there was no point in explaining either of those things to these guys.

They were gone in seconds, carrying the rest of the pizzas into the house. I wished I'd thought to make sure they were only taking their order, but there wasn't anything I could do about it after the fact.

Brody stood talking to collared-shirt guy for a bit longer before accepting a wad of cash, offering a wave, and finally returning to the car.

"What took so long?" I asked as he settled behind the wheel.

"Aw, miss me?"

"You wish."

"We gotta make a quick stop before we head back to get the next batch of deliveries," he said as he started driving. "Those guys gave me an extra hundred bucks to go get them more beer and some Black & Milds. They said I could keep the change." After a few seconds, his face lit up. "I'm going to get them Advil and Gatorade too. Go above and beyond to meet their hangover needs and all that shit."

I shook my head as if to make sense of his words. "So, they asked you to be their errand boy, and you agreed?"

He briefly took his eyes off the road to glare at me. "Yes."

"Why?"

He shrugged. "Why not? And I can probably get what they need for half of what they gave me. Fifty bucks is fifty bucks."

"Isn't that a line from a movie?" I asked. It sounded familiar.

"Yes, it's from the comedic tragedy entitled *The Sad, Sad, Sad Life of Brody Mason and His Even Sadder Friend Drew.*"

"Hmm, I feel like that title needs work."

"It was called *Dipshits* for short."

"Ah, much better." I shifted around to try to get my leg more comfortable. It was starting to ache from being cooped up in the car for so long. "Seriously, though, you do realize you don't need the money, right?"

I mean, granted, the guy had been dodging his parents for months, but it wasn't like they'd cut him off.

"I don't, but you do."

I felt... touched. "You don't need to knock yourself out on my account. It's more than enough that you're working this job in the first place. You don't need to go to more trouble on top of that." My voice was soft and heartfelt because I really appreciated what he was doing.

Not only had he opened his home to me and gotten a job to help support me, but now he was also running side gigs just to earn more money for me. I wasn't sure what I'd done to deserve friends like the ones I'd met at Lazarus, but I needed to get my head out of my ass and stop taking them for granted.

"Jesus Christ, stop looking at me with hearts in your eyes," he snapped, breaking me out of my sentimental inner-musings. "I didn't really do it for you. It was a rush...those guys looking at me all desperate and then like I was their savior when I said I could help them out—for a price. I was like the fucking Godfather of booze and cancer sticks."

So much for all those good feelings. I scoffed as I turned my attention back out the window.

"You're ridiculous."

"I know."

We were mostly quiet while Brody got the requested—and unrequested—items and returned them to the frat house. The guys all high-fived Brody, and the dope was grinning like some kind of loon at the attention.

It made me sad for him in a way—he was clearly basking in the adoration, and it wasn't hard to understand why. His own sister never missed an opportunity to remind him what a fuckup he was, and his parents seemed to have pretty low expectations.

Brody Mason was fulfilling a prophecy foretold by the people who were supposed to love him the most. But in the few instances where people had put some genuine faith in him, he'd come through: first with getting this job and now with the frat guys. It might not have been much to many, but it was something to him.

When he came back to the car, he sat in the driver's seat, hands flexing on the wheel as he stared out the windshield.

"You okay, man?" I asked.

He jarred a bit, as if he'd forgotten I was there for a second.

"Yeah, yeah, great," he said as he put the car in drive and pulled onto the street.

We traveled in silence for a while as Brody drove us back to the restaurant. It was a task that was especially uncomfortable for me because I'd have to lean my seat all the way back to stay out of sight since he wasn't supposed to have passengers while he was working.

When we were still about five minutes from the restaurant, Brody pulled over to the side of the road, threw the car in park, and looked over at me intently.

"I have an idea, and I want you to hear me out."

Brody's track record with ideas wasn't stellar, but the serious way he was regarding me, almost as if he were begging me to give him a shot, had me holding back any snarky comments.

Instead, I uttered, "Okay, lay it on me."

SOPHIA

"Drew? Brody? You guys here?" I shut the apartment door behind me and looked around for any signs of life.

Last night, we'd had a long planning meeting at the sorority house for an event next Friday, so I'd decided to stay there instead of coming back to Brody's apartment late at night. And while it hadn't been the first time I'd spent a night away, I was still anxious about not being able to check on Drew—a feeling I felt all the more acutely since we'd shared that kiss a week ago.

Maybe it wasn't fair to say I wanted to check on him. My motives weren't necessarily fueled by feelings of caregiving. Truth be told, I wanted to be near him, and saying it was to ensure he was okay was easier than admitting that I simply felt better—more me—when I was somewhere in his orbit.

"We're in here" came a yell from the bedroom.

I plopped my things down on a chair and made my way

toward them. When I pushed the door all the way open, I saw them both leaning against the headboard, hunched together as they looked at a laptop. There were a couple of notebooks and stray pieces of paper littered over the comforter.

If I hadn't known better, I'd have said they were doing homework, but neither of them was enrolled in any classes, and Brody had never given his assignments anywhere near the level of focus he was currently giving the laptop.

"What are you doing?"

"Starting a business," Brody answered gruffly. "You're not allowed to be part of it. Goodbye."

My hands went to my hips in irritation. "Like I'd want to go into business with you."

"That works out, then. Later."

Neither of them looked in my direction, and while that was incredibly infuriating, it also made me curious as hell.

"It's not illegal, is it?"

That made Drew's head pop up, and he graced me with a small smile. "Nah." Then his face contorted a bit as he seemed to mull something over. "At least I don't think so."

"That's encouraging," I muttered. "Spill."

They exchanged a look that did *not* make me feel better. They looked like two people trying to communicate telepathically when they didn't even speak the same language.

"You tell her," Drew said.

"Why do I have to tell her?"

"Because she's *your* sister." I ignored the fact that Drew didn't say this like it was a good thing.

"But she's your"—Brody waved his hand around vaguely—"whatever."

"She expects bad ideas from you," Drew whispered harshly.

"Are you guys unaware that I can hear you?" I asked, though they both ignored me.

"All the more reason for you to tell her. Because this is an amazing idea."

Frustrated by my lot in life that put me in the direct path of these two toddlers, I took a few steps toward the bed and grabbed the laptop.

"Hey," they both yelled in unison.

"Shut up." I looked at the screen, trying to make sense of what I was seeing. It was a website—a very ugly website with weird fonts and an orange, blue, and green color scheme. The top said *Nite Bites*, and there was a rambling mission statement underneath that said something about "servicing men and women without prejudice."

Glancing over at them, I asked, "Are you guys becoming vampire rent boys?"

Drew groaned. "I told you the website was unclear."

"It's just a rough draft. We can fix it later."

I dropped the laptop on the bed. "Seriously, what's going on?"

Drew scrubbed his good hand over his face. "Brody had this idea—"

"Which you're totally into," Brody interrupted.

"Which I've come around to," Drew amended. "I wasn't a fan at first, but the more we talked about it, the more viable the idea seemed. Anyway, when Brody and I were out delivering pizzas tonight—"

"Are you still doing that?" I asked. "You're going to get him fired."

Drew glared. "Do you want to hear this or not?"

I held my hands up in a placating gesture and waited for him to continue.

"He had a delivery at a frat, and the guys there gave him some money to run to the store and pick up a few things for them." He paused, as if he could tell I desperately wanted to throw my two cents in, but I managed to restrain myself. "They tipped like fifty percent because they were so grateful. That's when Brody came up with the idea for Nite Bites, a service that would deliver care packages to people with things they were either too lazy to get themselves or needed last-minute and could benefit from having them delivered quickly."

"Just think about it," Brody added eagerly. "How many times have you woken up with a hangover and realized you were out of Advil or Gatorade or whatever? And you end up just going without because you can't pry yourself out of bed to go get any? We could solve that problem and make a profit while doing it."

It was perhaps the most excited I'd ever seen him, which almost made me feel bad that I was about to dash his dreams.

It wasn't that I thought it was a horrible idea necessarily, but I also didn't think it was okay to be delivering random shit to undergrads. What if someone in a frat said they had a cold, asked Brody to bring them Sudafed, and then they used it to start a meth lab in their basement? Or maybe, more likely, someone got alcohol poisoning from the beer he brought them? I wasn't aware enough of the law to know if Brody would be culpable for that, but I also wasn't sure it was worth the risk.

"Look at her face. She's cycling through all the reasons it's a bad idea," Brody said. "Well, keep them all to yourself. We didn't ask your opinion."

"I don't think it's the *worst* idea you've ever had," I started.

"La la la, not listening," Brody said like the baby he was.

"But I also think it can go wrong in a lot of ways."

"What kind of ways?" Drew asked, causing Brody to give him a murderous look.

"I think that people could order things that could be used illegally for one. And then that could come back on you because you provided it."

"We were going to put an age restriction on our page," Drew said. "We won't work with anyone under twenty-one. And everyone will have to accept our terms of service, which will make them sign off that they won't share their care package with anyone underage. Brody had a prelaw buddy draft something that makes us not legally responsible for what someone does with the box after we deliver it."

Okay, well, that was good. I was sure someone could find a work-around to whatever language was in their terms of service, but at least they'd thought of it. But . . .

"The campus also works by its own set of rules. You may be legally okay, but I don't know if there could be other issues or something."

"How? We're not students," Brody said.

"True," I murmured. "I'm not going to lie. I don't have a great feeling about it. But you seem to have done your research, and if you think you can make it work . . . " I shrugged because I didn't necessarily want to give them my blessing, but I didn't want to *not* give it to them either. I was sure they could make some decent money doing it, and they both seemed motivated by the idea.

Drew hadn't been into much of anything since he got out of the hospital, and Brody hadn't been into much of anything since . . . ever. Was I really going to quash something that could maybe lead to better, more promising endeavors in the future?

"Are you marketing it to only students or people in

general?" I asked because I was curious despite myself.

"Everyone, though we'll probably focus a lot of our marketing on students because they'll probably be more likely to use us," Drew explained. "But we'll definitely offer the service to anyone who's interested."

That actually made me feel a little better—that it would be a business that targeted all people but just so happened to be used by students instead of one geared just toward them. If shit did hit the fan, their business would probably seem more reputable that way.

"How were you going to market it?"

"We haven't gotten that far yet," Brody grumbled, back to pecking away at his laptop.

Drew turned a dazzling smile—one I hadn't seen in far too long—on me. "If only we knew a marketing major who could help us." He batted his eyelashes at me, as if I could be swayed by a pretty face.

"No way. You guys are on your own."

He pouted dramatically and sighed. "You'll come around."

Nope. No way. "I'll leave you guys to it, then."

They gave me distracted waves as I made my way to the door.

"You know what I think we need?" said Brody. "A little pink. Really make it pop."

Oh, hell no.

I turned abruptly, went over to the bed, and grabbed the laptop again. I sat on an open space by their feet.

"You guys are seriously the worst," I muttered as I began fixing the disaster that was their website. I chanced a glance over at them when they remained silent. They were both regarding me with shit-eating grins on their faces, and I felt like I'd just been played.

"What?" I asked, hostility clear in my voice.

"Nothing," Brody said.

Drew's smile widened. "Welcome to the team."

I growled a little, forcing myself to ignore how hot he looked when he was happy, before turning my attention back to the website.

I guess I'd come around after all.

Chapter Thirteen

DREW

It didn't take Sophia long to get the website ready and looking a thousand times better than the dumpster fire we'd created.

Our inexperience also had the added bonus of getting her to think we were helpless without her. And now that she had some time and effort invested, she was fully on board, which I couldn't have been happier about. Not only did that mean we had a common goal, but it meant I'd get to spend more time with her.

Brody and I waited not-so-patiently for a few days while Sophia finished the website and plugged in whatever weird codes and targets or whatever were required to get the site up and running.

I didn't understand any of what she was doing, and I was sure Brody didn't either. All I knew was the site looked professional and eye-catching, and she'd even gotten our social media going and was already posting and hashtagging to get interest before the site went live.

"So what happens now?" Brody asked once she finalized everything and the site was accessible to the public.

"We wait," Sophia said. "I have the link on all of your socials, and I've been posting pictures of the items we'll offer. People have been messaging to ask when they can start placing orders, and I told them we'd be ready to start filling them soon."

"Why didn't you just let them order?" Brody asked.

"Oh, my brother, how little you know."

"Shut up, Yoda. It's not a dumb question. Money's money."

Sophia smiled, beaming with a confidence that made her look even more beautiful. "Money it is not. Generate interest you must," she said, clearly trying to sound like Yoda but not really succeeding.

I tried to hold back my laughter, but Brody just shook his head and said, "Don't ever do that again."

"Fine. *Star Wars* is for nerds anyway."

I jerked my head back to show her how offended I was. "Excuse me," I said, putting a hand to my chest at the insult. "*Star Wars* is an epic that can be enjoyed by everyone. It brings people from all walks of life together. You don't have to be a nerd to enjoy it."

Sophia just stared at me as Brody nodded.

"Anyway, back to things that matter…" she said. "It's important to get people talking about the service before you officially offer it. People want what they can't have, and you want them to be waiting for its release. Teasing them is important. Then when it's finally available, they'll be all over it."

I tried to remind myself that she was talking about our business venture, but it was difficult to keep my mind out of the gutter when she was using words like *service*, *release*, and *teasing*.

"Okay, that does make sense," Brody agreed, surprising even me. "I guess I should say thank you for helping us with all this."

Sophia smiled and settled back into the chair with her hands across her chest. "That'd be great."

Looking confused at her comment for a few moments, Brody finally said, "Oh, that *was* my thank-you."

Rolling her eyes, Sophia said, "You're welcome."

"Thanks," I told her. "I mean it. We couldn't have done this without you."

"We *could've*," Brody said. "It probably just would've taken us three times as long."

"Would you stop?" I begged him.

Brody seemed to concede when he held up the Red Bull he'd been drinking in a toast. "To owning our first business."

"To Nite Bites," I added, lifting my bottle of water.

We both made a silent promise with our eyes that we'd wait for Sophia to join before we'd clink our drinks together, so we stood there holding them for a few seconds before Sophia finally picked up her large iced coffee and sighed.

"To Nite Bites," she said with a smile she couldn't seem to suppress.

SOPHIA

I wasn't sure what kind of reaction I'd get when I asked Aamee if I could distribute some Nite Bites business cards at the party Zeta Eta Chi was hosting at our house this weekend. We hadn't thrown a party since before winter break, and I knew Aamee and...well, pretty much all the girls, myself included, were looking forward to the bash.

Though it was far from warm weather, the party was a sorority tradition and an informal kickoff to the spring and usually held the weekend before Valentine's Day. Before we knew it, it would be April, and people would be preparing for graduation.

I didn't want to muddle the party's intention by suggesting that I take advantage of the people attending by passing out our cards. Ultimately, it was Aamee's call, and though I was pretty sure her answer would be a negative one, I'd promised the boys I'd ask. The worst she could say was no, right?

"Sure!" she said.

I continued drying the bowl she'd just handed to me after washing it. "I understand. Just figured I'd ask, but—"

"Do you need your hearing checked? I said it was fine."

I looked around, wondering if there were hidden cameras nearby and someone ready to jump out to tell me Aamee was just messing with me. When I was certain we were the only ones on the entire floor, I put the bowl away and stared at her.

"Seriously? You really don't mind?"

"Mind? I think it's a great idea!" She sounded so elated I wondered if she'd accidentally taken some of Bethany's Ritalin.

"Um, okay. Thanks," I replied, sounding hesitant. "I didn't expect you to agree so easily. I thought you might think it took away from the focus of the party or something."

She handed over another bowl. "It's a good thing you're not prelaw, because your arguing skills are shit. I said yes, and now you're giving me reasons to rescind my offer."

"No, no, I'm not. Thank you, really. I owe you one."

"You don't owe me anything," she said with a smile so sweet it barely looked like her face. "Now Brody, on the other hand..." Her voice trailed off without finishing her sentence, and she stared out the window as she washed the next dish. I wasn't sure what she was thinking about, and I didn't want to know. "Make sure he knows he's invited. I'd love to see him again."

Afraid that she might have second thoughts about letting us promote the business at the party, I didn't chance a glance in her direction because there was no hiding the disgust on my face. I could see it in the reflection of the window.

"I'll be sure to tell him" was all I said.

Chapter Fourteen

SOPHIA

"These look awesome," Drew said, handing over the matte black business cards. In silver, *Nite Bites* was written in a playful script, and below the name of the company were the founders' names: Brody Mason and Drew Nolan.

"Why didn't you put your name on here too?" Drew asked. "We're a threesome."

Brody didn't miss a beat before speaking. "As someone who's familiar with threesomes, they don't usually involve siblings."

"You're disgusting," I told him.

Drew laughed. "You know what I mean. Trio, triad, whatever. We're a team. You could've put your name on there too."

"I know. I kinda think it'll help you get business if I'm not involved, though."

"Because no one likes you?" Brody said.

Rolling my eyes, I handed the guys each a small stack of cards. "Not because no one likes me. I feel like having you guys be the public faces will be better all around."

"That's so sexist," Brody said, acting appalled.

"I also won't feel as weird promoting it at the party if people don't know I'm part of it. Something about promoting myself seems strange to me."

"Well, you gotta get used to it," Drew said, putting his good arm around my shoulder. "If you don't believe in yourself, how do you expect other people to?"

"He does have a point." Brody grabbed his jacket and slipped it on. "Sorry you can't go, man."

"Eh," Drew said with a shrug. "I'm all right with it. I got my fill of sorority events with the bachelor auction and Aamee's costume party."

"Okay, we'll see ya later tonight, then," Brody told him. Then he turned to me. "We should probably go. I told Aamee I'd be there before it started to help set up."

"You talked to Aamee?"

"Well, texted, but yeah."

"When?"

"What's with all the questions, Nancy Drew? Do you have a little crush on your sorority president?" Brody was obviously teasing, but I found myself getting defensive. The last thing I wanted was for anyone to think I had a crush on Aamee—especially Aamee herself.

"Ew, gross," I said, sounding like an elementary school kid who'd been accused of chasing someone on the playground because they secretly liked the person. "Let's just go."

"So you can see your girlfriend?" Brody practically sang. Even as an adult, he didn't miss an opportunity to make fun of me if one presented itself.

Then again, neither did I. "No," I said. "So you can see yours."

The comeback wasn't well thought out, and I regretted it the moment I said it. It didn't help that Brody knew it too. He grinned at me with the sort of smile that made my skin crawl. The only thing that could bother me more than Brody and Aamee was Brody and Aamee—together.

"Come on," I said, already heading out the door without waiting for him.

When we got to the sorority house, most of the girls were in the kitchen, including Gina, who was holding a bottle of Tito's and licking a popsicle.

"Hey," she said when she saw me, jumping up to wrap her arms around me.

"Careful," I said, trying to avoid getting a red stain on the back of my cream sweater.

Gina hugged me like she hadn't seen me in years before pulling away and finding a seat at the counter again. Though she misjudged its height and almost missed it entirely.

Brody offered a "What's up?" to the other girls in the kitchen, and they replied with a hello to both of us, though none of them seemed as pleased to see me as Gina.

"She's been drinking since noon," Aamee said. "It's your turn to babysit."

"Maybe getting the alcohol approved was a mistake," I offered.

There'd always been loopholes to get around the university's alcohol policies concerning sororities—loopholes we'd often exploited—but with the new semester had come an easing on this rule, allowing us to not go to such extremes to serve liquor. Penalties for serving underage people were still severe, but that was a risk all the houses seemed willing to take.

"Ya *think*?" Aamee grabbed the bottle from Gina's hands

and put it back in the freezer. "That's enough, Hasselhoff. Go get ready."

Gina slid off the bar stool and wandered into the living room toward the stairs, but I didn't watch closely enough to know if she actually went up them.

"When I suggested it, I didn't really think they'd ever overturn the rule. It was just kind of a pipe dream," I said. "Like the 2020 version of the women's suffrage movement."

"Yeah, I know. I couldn't believe your mom and some of the other legacies were on board with the idea, but I guess even they thought the rule was outdated and sexist too. Other schools have updated the regulations. I guess Lazarus was feeling the peer pressure."

"Nice!" Brody smacked me on the back. "I was worried this would be a dry party since it was at your house." Though it hurt, I knew he meant the gesture as a compliment of sorts. "And Mom helped with this? *Our* mom?"

I nodded. He sounded shocked, and I can't say I blamed him. I didn't even know she had anything to do with it until she told me after the fact. It'd surprised me more that the rule could be overturned so quickly, but I wasn't a stranger to money buying more than material possessions.

I didn't exactly think my mom or the other legacies had *paid* anyone for the amendment, but the pressure of knowing some of its biggest donors thought the regulation was sexist had probably been enough to change some important minds. There was no harm in that. Well, other than Gina's impending alcohol poisoning.

"Hey, Brian," Emma said as she walked into the kitchen. Looking at her phone, she barely chanced a glance at Brody. She was clearly trying to be casual but seeming anything but.

At least to those of us who knew her. I'd forgotten the other girls had even seen Brody before, much less that they thought his name was Brian.

Brody's face contorted into full confusion. "Who's Brian?"

That got Emma's attention, pulling her focus from whatever she was pretending to be busy doing on her phone.

"Um, you?" Then she looked to me. "You said Brian, right? With an *i*?"

"Why'd you tell her my name was Brian?"

Aamee chimed in with, "I think I was actually the one who said that. I must've been mistaken." I appreciated her taking the fall for this, even though it had been me who said it.

Brody's eyebrows pushed together in a way that made him look like a dog that had just been surrendered at a shelter. "You forgot my name?" he asked Aamee.

"Oh, for fuck's sake," I said. "She didn't forget your name. You're such an idiot."

Emma's gaze darted back and forth between Aamee, Brody, and me. "Can someone tell me what's going on?"

I sighed loudly, raising my palms to my face so I could rub my eyes. This had gone on long enough.

"Yes," I said. "I'll tell you what's going on. I'll tell everyone, actually." I went to the living room so I could call up the stairs and ask the remaining girls to come down. Gina was still in the living room, now lying on the couch and playing with her hair above her face. "Can you all come down for a minute? I have to tell you something."

I waited for everyone to arrive before I took a deep breath. I'd lied to them for a semester, and I'd felt guilty as hell doing it. But I'd done it for my brother, which seemed like the right decision, even if I couldn't stand him most of the time. But now there was no reason to lie. Brody was home and hadn't re-enrolled, and Drew, well...Drew was *not* related to me, and I couldn't deny I was a bit excited to tell people that.

Once everyone was in the room and I seemed to have their attention, I said, "There's something I need to tell all of you, and I hope you'll forgive me." I intentionally avoided eye contact with anyone except for Aamee, who gave me a little nod like she was encouraging me to continue. "Last semester, I lied to all of you," I said, ashamed. "The person I told you was my brother Brody was really a guy impersonating him because my real brother is a cowardly moron who took off for Europe instead of staying here like a responsible adult."

I looked to Brody, who didn't seem at all insulted by the comment.

I extended a hand toward him. "This is the real Brody Mason. The guy who was pretending to be him is named Drew Nolan. He's the one who got into the horrible motorcycle crash, and he's also recuperating at Brody's apartment. He's on the mend now, but I moved back to help him."

A few of the girls exchanged glances with each other during the silence. I tried to decipher the meaning of them but couldn't.

"I'm so sorry I didn't tell you the truth. All of you deserve better than that." Giving them a small contrite smile, I said, "You're my sisters."

There was a long moment of silence, which I was now scared to fill, before Macy spoke.

"So you *weren't* fucking your brother?"

"No!" I practically yelled.

Brody laughed but seemed equally disgusted.

"Okay, I'll make a note of that." She got up from her seat

on the couch and reached over to grab her computer off a bookcase. "Excuse me. Sorry."

"You're writing that down?"

"Of course," Macy said. "I'm sorority secretary, and I plan to keep that position until I graduate next year. I can't have information that is incorrect."

"You put on record that I was fucking my brother?" I shook my head, confused. "When? Why?"

She seemed a bit flustered as she woke up her laptop and began to click around. "We had a meeting about it when you weren't here. I can tell you the exact date if you give me a minute."

"Oh my God! Never mind. Just make sure the record reflects that information is incorrect."

Macy nodded and quietly typed.

"So is that it?" Sam, the vice president, asked. "You just wanted to let us know that this guy is Brody and the other guy wasn't?"

"Yeah, um, I guess."

"Okay, so can we go back to getting ready? People will be here soon."

"Yeah, um, I guess," I said again.

The rest of the girls muttered to each other, and some introduced themselves to Brody before returning to whatever they'd been doing before I'd called them to the living room.

Once most of the room cleared out, I headed back to the kitchen with Aamee, Emma, and Brody.

"Well, that went well," I said slowly. "I wasn't sure how everyone would take it, but it seems like they don't really mind that I lied to them."

"Yeah, I'm not surprised," Aamee said, tossing a bag of

pretzels to Brody to pour into a heart-shaped bowl. "I've told you before no one gives a shit about your personal life, Mason."

"Right," I said on a laugh. I wondered when people were going to start arriving so I had something to focus on besides my disaster of a life.

Chapter Fifteen

DREW

"Isn't there a better way to do this?" As I cross-checked the online orders against the handwritten list I'd created in a notebook, I scrutinized the spreadsheet on the iPad Brody had put in front of me.

"Like what?"

It was a good question and one I didn't have an answer to. "I don't know. Just seems like there should be an app or something that does this automatically."

Brody's eyes lit up.

"Don't even think about it," Sophia said. "We should focus on one venture at a time."

"Fine," he replied, obviously disappointed.

Carter, Toby, and Aniyah seemed oblivious to our conversation as they opened Prime Pantry boxes and attempted to organize household items, food and drinks, and toiletries, among other things that had recently been ordered in due to special requests from some of the recurring customers.

Impressed by our success, Cody asked to come by to see

the process in action, and I'd given him the task of putting together the orders that were scheduled to go out next.

We'd been in business less than a month, and word had spread quickly that we were running a customizable delivery system. The first few days, we fielded a few calls—food and beer mostly—although one guy asked us to bring condoms and offered a twenty-dollar tip if we could get them there in fifteen minutes. He was too drunk to drive but apparently not too drunk to realize he shouldn't be procreating as a sophomore. A few people had even asked us to pick out Valentine's Day gifts for their girlfriends.

Unsure of the most efficient and economically sound way to purchase items, we originally treated each order as an errand—going to drugstores or convenience stores as needed. But we quickly realized that not only was that a complete waste of time, it was a huge money suck.

It didn't take us long to begin ordering most items in bulk online and picking up some specialty goods at local stores, like the bakery below Brody's apartment and the vape shop a few blocks away. And though we were completely overwhelmed, we weren't complaining, because business meant money.

The idea was so good, it was hard to believe it'd been Brody's.

"You know what you should do?" Carter asked, but it was clear he didn't expect anyone to actually take a guess. "Create theme packages. Like Hangover Helper or Sexual Success or something. You can just have a bunch of them ready to go. Then you don't need to worry about customizing them as much. Like you could just have Tylenol, Gatorade, ginger ale, stuff like that."

"That's actually a really good idea," Sophia said, looking up from her computer.

"Thanks," Carter said, sounding almost as surprised at her compliment as Sophia had been at his idea.

"What would you put in the Sexual Success package?" Aniyah asked.

"I don't know. I didn't think that far ahead. I've never really had trouble getting laid, so I don't actually know what you'd need."

"I think we should call it the Sexcess Package," Toby said. "It's catchier."

"It's a good idea no matter what we call it," I told him. The fact that this could really turn into something surprised me, even though we'd already begun making money. "I bet we could come up with another theme or two and get a good amount of orders from those alone."

"Soph's gonna have to start delivering soon," Brody said, his eyebrows raised at his sister.

We both knew that would never happen. Neither one of us was going to let her show up to random houses and apartments by herself, especially late at night, which was when a lot of the orders were placed. But maybe with the theme box idea, we'd be able to get a more solid routine going so that we could get ahead of the orders instead of throwing shit together as it came in.

"No way," she said, probably knowing she wouldn't have to put too much effort into resisting.

"I'll do it," Cody said. "If you're serious about needing another driver."

There was no way I'd let him take on another job when he was already struggling in school.

"You can't keep your grades up with *one* job," I told him. "No way I'm letting you take another."

"I'll quit my job at the Donut Dive."

He spoke like the idea was a foregone conclusion and one that I didn't have much say in. Cody was like me in that way. Once he got an idea in his head, there wasn't much, if anything, anyone could do to stop him. But I'd try anyway.

"No. It's out of your way, and it'll be a gigantic waste of gas. You'd have to work late—"

"I work late now. And that's what they make gas stations for."

Rolling my eyes, I said, "You know what I mean. We're just starting out, and we can't pay you much. Most of what you'd make would go to gas money."

"Maybe at first. But if this thing takes off, we could all be millionaires."

"I think millionaires is a stretch. Especially since there'll be four of us by that point." I had to hand it to Cody; he knew how to dream big, and he didn't let anyone crush those dreams. "Maybe just tens of thousandaires," I said, letting my words concede the argument.

Cody's smirk shifted into a genuinely happy grin. "This is gonna be big. You guys watch."

"You said that when you tried to get Mom to sell cupcakes with pot in them for your freshman football fundraiser."

Carter laughed. "Seriously? That's awesome."

"Hey," Cody said, a finger pointing in my direction, "it would've worked if you hadn't warned her. I was ahead of my time. That was before edibles became super popular. I could've been a trendsetter."

"You could've been a felon. *Children* bought food at that fundraiser."

"Whatever," Cody said, brushing me off with a wave

of his hand. "I didn't think it all the way through. And it probably would've been Mom who went to jail anyway. It's not like it would've been her first time."

"You're horrible."

Brody finished tagging the box he'd just packed before he stood. "I think you're awesome. We could use an innovator like you," he said, extending a hand as he walked toward Cody. "Welcome to the team."

SOPHIA

With our brothers out doing deliveries, Drew and I had been in the apartment for a few hours together. I wasn't used to having this much alone time with him, and it seemed neither one of us knew quite how to fill it.

We'd begun the night by catching up on some of the order sheets, and since the two of us made a good team, the task didn't take more than a half hour before we'd done just about everything we could do for Nite Bites.

"Now what?" Drew asked, flipping the case of Brody's iPad closed and setting it on the coffee table.

I shrugged, trying to think of a suggestion that seemed normal. I wasn't exactly sure what normal was for two people who used to be together but were now business partners who were currently trying to ignore the sexual energy charging between them. I wondered if Drew could feel it too.

How could he not?

But it was hard to tell. Drew was calm and collected while I was all alert and tingly whenever I was around him, like I was hyperaware of his every movement and breath. It reminded me of the time Taylor and I had Four Lokos for breakfast during our senior trip after graduating high school.

"Netflix and chill?" I asked.

Drew laughed, making me feel even more uncomfortable in my skin.

"What?"

"You know what that means, right?"

"Yeah. Hang out and watch movies."

"It means hook up."

"Oh" was all I could get out. Not wanting to make eye contact with him, I stared straight ahead at the TV and rubbed my hands over my thighs nervously. Why was I always so awkward?

"Netflix is good, though," Drew said.

Out of the corner of my eye, I saw him smile, though I wished I hadn't. His smile did things to me that I'd been trying exceptionally hard not to think about lately. It was something about what it did to his eyes…and really, the rest of his gorgeous face. His smile lit his entire aura until he seemed like he was glowing. And then I'd feel all warm and antsy again.

Drew leaned behind me to grab the remote from the back of the sofa, his arm grazing the back of my neck so lightly that I almost didn't feel it.

I wondered if Drew could tell what he did to me, especially when we were alone, which, thankfully, wasn't that often. I wondered if he could see my face heat up when his eyes locked with mine or see the goose bumps on my skin when we were close.

I wanted him to touch me—*fantasized* about him touching me. But he'd made it clear that even though he wanted the same thing I did, now wasn't a good time to act on those desires.

"What do you wanna watch?" he asked.

You without any clothes on.

"Oh, um, whatever. I'm not picky. Any movie's fine."

"Thriller? Comedy? Horror?"

"Comedy's good." I figured maybe laughing at something other than my own life might be cathartic for me.

Drew turned on the TV guide channel, and it didn't take us long to decide on *Step Brothers*. We'd both seen it numerous times, but we also both agreed it never got old.

After a few minutes, Drew turned to me. "You know what this apartment needs?"

"Another bed?"

Chuckling, he said, "Well, yeah. That'd definitely be nice. I'm sure Brody's getting tired of sleeping on the floor."

Most of the time, Brody never even made it into the bedroom to the makeshift bed he'd created for himself out of extra pillows and a sleeping bag. Sometimes he passed out on the love seat, and other times he must have sweet-talked some unsuspecting girl into letting him stay with her, but I hadn't really bothered to think about it much until now.

"I was thinking a drum set," Drew said.

"That will *never* happen."

"I can play, though."

"You can?" I raised an eyebrow skeptically.

"Why do you look so surprised?"

I shrugged, unsure myself. "I don't know. You never told me."

"Never came up. I guess I was too focused on being your gay brother to let you know who I really was."

He laughed after he said it, but I couldn't help but hear the truth in it. So much of what we knew about each other had been overshadowed by the lie we'd been a part of. Sure, somehow living together now—even with Brody nearby most of the time—had allowed us to find out more about the other person without that knowledge getting clouded by all the sorority and school bullshit.

But it became suddenly clear to me just how little we actually knew about each other. All the small details had been pushed aside for more major concerns at the time, and now that those concerns didn't exist, I wanted to know Drew Nolan like I'd never known him before.

"Well, you're not my brother anymore," I said quietly.

There was a silent moment between us before a smile spread across his face. I'd tried to suppress my own, but I felt myself failing miserably.

"I swear I didn't mean for that to sound as creepy as it did."

We both laughed loudly, and when we calmed down, Drew said, "I didn't think you did."

"Try again?" I asked, heat radiating up my cheeks.

"Go for it."

The way he stared at me, his eyes fixed on mine like they never wanted to look anywhere else, had my pulse speeding up.

I swallowed hard, clearing my throat before I said something stupid again.

He waited patiently, his body square with mine and an elbow propped on the back of the couch.

"Tell me about yourself, Drew." This time I could tell the words came out as I'd intended for them to—low and as sexy as I was capable of making anything sound. I hoped Drew heard them the same way.

"What do you wanna know?" His voice was low too and huskier than usual.

"Everything."

As he thought, Drew's tongue slipped out of his mouth and over his lips, but he didn't say anything right away. I wasn't sure if he was overwhelmed or just unsure of where to start.

"I'm not letting you off the hook."

"Didn't think you would," he replied with a smile. "I wanna know about you too."

His eyes never strayed from mine, and it somehow felt like we were silently communicating all the things we never got the chance to say to one another.

I was just about to tell him he didn't really have to tell me *everything* or that we could do this another time—though that was definitely not me letting him off the hook—when he spoke up.

"Never have I ever had a family holiday where someone didn't fist fight."

I shouldn't have been surprised that he was choosing to turn this into a game. It no doubt made him feel more comfortable and probably brought a lightness to my request that wouldn't have been there otherwise.

"Your family really has physical altercations at every holiday?"

"Well, maybe not *every* one. I'm sure there was a Flag Day or something that we missed. It's a blast," he said dryly. "You'll have to come check it out sometime, fiancée."

I rolled my eyes. "That was *your* fault."

"Most things are," he answered. "I'm okay with it. You're up."

I wanted to tell him that wasn't true, but I knew better than to try to convince Drew not to get down on himself.

"Never have I ever slept with an ex."

"Shouldn't we get something to drink?"

"No alcohol for you until you're completely off the painkillers, right? We can play with our fingers."

His eyes widened, and I wondered when I'd learn to think before I spoke. Sighing, I tried to clarify.

"It's how the kids I used to babysit for played. You hold up five fingers, and every time you've done something that someone says, you put one down. First one without any left loses."

"I like it."

"Guess we're both at four now," I said.

"You're at four. I've still got a full hand."

I knew I looked surprised, but there wasn't anything I could do to hide it. "You never fucked one of your exes?"

"Whoa, what's with the harsh language? It sounds so dirty when you say it like that."

I gave him a shove with my free hand before recognizing it probably hurt way more than I'd meant for it to. I never seemed to remember just how fragile Drew was.

"Seriously?"

"Seriously," he said. "I didn't say I never wanted to, just that I never have." He let his comment settle between us before saying, "My turn. Never have I ever applied to college."

"That's totally not fair. You already know I have."

"Better put another finger down, then."

I put another down so there were only three left.

"Fine. But two can play that game. Never have I ever peed standing up."

"Wrong. Everyone does when they're babies in a diaper. Go again."

"Never have I ever . . ." I looked around the apartment for

some sort of inspiration, but nothing I looked at sparked any good ideas. "Never have I ever liked living with a guy before you."

Drew looked pleased at the compliment. "Remember the first few days when we were arguing about everything and driving each other nuts?"

"I remember."

"Guess we've come a long way since then," he said.

And I had to agree.

Drew put a finger down. "Guess I should play fair. I liked the two roommates I've had before you, and both were guys." Drew bit down on his bottom lip as he thought about what his next statement would be. "Never have I ever been to another country."

I put down a finger. "I've been to so many, I don't think I could name them all."

"Sometime you'll have to try eventually," Drew said, and I could tell he meant it.

"Deal," I told him with a smile that felt sad somehow. "Never have I ever been good at math."

"I was pretty good at it as a kid," he said, dropping his fingers down to three. "Never have I ever fantasized about a man."

He smirked as I put a finger down.

"You're such a cheater."

"Was it me?" he asked.

"Huh?"

"That you fantasized about."

"This isn't how the game is played," I replied in an effort to avoid the question.

His stupid dimples let me know he knew exactly what I was doing.

"Never have I ever fantasized about a woman."

One more finger went down, leaving him with two and me with one.

"Never have I ever been as happy as I am when I'm with you." His eyes darted to my hand as he clearly waited to see if I felt the same. When my finger stayed up, he said, "Never have I ever wanted someone as much as I want you."

I wanted to ask him why he was doing this. Why was he telling me how he truly felt if he had no plans of acting on those feelings?

But instead I said, "You can't do two in a row."

"I did, though."

"I think you should be disqualified," I joked, trying to ease the tension.

"Nah, your turn. You can just forget about the last one."

I was sure Drew didn't realize the implications of telling me to forget about what he'd just said. He'd meant to forget it in regards to the game. But asking me to forget what he'd said was like telling a jury to disregard evidence they'd heard so they could make a fair and unbiased decision.

It was too late. I couldn't unhear that, and I didn't want to.

I just wondered if I'd ever get to say it back.

Chapter Sixteen

SOPHIA

I came home from class to find Drew packing boxes with various things.

He was whistling happily as he plopped pain relievers, condoms, and other collegiate necessities into some boxes and formula and burp cloths into another for one of our nonstudent clients. That part of the business hadn't taken off as much, but we were starting to see growth in the new-mom circles.

"Hey," I said warily, worried he'd been body-snatched or something. Granted, he'd been in a much better place lately, but whistling—was that a Taylor Swift song?—was maybe a bit extreme. "How was your day?"

"Pretty good," he replied, offering me a smile before returning his attention to his work. "My physical therapist talked to my doctor, and they both agreed that I could start bearing more weight on my leg. I've been doing that with my PT for a while, but it'll be nice to be able to do it all the time. No full-out walking, and I still need to use the crutches, but I don't have to keep all weight off it."

"That's great news," I said, happy to see him happy.

He'd been making steady progress over the previous weeks. His arm now only needed a brace, and most of his bruises were totally gone. There were still a few purplish and raised scars, but overall, his leg was really the only major injury left to contend with.

"Need help?" I asked as I sat beside him on the couch.

"I don't think so," he replied. "I only have two more boxes to go."

"'Kay." I settled in and watched him.

Things between us were getting better every day, and while I wasn't sure what we were moving toward, I did know we were moving forward. So I didn't stress about letting my eyes linger on him. I didn't care if he noticed the way I tracked his movements with obvious appreciation.

It was fine if he noticed the million little reasons I found to touch him and be near him every day. Life was good, and time spent with Drew was even better. I wasn't going to pretend to believe a different truth.

"How was class?" he asked.

"Riveting," I said dryly.

He looked over at me, raising an eyebrow. "Oh yeah?"

"I think I hate one of my professors."

"You're not sure?" He looked amused, which made me smile.

"He wears tweed jackets with elbow patches."

"Is that the reason you hate him or the reason you're not sure?"

"Yes."

Drew laughed aloud at that. "You're so weird."

"I seriously can't tell if he's a pretentious prick or an

endearing grandfather. Though with the comments he left on my last paper, I'm leaning toward the former."

"Eviscerated your writing, huh?"

"He said I lacked creative insight but complimented me on my knowledge of proper comma usage."

"Ah, I see your predicament."

We fell into companionable silence while he finished packing the last of the materials that would be delivered by Cody later. After he closed the final box and set it aside, he leaned back on the couch, which brought his shoulder into contact with mine as we sat side by side.

"How's your arm?" I asked, unable to keep my fingers from tracing over his brace and then up and down his arm.

"Feeling better every day."

"That's good."

"I'll probably be able to get out of your hair soon. We're pulling some decent money in, and I'm almost done with being an invalid."

I felt a pang in my chest that nearly made me wince.

"Sounds like you're in a hurry to leave."

He paused for a second, but I didn't look up at him, preferring to focus on something immovable and secure.

"Not really. But I figured I was starting to overstay my welcome." His statement sounded like a question and had me wanting to be completely honest, even if it also made me feel extremely vulnerable.

I shook my head slightly. "I like having you around."

He breathed deeply. "I like being around."

At that, I did look up at him, my eyes locking on his with intensity. It made me grateful when I saw the same want and passion I felt reflected back at me.

He wanted this, me, *us*, just as much as I did, and contentment washed over me at the realization that we were finally on the same page, emotionally and physically.

"Then stay."

Rather than utter a promise with words, he used his lips instead. He brought his mouth to mine with a slowness typically reserved for replays of sports highlights. It was both frustrating and arousing.

Mostly arousing.

The second his lips touched mine, we both groaned. It was the kind of sound someone made after a long day at work when they finally got to relax into the couch. It sounded like coming home.

We pressed closer together, his good hand cupping my jaw and angling my head so he could deepen the kiss.

I fisted my hands in his T-shirt like I was never going to let him go. Maybe I wouldn't.

His tongue danced with mine, a dirty grind that moved to a primitive rhythm. His hand moved from my face and trailed lightly down my arm, causing pinpricks to bloom on my skin. It heightened my arousal, creating a pulse in time with the thrust of his tongue into my mouth.

My hands untangled from his shirt enough to dive beneath it, sliding under the hem and rubbing over the coarse hair that led down from his navel. He was thinner than he'd been before, but he wasn't frail. It made me want to touch him with more fervor so I could remind my senses that he wasn't broken.

He was strong and solid and *here*.

We were both panting, and it would've been easy to let the moment build to a crescendo. To let the fire between us burn until we both combusted. But those feelings were fleeting.

I needed something else first. Something that would let me know I could count on this. That I could rely on its permanence.

"Wait," I said abruptly as I pulled away from him.

He jerked back as if someone had told him I was a live wire. "What's wrong?"

"Nothing," I said, receiving a skeptical look in return. "I just ... I need to know."

"Know what?"

I looked intently into his eyes, hoping forcing him to answer the question he'd previously evaded didn't push him away.

"I need to know why you left. The full reason," I quickly added as he opened his mouth to reply.

He hesitated for a moment, and I watched indecision flit across his face. Then, his look transformed into something more akin to determination. And he promptly rose from the couch, grabbed his crutches, and limped away.

DREW

I'd cowardly hoped I could avoid this question forever. But Sophia deserved an answer, so I needed to give her one. Unfortunately, I didn't quite know how to explain the rush of feelings I'd been assaulted by that day, all of which had continued to fester in the guilt and regret that had consumed me every minute since I'd left her.

I hobbled over to the table by the hallway and retrieved my wallet before returning to the couch and easing down beside her. She looked at me curiously, but I stayed quiet as I took the check from my wallet and handed it to her.

Sophia looked at the paper in my hand before tentatively reaching out and taking it from me, unfolding it as if it were some kind of bomb. And perhaps that was exactly what it was. It'd blown things apart for us months ago and might very likely do so again.

As she read it, her forehead creased and her eyes narrowed.

"What the hell is this?" Her voice was harsh and demanding, but I didn't miss the wobble of emotion in it.

"It's what it looks like it is."

"My dad gave this to you the day you left?" she asked, though she had to know the answer.

I chalked it up to shock.

"Yeah, he told me I'd never be good enough for you and gave me that to go away."

Sophia sat there for a moment, looking over the check as if it would somehow magically say something different if she stared at it long enough.

"But you didn't cash it." It wasn't a question.

"No, of course not."

"So you left me for free?"

I couldn't control the scoff that escaped. "Free? Leaving you cost me everything. Everything that mattered at least."

"But... I'm so confused. Do you *plan* to cash it? Or *did* you before the accident?"

"*No.*" The word ripped out of me. I had no place to feel offended since this whole mess was my fault, but I did anyway.

"Then why do you still have it?"

I sighed. Her voice was smaller and more wounded than it had been when this conversation began, and I hated that I'd made her feel that way.

"Because I wasn't sure what your dad would tell you. And I wanted to have proof that I didn't take his money. I'd never do that."

One side of her face contorted as if she were completely confused. "Why would it have even mattered? Either way, you left. You may as well have taken the money if you were just going to skip out on me anyway."

"I … What?"

Sophia stood from the couch and began pacing in front of me. "You're really an idiot, you know that?"

"Uh, yes?" I asked, because I did know it but wasn't sure how it applied to this moment.

"Like really, epically, *you should win an award* type of stupid."

"Okay," I stated more firmly because I didn't want to argue with someone who looked like they were contemplating skinning me alive.

Suddenly, she stopped moving and threw her hands up. "If you weren't going to take the money, why did you leave?"

"Just because being bought off didn't appeal to me doesn't mean what he said wasn't true. I'm *not* good enough for you. You deserve someone who can give you so much more than I'll probably ever be able to give you. But I'm also fairly certain no one will love you more than I do, and I'm starting to think that might be enough. At least I'm hoping it is."

She stared at me for a long moment before tilting her head toward the ceiling and yelling, "Extraordinarily fucking stupid!" Then she took two steps forward and dropped onto the couch, burying her face in her hands.

It took me a second to realize she was shaking, and I wanted to re-break my own leg for making her cry.

"Hey, Soph, Jesus, I'm so, so sorry. If I could take it all back, I would." I slid closer so I could put my arm around her, but that's when she lifted her head, allowing me to see that she wasn't crying. "Are you . . . are you *laughing*?"

That set her off with renewed vigor, her hearty laughter making tears leak from her eyes. After a minute or so, she calmed enough to speak, though her words still came in gusts between chuckles.

"So, let me get this straight. Not only did you leave me for the most clichéd reason ever, but you also just seriously told me you loved me in the most blasé way possible. You are such a douche sometimes."

I would've been insulted by her assessment of both my character and my timing, but she was still laughing, so I decided it was best not to rock the boat.

"It wasn't clichéd. It was honest. I just wanted you to be happy."

"So you made me miserable?"

"I figured that was temporary. Eventually you'd meet someone else and forget all about me."

That dried her laughter up, and my brain began whirring with ways to backpedal. She leaned closer, and my mind screamed *Abort! Abort!*, but with a busted leg, there was no way I'd be able to get away quickly enough.

"You know what? I can't even address that right now. There's only one thing I need you to tell me, and I need you to be honest about it."

"Okay, yes, I can do that."

She released a short puff of air before putting her hand on my cheek and letting her fingers tease over my skin.

"Are you done making decisions for me?"

"Yes. Especially since I seem to be really bad at it."

"The worst," she whispered, her mouth hovering just in front of mine.

I wanted to close the distance between us, but I also wanted to leave this next move in her hands.

"You really love me?" she asked.

I pulled back slightly so she could read the truth of my words on my face. "I love you more than I thought it was possible to love someone. I'm sorry I almost ruined everything. Walking away from you was the worst decision I ever made. Thank you for coming to me even though I hurt you. I didn't deserve it."

"Maybe you shouldn't make decisions about what anyone deserves anymore either."

I smiled. "I'll take it under advisement."

"Good. And for the record, I love you too. Now hurry up and kiss me, dumbass."

Who was I to ignore a directive like that?

Chapter Seventeen

DREW

I'd convinced myself I'd never have this again. And as I took in the way her body fit perfectly against mine, I was happy to have been wrong.

We had to unfuse our mouths so I could hobble down the hallway toward the bedroom. But that didn't bother me much because we'd finally found a common page in this misadventure we'd been on.

There was no getting around the fact that I still had my doubts about how long this would last—how long it would take for her to move on to someone more in her league—but those thoughts were quieter now. They thrummed low in a background that was overwhelmed by want and need. With enough time, I hoped they'd disappear completely.

The desire I felt for her was unlike anything I'd ever experienced, which perhaps explained why I'd been rudderless in life for so long. If this was what passion felt like, then I'd need to work harder to find it in all aspects of my life. But for now, I was going to focus on what was in front of me.

We hurried through the slightly ajar door of the bedroom, and I stumbled a bit as she backed awkwardly to the bed, obviously caught between wanting to help me and wanting to leave my pride intact.

It made our dance strange and off-balance but somehow all the more perfect for it. I leaned in to kiss her quickly before our lips broke apart so we could each breathe a short laugh before we dived back in, tasting each other as our tongues tangled.

I belatedly thought about how Brody would not appreciate walking in on this and that we should probably at least have locked the door, but I quickly dismissed the concern because it wasn't even in the same stratosphere of importance as getting Sophia naked and under me.

I eased her back on the bed, giving her space to scoot up a bit before I somehow hauled up after her, blanketing her clothed body with mine. Thank God I'd gotten clearance to put some weight on my leg, though I did my best to angle my body enough to accommodate it.

I was desperate to get her naked, but I also didn't want this to be over too soon. I wanted to savor the fact that I could kiss this girl—my girl—again. Despite the brace on my arm, I was able to prop my upper body on my elbows so I didn't crush her.

But I did let my hips fall to make contact with hers. My sweatpants did little to hide my excitement, and I was glad for the give in the extra material.

She pulled her mouth away from mine on a gasp, her fingernails digging into my biceps in a way that was grounding instead of painful. With her eyes closed, she began to writhe and whimper beneath me.

"Please. Drew, please."

"I got you."

Her eyes opened, and she looked at me intently. "You promise?"

I knew she was asking about more than the here and now. It wasn't about getting off—well, not *only* about getting off at least—but about having her back for as long as she'd let me be there. It was about not running when things got complicated and messy. It was about loving her even when I didn't think I deserved her love in return.

"I promise." It was the easiest, and scariest, oath I'd ever made.

She pulled me back down for a kiss as if we were searing our pact. But she quickly let go, letting her hands drop to the bed beside her head.

"Show me."

Challenge accepted.

There was no finesse to what happened next. My only mission was to get us both naked as quickly as possible, and with a bum leg, it was sadly not the sexy strip tease I'd hoped for.

Thankfully, she shed her own clothing while I struggled with mine, because time was of the essence. For better or worse, as hot as she looked laid out for me—the flush that ran down her neck and spread over her chest and the way her toned belly rose and fell with every breath—I wasn't going to last long.

We were going to have to go for slow and sensual another time. Right now, it was all about satisfying a carnal need.

"Fuck, you're beautiful." The words came out of my mouth almost harshly, my voice raw with how turned on I was.

Settling down on my side, I took in her body.

I skimmed my fingertips down her perfect skin, enamored by the goose bumps that popped up in the wake of my touch.

A small, serene smile spread across her lips, and as my fingers ghosted over her pelvic bone, she arched her back a bit, clearly preparing herself for the pleasure that was about to jolt through her body.

Unable to help myself, I leaned forward and began kissing her skin wherever I could reach.

She slid closer to me so I had better access, and I took full advantage.

I was torn between wanting to move things along and drag them out forever. But it wasn't long before need won out.

"I'm not sure of the best way to do this," I admitted, my voice a bit more vulnerable than I intended. There was nothing I wanted more than to climb on top of her, but I was limited by my injuries.

I'd never felt more like the idiot Sophia claimed I was than in this moment. What type of man jeopardized his ability to have sex because he thought it was okay to ride a motorcycle in a snowstorm?

She smiled sweetly. "What do you think would be easiest on you?"

"Get over here and we'll find out."

"I'm not sure if that's incredibly cheesy or incredibly hot."

"Definitely hot," I replied as my hands went to her hips.

"Do we need protection?" she asked.

I darted my eyes up to hers and let her see the truth written there. "I haven't been with anyone else."

"Me neither."

I couldn't stop a smirk at hearing that. It made me supremely happy.

Her slapping me on the chest ruined my moment though. "Stop looking so smug," she ordered.

I scoffed. "I have the hottest girl in the city sitting naked on my lap. I've earned the right to be smug."

"Such a sweet talker."

"One of my many talents."

She put her hands on my chest and began to grind down. "I'm hoping not all of those talents involve your mouth."

I wagged my eyebrows. "Some definitely do."

She moaned. "Okay, God, you can show me those later."

I gripped her hips to anchor her on top of me.

"Mm, I almost forgot how good you feel," she whispered.

"Glad I could remind you."

"Me too."

We kept it slow and lazy at first, me doing my best to make her feel as good as she was making me feel. Though I was limited, I was determined to do as much as I could.

But soon, the passion between us could no longer be contained, and we both dissolved into madness as we let ourselves be consumed in the feeling of getting to know each other's bodies again.

SOPHIA

Drew and I hadn't had a ton of sex before he'd left. Our relationship had been too new to put in any serious sexual mileage. But despite how relatively new things had been between us, I'd missed sleeping with him instantly.

Drew Nolan, even with a broken leg and a host of other injuries, was still a spectacular fuck. And while I'd initially gone slowly because I'd been afraid I'd hurt him, it hadn't taken long for my concern to fade.

"That's it," Drew said, his voice low and raw as he gripped my hips so he could control my movements. "Fuck, you feel amazing."

I preened at his words, letting my head fall back and pushing my chest out as I became almost frantic in my need to make it good for him.

He touched me in all the right places, lighting up my insides as if I were a pinball machine. I was nearly overwhelmed by the feeling. My mind was consumed with thoughts of *faster*, *harder*, *deeper*, and I let those thoughts drive my actions until I was a writhing mess atop him.

If the look on Drew's face was anything to go by, he had no objections. He looked just as ravenous for me, with his eyes blown wide, his jaw set, and the muscles in his arms straining to keep me from bucking off him.

The sex was frenzied and wild and spoke to the primal level with which we'd missed one another. And while I knew that this was likely not an intensity we'd be able to maintain forever, I was more than happy to revel in it for the time being.

"I'm getting close," he gritted out, as if he were angry at the words.

"Me too."

Drew growled, his gaze locked on where I was playing with my breast. He slid one hand around so his thumb could toy with me.

I couldn't help the cry that escaped me. I hadn't thought this union could get much better, but he'd proved me wrong.

"Come for me," he ordered.

This time there was no question: the words were

undeniably hot, as was the man beneath me. My vision nearly whited out as I did as he'd said, my body quaking and convulsing.

I was still tense with release when he rocked into me one more time. His muscles bulged as he finished, his upper back rounding and causing his shoulders to lift off the bed with the force of his orgasm.

His whole body went limp, and he plopped back onto the mattress.

I let gravity take me as well, letting my body hunch forward so my skin brushed against his without applying any more pressure to his body.

His hands roamed over my back as we caught our breath.

"Wow," he said.

I lifted up my head so I could look at him. "Yeah." I shimmied around a bit, shifting my weight off him. I was instantly disappointed at the loss.

We looked at one another for a moment before he ran a hand through my hair.

"I'm sorry."

I narrowed my eyes at him playfully. "I'm pretty sure it's a bad sign if you have to apologize after sex."

He laughed at that. "Smartass." Then he sobered. "Seriously, though, I'm sorry for not talking to you. For letting your dad prey on my insecurities. For not being...better. Smarter. I almost cost us this, and—"

I had to put my hand over his mouth because we didn't need to rehash all of this. He'd already explained and apologized. That was enough looking backward. From now on, I was only interested in moving forward.

"You're ruining my afterglow with words."

He smiled widely, transforming his already handsome face into something even more breathtaking.

"We don't want that."

"Nope."

"Though I guess if I ruin the first one, I can always give you a second afterglow."

"Oh yeah? You think you're up for that?"

He smirked. "Parts of me are definitely up for it."

"Thank God you didn't hurt your penis in the accident," I told him solemnly before leaning down to kiss him.

He laughed against my lips.

I guess he thought I was kidding.

Chapter Eighteen

SOPHIA

I had to give Drew credit. Despite how busted his body was, he could still fuck like a champ.

Whenever we could find time alone, we made the most of it. Part of me thought we should slow down and talk more about…whatever people who weren't having amazing sex talked about. But since that part was clearly a deranged lunatic, I ignored it.

One thing I couldn't ignore, though, was the shit my dad had pulled with Drew. While I knew Drew was a grown man in charge of his own life and choices, I couldn't help but be livid at my parents for trying to buy off one of my boyfriends. Who *did* that?

And it was the desire for an answer to that question that had prompted me to borrow Carter's car and make the hour drive home to my parents' house after my last class Thursday afternoon. I had a late start Friday and wanted to spend the weekend with Drew, so it made the most sense to get it over with.

I'd contemplated calling ahead and letting my mom know I was coming, but they hadn't let me know they planned to bribe my boyfriend, so I figured I didn't owe them the courtesy.

Pulling into our driveway, I saw my mom's car through the open garage door, but my dad's was absent. I looked at my watch and noticed that it was still a bit early for him to be home, which would maybe work to my advantage. I could reason with my mom before adding him to the mix.

After I climbed out of the car and shut my door, I stood there for a second and took a deep breath. *Here goes nothing.*

I climbed the two stone steps to the matching path that led to the side door that opened into the kitchen and was the one we used most often.

"Mom? It's me," I yelled as I shrugged out of my coat and hung it on the hook behind the door.

"Sophia?" I heard my mom call from another room.

"Yup," I replied as I walked over to the island and took the lid off our Cookie Monster cookie jar.

For as long as I could remember, my mom had kept it stocked with some form of homemade cookie, but today I found it empty. When she entered the room, I glared at her accusingly, my hand still inside the jar.

"How could you?"

She rolled her eyes and moved to a cabinet and withdrew a bag of Oreos. "I only fill that when you kids are home." She slid the package across the island to me, and I snatched it up like Gollum grasping for his Precious.

"That's sad. What if Dad wants a cookie?" Not that I particularly cared if my father ever had another cookie in his entire life after the stunt he'd pulled, but still. It threw me a little to hear that my parents lived different lives when I wasn't looking.

"Then he can open a cabinet and get one."

"But . . . they're better when they're in Cookie Monster."

She sighed. "As happy as I am to be having this inane conversation with you, do you want to tell me what brings you home unannounced?"

"Is that another new thing happening here now? I have to announce my intentions to come to my own home? Should I start calling you Kate instead of Mom?"

My mom tilted her head and regarded me. "You and your brother's brains work so strangely."

"It's a curse and a gift," I said before pulling apart my Oreo and eating the side with icing on it.

She leaned forward so she could put her forearms onto the counter and looked at me with green eyes that looked exactly like my own. In fact, with her olive skin and pronounced cheekbones, she was basically me in thirty years. If I aged half as well as my mother, I'd be set.

"This was a long way to come on a school night. What's wrong, Sophia?"

As crazy as my mom drove me sometimes, when she looked at me with genuine concern, it made me melt a little. This woman really loved me. Which made it even harder to understand why she'd want to make me so unhappy by chasing off Drew.

I looked at her for a second, trying to figure out how to phrase my feelings delicately.

"Why would you think it was a good idea to ruin my life by offering my boyfriend four hundred grand to leave me?"

Okay, so maybe that hadn't been the most tactful phrasing, but at least it was honest, which was more than I could say for her.

She'd comforted me for the duration of winter break with small, thoughtful actions: buying me my favorite candy, making me delicious breakfasts, letting me pick movies to watch—all the things a mom did to make their heartbroken daughter feel better. Granted, I hadn't told her much about what had gone down with Drew, but she wasn't stupid. What kind of sociopath soothed their daughter after a breakup she caused?

She froze for a moment before standing up slowly. "What are you talking about?"

"Oh, come on. Don't pretend you don't know. I saw the check. I can't believe you guys would do that. I mean, I knew you were snobs, but this is low even for you."

Her eyes narrowed. "I don't have a single idea what you're talking about. Start from the beginning. What check?" She put up a finger and wagged it in my direction. "And don't think I'm going to let that snob comment slide either."

I watched her, trying to figure out how she could possibly *not* know what I was talking about.

"The check Dad gave Drew," I said uncertainly. "Dad told him he wasn't good enough for me and then wrote him a check for four hundred thousand dollars to leave and not come back."

Her eyes widened, and genuine surprise was written all over her face.

"You really didn't know?" I asked.

"No," she said coldly. Just then, we heard the garage door opening. "But I'm going to get to the bottom of it right now."

We stood there silently until my dad came in, dropping his briefcase by the door and hanging up his coat before he looked up and saw me.

"Sophia. What a wonderful surprise." He came over and

160

kissed my temple before walking around the island to where my mother was and pressing one to hers as well. But he must have noticed how rigidly she was holding herself because he pulled away slowly. "Something wrong?" he asked, his gaze darting between the two of us.

"That depends." My mom's voice was unnaturally bright in that way she had that let you know she was about to enjoy eating you alive. She turned toward my dad before continuing. "Do you think it's wrong to not tell your wife that you offered her daughter's vagabond boyfriend hundreds of thousands of dollars to disappear into the ether?"

"Hey!" I yelled, ready to defend Drew's honor until my mother shot me a dark look for interrupting that quite frankly scared the shit out of me.

"Oh, um, well, ahem, I . . . I guess that could perhaps be interpreted as wrong."

"Could perhaps?" she repeated, arching an eyebrow at him in such a way that defied the laws of Botox.

My dad threw a desperate glance around as if magically there was someone else here who might have a life raft to throw him.

"Well?" my mother asked, her hands cocked on her hips, making her look like some kind of designer schoolmarm.

My father did a dying fish impersonation for a minute before his eyes narrowed. "How do you know about the money?" he asked me.

"He told me."

I briefly wondered if the fact that I was back in contact with Drew was news I truly wanted to break to them right then. It was a much stronger tactic to keep the attention focused solely on my dad, but I didn't have it in me to deny Drew either.

It had taken us long enough to get back to where we were, and I wanted to celebrate that we'd finally made it.

I also wanted my dad to know his plan to break us up hadn't worked. Well, hadn't worked for *long*.

His lips pursed. "I should've known when he didn't cash the check right away that he wouldn't be able to keep up his end of the bargain. A kid like that has no scruples."

"Are you really bashing someone else's integrity?"

My dad looked unimpressed by my comment but didn't dwell on it, probably because he wouldn't have been able to adequately argue it.

"You honestly think it's pertinent to continue to spend time with someone who can be so easily persuaded to stay away from you?"

"Can he? Tell me, Dad, when did he cash the check you gave him?"

His face was unreadable except for a slight tic in his jaw, but that tiny muscle movement was enough.

Game, set, match.

Everything he'd been telling himself about who Drew was came down to one irrefutable fact: Drew hadn't taken the payoff. He'd been offered a better life on a smarmy silver platter, but he hadn't taken it. That wasn't who Drew was. And if my dad had taken a single minute to try to get to know him, he would've seen that.

But as it was, my dad had only seen a problem, and it was my dad's MO to, when all else failed, throw money at something until it was resolved. But this issue wouldn't be resolved, because it wasn't actually a problem. At least not for me.

As for my parents, they could get the hell over it.

I dug my hand into the pocket of my jeans and withdrew the check, flattening it on the island and pushing it toward him.

"Drew would never cash this. He's a better man than that."

My dad cocked an eyebrow. "Then why'd he keep it?"

"Insurance," I replied calmly. "So you could never claim differently."

"You do realize you can direct deposit a check from your phone nowadays, don't you? His having this doesn't prove he didn't cash it."

"That's true," I replied, keeping my voice even despite his words throwing me a bit. Because I *hadn't* thought of that. Not that it mattered. If Drew said he didn't cash it, then he didn't. "But we both know, for different reasons of course, that he didn't. Don't we?"

He looked at me for a second before he spoke again. "What reason do you have for believing him?"

I shrugged. "I know him."

My dad scoffed. "Hardly incontrovertible evidence."

"Maybe not. But it's enough for me."

"And if it's not enough for us?" my mom asked.

I'd almost forgotten she was here in this detente with my dad, and her words jolted me slightly.

I looked over at her and was relieved to see only concern on her face. She wasn't making harsh judgments. Well, she probably *was*, but she wasn't letting those things make up her mind for her. And while I wasn't thrilled at having my judgment questioned, I'd take that over someone who made decisions for me without ever consulting me about them.

"Then maybe you should get to know him so it can be."

My mom nodded slightly before smoothing a hand through her hair. "Did you want to stay for dinner?"

"Not particularly," I answered.

"That's probably best. Your father and I have a lot to discuss." Her tone sounded like she was a CIA agent preparing to torture a confession out of a terrorist, and I felt immense satisfaction at the prospect.

"Then I'll leave you to it." I walked toward the door, collecting my things on the way. After I pulled on my coat and opened the door, my dad's voice stopped me.

"Sophia."

I turned and looked at him expectantly.

"He's not living at the apartment, is he?"

"Of course not," I snapped before slamming the door closed and hurrying to the car.

As I put the car in reverse and pulled out of my parents' driveway, I assured myself there was no harm in telling one tiny white lie.

Chapter Nineteen

SOPHIA

The coffee table in the sorority house was covered in different polishes, removers, and cotton balls—most of which had been tossed back onto the table after they'd been used t o take off whatever polish we'd had on.

Most of the girls were stationed somewhere around the living room on furniture, the floor, or even the edge of the wooden stairs. The night consisted of pizza, soda, and so many ice cream toppings, I was actually concerned I'd need an insulin pump before the night was done.

I wasn't sure whose idea it'd been to have a middle school–style sleepover, but I was happy someone had come up with it. I hadn't spent much prolonged time at the house since I'd started helping Drew, and though I did miss him—and for some strange reason, Brody too—it felt good to hang out with the girls. It was a strange paradox where I felt relieved that I didn't need to be responsible for them but also wished they were both here.

I figured this must be what it felt like to have a girls' night out when you have kids. Only in my case, my two boys were in their mid-twenties. After finishing with the top coat on my toes, I closed the bottle and put it on the end table next to my chair.

"Emma, can you toss me that wine-colored one?" I asked, pointing at the nail polish that was sitting in front of her.

Emma grabbed the small bottle and tossed it to where I was seated about five feet away.

"Wait, the lid's not on all the way." I tried to shield my head with my arms while still trying to catch the bottle, but the result was some of the polish splashing onto my jeans as well as the old recliner I was sitting on, which I cared significantly less about.

"Sorry," Emma said, cringing. She grabbed a roll of paper towels from the floor and chucked them at me without warning. "Did it get on your clothes?"

I sighed as I tore off a paper towel and poured some nail polish remover onto it.

"Yeah. It's okay. It'll probably come out," I told her, even though I didn't think it would.

I didn't want her to feel worse than she already did, and it wasn't like I didn't have other pairs or the ability to get them.

Aamee hadn't even bothered to look up from her nails when it had happened, but once she'd heard about the polish staining my jeans, she took interest.

Craning her neck from her perch at the end of the couch, she said, "You'll probably have to throw those out."

"Or we could just tear them where the spot is," Sam suggested.

"I don't know if I'll be able to make it look like the rip was supposed to be there, though."

"Take 'em off," Sam said, already standing in excitement. "I've done mine before. My mom thought they looked trashy, so she'd never buy me ripped jeans. I used to do it myself."

"Didn't your mom flip out when she saw you cut up the jeans she bought?"

I tried to imagine what my own mother would've done if I'd taken scissors to an item of clothing she'd purchased for me, but I decided I didn't want to ruin a good night with thoughts of my mom and her murderous rage.

"I just told her I bought them with my own money. She had no idea they were the same ones she'd bought." Sam went into the kitchen and came out with scissors and a razor blade. "They'll look better than they do now. I promise."

She made a motion with her hand for me to stand, so I did. I figured the jeans would be ruined because of the stain, and they were currently wet from where I'd tried to scrub it out, so I thought it would at least be more comfortable without them on. And it was a sleepover, so what the hell?

I removed my jeans slowly, careful not to smudge the polish on my toes, which I didn't think was dry yet, and handed them to Sam. She began immediately, spreading my jeans out on the floor and describing in detail what she was doing as if she were a surgeon instructing a roomful of medical students.

We watched her work, paying more attention to that than we were to painting our nails. A few minutes passed before the doorbell rang.

Aamee jumped up to answer it. She'd already pulled the door open before I remembered I didn't have any pants on, so I quickly grabbed a blanket that was draped across the couch and pulled it over my lap.

From my chair, I couldn't see who was at the door, but I

recognized the voice immediately.

"Someone order a Nite Bites package?" Brody asked, clearly trying to sound smooth but sounding creepy instead.

Or maybe it just sounded creepy to me, because the rest of the girls seemed to light up at his words. They combed their hair with their fingers—careful not to smudge their nail polish—adjusted their clothing, and gazed at him.

"Come on in." Aamee pulled the door open farther so Brody could enter.

"That's a big package you have there," she said.

Brody put the box down on the ground before replying, "Yeah, I get that a lot."

Aamee was right beside him, and as he returned himself back to an upright position, he grabbed a handful of her hair and brought it to his nose to smell.

"You smell so good. What is that?"

I was sure the way he looked at her as he inhaled her smell must've seemed sexy to her. But to me it was predacious—reminiscent of that scene from *Jurassic Park* where the raptor gets the scent of the kids hiding in the kitchen and chases them around, snarling and drooling.

"Thanks. I haven't washed my hair in two days."

It was, no doubt, a strange response, but Brody just laughed like she'd been kidding. I thought I saw Aamee blush, which made her seem more innocent than usual. She always exuded such dominance, so it was strange to watch how a male could affect her.

Not to mention disgusting. It was a struggle to keep the vomit from rising up my throat, but I managed. Aamee and Brody were clearly into each other, but I didn't know if the mating ritual was for show or thoroughly authentic.

"What'd you order?" Gina asked, nodding at the box.

"Oh, just some things for upstairs. Body wash, shaving cream, stuff like that."

"You know you don't need Nite Bites to deliver things you can easily get from Amazon, right?" I said.

Sure, people included those types of products in their orders, but they were usually combined with some sort of alcohol or local food.

Aamee put her hands on her hips and gave me a glare she'd probably perfected on an elementary school playground over a decade ago. "Amazon doesn't guarantee hot delivery guys."

Sighing, I pulled the blanket up higher. "Don't you have somewhere else to be?" I asked Brody.

He laughed and ran a hand over his messy hair before shoving both hands in his coat. "I'm going, I'm going. Relax, I have more orders to deliver." He began walking backward to the door, giving the rest of the room a smile and a "Bye, ladies" on his way out.

"Thanks for bringing me your package," Aamee said.

Brody winked and replied, "Next time I'll stay long enough to help you open your box."

This time I wasn't sure the vomit would stay down.

DREW

I'd woken up to an empty apartment for the first time since . . . well, probably since last semester when I'd first moved into Brody's place and pretended to be him. It felt strange to hear the silence that came with being the only one home. I had no idea where Brody was, but I knew Sophia had stayed at the sorority house last night, and I wasn't sure when she planned to be home.

Against my better judgment, I texted her to see. I didn't want her to think I was trying to rush her or that I was trying to give her some sort of misplaced curfew, but I wanted breakfast and thought if she was planning to be home soon, I would wait for her. Plus, there was something I wanted to ask her, and I thought it might be harder for her to say no if she had food in her mouth.

Taking out my phone as I waited for the coffee to brew, I leaned against the counter. I hadn't even started typing when I heard the door open, and a weary-eyed Sophia shuffled into the apartment.

She groaned as she crashed onto the couch and pulled the blanket over herself.

"Didn't get much sleep, huh?"

I took down a mug from the cabinet and pulled out the coffeepot, stopping it mid-brew so I could pour her a cup. I put in a splash of whole milk and a teaspoon of sugar—just how I knew she liked it—and then headed over to the couch.

She was nearly asleep by the time I got there.

"I have coffee," I practically sang, leaning down to place a soft kiss to her temple.

She let out something that could best be described as a growl of appreciation and slowly pulled herself upright enough to take the cup from my hands and drink a little.

"Thank you," she said. "It was a long night."

"Long good or long bad?"

"I'm not sure. Just long, I think. Is Brody still asleep?"

"Nah, I don't know where he is. If he came home last night, I was already asleep. If he made it home, he was gone again before I came out here."

"Huh," Sophia said, looking more thoughtful than I'd expected her to.

"Aww," I teased. "You're not worried about your big brother, are you?"

"Of course not," she replied.

The look of concern on her face made me wonder if she was telling the truth. I knew Brody drove Sophia nuts, and vice versa, but lately I'd been sensing that their sibling rivalry had been losing its fire. Though I'd never explicitly say that to either of them.

I was pouring myself a cup of coffee a few minutes later when Brody walked in. He looked like he'd gotten about as much sleep as Sophia, but he didn't look nearly as pretty.

"Where were you?" Sophia shot at him.

"Out," he replied casually as he tossed his keys onto the table by the door and kicked off his sneakers.

"All night?"

"Yes, Mom." He rolled his eyes at her, and though he was already heading for the kitchen, I was pretty sure Sophia didn't miss the gesture.

"With who?"

"Jesus, what's with the interrogation? I didn't think I needed to let you know what my plans were." Brody poured way too much cream and sugar in his coffee and tossed the spoon into the sink with a loud clang.

"I was just asking."

Sophia's voice had softened a little, and the exchange made me wonder why she was suddenly okay with showing her concern. She usually acted like she didn't give a shit if Brody might by lying in a gutter somewhere bleeding out from a stab wound, and suddenly she was questioning him about where he was and who he was with.

I had to admit, it confused me too.

Brody drank a little more of his coffee before he set it down and smirked. "'Kay." Then he headed down the hall and into the bathroom.

Once I heard the shower turn on, I couldn't help it. "So are you gonna tell me what *that* was about?"

Sophia looked like she thought about trying to tell me it was nothing but then thought better of it. I knew her better than a lot of people, probably her brother included, and I knew for sure she wasn't asking about his night because she was interested in actually hearing about it.

I sat down beside her on the couch and raised my eyebrows. "Out with it."

"Fine. This is like . . . God, it's like the stupidest thing ever."

"I don't know. Remember, I once kissed a guy in the middle of campus to keep up the illusion that I was gay."

Sophia laughed. "Okay, so maybe not as dumb as that. I don't even know why I care about this, but last night Brody delivered something to Aamee, and they were all lovey-dovey and flirty. He stayed a few minutes and then said he had to make some more deliveries."

I thought she'd have something more to add, and when she didn't, I said, "And?"

"And there's no way he delivered all night."

"Okay," I said slowly as I tried to process the importance of what she was saying.

"So where was he?"

"I feel like this is a rhetorical question since I already said I don't know."

"It is a rhetorical question. For *you*. I wish Brody would've answered me, though. Why the hell is he acting like he wants to get in Aamee's pants every time he sees her and then staying over at . . . who the hell knows where he was?"

My brain was turning over the pieces of the puzzle as Sophia talked, but it took me a while to put them together into any sort of picture.

"So you *care* about Aamee?"

"No! Of course not."

"What am I missing?"

She released a sigh that sounded like it stemmed from annoyance. Whether it was because I asked if she cared about Aamee or because Sophia had to explain herself because evidently I was too fucking dumb, I wasn't sure.

"I don't care what happens to Aamee, but if Brody's acting all Netflix and chill when he's with her and then sliding into some other girl's"—she gestured wildly—"DMs—"

"I'm so happy you said DMs."

Sophia stared at me blankly for a few moments until she realized why I'd said that.

"Ew!"

"Sorry," I laughed. "Keep going."

"I just don't want to give Aamee another reason to hate me. I know I don't control Brody, but he's *my* brother, and if he fucks her over, she'll take that out on me."

I nodded. "Oh, gotcha. That makes sense. You want me to talk to him? I'll let it come up naturally, just see what his thoughts are and what he's been up to lately, that kind of thing."

"Yes, thank you! That's a good idea, actually. Aamee's level of hatred for me seems to have dropped a degree or two this semester, and I don't want a sudden spike in temperature because of something I had nothing to do with."

"Yeah, totally. I'll talk to him after we go to dinner at my parents'."

I knew Sophia was too sharp to let me slip that in there unnoticed, but I tried anyway.

"Like, you and Brody are going?" she asked, though from the look on her face, she already knew the answer.

"No-oo?" I dragged out the word like it was more than one syllable and also a question. "My mom called to apologize for never actually coming here to check on me like she promised, and when she heard I was doing better, she wanted to know why I hadn't brought my fiancée over for dinner yet."

Sophia just stared at me, lips pressed together. I couldn't figure out if she was trying not to laugh or attempting to stop herself from piercing a hole through my jugular with her teeth.

"So we're doing this tonight?"

"Only if you want to." And since I'd already told my mom yes, I sincerely hoped she'd want to.

"*Want* is a strong word."

"I'm thinking that's as close to a yes as we'll get, so thank you. I owe you one."

"You owe me way more than that."

I couldn't disagree.

Chapter Twenty

SOPHIA

I wasn't sure what I expected Drew's childhood home to be like, but I knew as soon as I saw it, it wasn't how I imagined it.

A brick Cape Cod that would probably have been described as quaint in a real estate ad sat nestled in between two others exactly like it on a quiet street. The shutters were black, although noticeably faded, and it had a black door to match—the kind with three tiny diamond windows running down at an angle that were popular in the nineteen eighties.

When one of Drew's sisters opened it for us before we'd made it to the front porch, it was oddly reminiscent of Kelly Bundy's entrance on *Married with Children*. Since I'd only met Drew's sisters once before and they were all blond with freckles and curvy bodies, I had no idea which one had just greeted us.

Had I been a better "fiancée," I would've stalked their social media, scouring every picture until I found a way to distinguish them from one another. But since I hadn't thought of it until now—mostly because I also didn't know we were coming until earlier today—I had to hope I either didn't need to know their names or Drew would discreetly tell me them again.

"Hi," Sister One called, holding open the storm door for us even though we were still about ten feet away.

The other two appeared at the door behind her, stacked like dominoes as they peered around each other to watch us walk up the concrete path that was flanked by flower beds that I was sure in the spring would have actual flowers in them.

Without warning, two gigantic dogs came racing out the door, not even bothering to use the four steps that led to the house, instead jumping off the small porch and landing midstride on the path. They wiggled their muscular bodies and wagged their tails as they greeted Drew like he was a soldier coming home from overseas.

Drew reached down to pet them as best he could, and I put a hand on his bicep to try to help steady him.

The dogs seemed to notice me as an afterthought, and I was thankful for it. Both had enormous heads and looked to weigh close to a hundred pounds. I was glad they didn't jump, but they both sniffed me forcefully, and I didn't know whether I should pet them or remain perfectly still.

"This one's Daisy," Drew said, pointing to the white one with brown spots, "and the other one is Tulip."

Tulip was mostly black with some white on her paws and tail. Neither one really struck me as a delicate flower, but I tried not to judge too soon.

"Cute. Did your mom name them?" I knew Pam liked to garden, so it made the most sense.

"My dad. He thought it'd be funny to name two pit bull mixes something really nonthreatening."

A few seconds later, we were out of the cold and in the living room. The home was clean, but I could tell they'd probably had the same furniture for most of Drew's life, if not longer, and the faded teal carpet was flattened in most places.

Drew's dad was sitting in a recliner near the TV, watching a basketball game.

He barely looked in my direction, but he raised a hand and uttered a "Hey."

Not that I minded the lack of attention. Judging by all the faces currently staring at me like I was about to put on some sort of one-woman show, I'd be getting more than my share.

"Courtney, go get the magazines," the tallest of the blondes ordered.

I made a mental note that the tallest one was *not* Courtney. This one was clearly the alpha of the group. Her face could be described as permanently hard, rough in a way that let people know she wasn't taking their shit. She struck me as one of those people you'd love to have on your side but be scared to have against you.

One of the other sisters—presumably Courtney—had already gotten up and walked to the kitchen, so I at least knew who one of them was.

Courtney has a butterfly tattoo on her forearm, butterflies were once caterpillars, and caterpillar starts with a C like Courtney. Got it.

I'd never needed to use a mnemonic device for remembering names, but I'd used them for years to study, so it was a natural progression and one that would hopefully help me not look like a moron in front of Drew's family.

While she was gone, I studied the other two, making distinctions where some could be made. Tall Alpha was heavily made-up—too much foundation, lipstick that was too red for her complexion. The other I mentally referred to as Fifty Shades of Blond because her blond hair, now that I was close enough to see, was dyed various tones ranging from platinum to a light bronze.

She was petite in every way—lean with sinewy muscles most women would die for. I suspected Fifty's physique was probably genetic since Drew had told me he was the only one in his whole family who ever attempted to eat healthy or work out.

Several seconds later, Courtney returned carrying a few magazines. It surprised me anyone bought print anymore when everything was so easily accessible online.

"We've been dying for you to come over," Courtney said. "We have so many styles picked out, and we need your input."

She thrust one of the magazines toward me, holding it open and so close to my face that I couldn't even see what I was supposed to be looking at.

"Heather likes this one," she said, "but it's asymmetrical, and I don't really look great with that."

"It doesn't matter what you look good in. The bridesmaids' dresses are Sophia's decision."

I assumed that comment had come from Heather since it would make the most sense that she'd be on the defensive.

Okay, Fifty is Heather, which makes Alpha Amber. And Courtney's the caterpillar. Got it.

"I also have some pinned," Heather added, picking up her phone from where it lay on the coffee table.

"Did you have a color in mind?" Amber asked. "Did you even pick a date yet? Or a season?"

Thankfully, those questions seemed to be directed at

Drew, so I let him field them.

"Um, no. We haven't really talked about it much. Sophia's still in school for another year after this. We don't have to make any decisions today."

"Of course not," Drew's mom added. "But since you're finally both here, we can talk a little bit about it. I wanted to come by and see the two of you and discuss it before, but you know how time can get away from you sometimes."

I actually didn't know how time could get so far away that a mother couldn't check on the son she'd almost lost, but I didn't think it would be wise to ask. I was getting the impression that Drew's family voiced intentions they never put action behind. And the saddest part of that was how Drew rolled with it as if it were normal.

I guessed to him it was.

"Maybe later," Drew told her, shaking me from my thoughts. "Can I at least let Sophia breathe for a second? We barely stepped in the house before you started throwing magazines in her face. She hasn't even met everyone yet."

I assumed the person sitting on the arm of the couch was Ryan, Amber's boyfriend, but I hadn't actually met him yet. Once Drew's mom and Heather headed into the kitchen, the living room felt significantly bigger. It also allowed Ryan to get up and move toward me unobstructed.

"Hi, I'm Ryan." He then looked around the room. "My daughter's around here somewhere. She might still be out back."

"No," a small voice called from the top of the stairs. "I'm up here playing with Amber's makeup."

I caught a glimpse of Amber looking beyond annoyed, though she had enough courtesy not to voice it.

"I'll help you with it later," Amber said. "Why don't you come downstairs? It's almost dinnertime."

The girl was already halfway down the steps by the time Amber was finished talking.

"Are you Sophia?" she asked.

"I am. Are you Hazel?"

"Yeah." She smiled broadly. "How did you know my name?"

"Drew's told me a lot about you."

"Probably how you can't stand me," Amber said.

Ryan put an arm on Amber like the simple touch might calm her down. "Stop," he said softly. "She doesn't hate you."

"I never said she *hated* me. Jesus."

Hazel did nothing to imply that either statement was false. She just stood there, staring at me like she was waiting for me to speak again. Even through her sweatshirt, I could tell that she was long and lean but not skinny exactly. Already at eight, Hazel had the build of a budding athlete. A swimmer maybe, or perhaps basketball would be her sport. Something that would allow her to use her long limbs as an advantage.

"So are you in second grade, Hazel?"

"Third," she said, standing a bit taller and somehow more confidently.

I'd never seen a child more self-assured in my life.

"I turn nine in March."

"Wow! Nine's a big birthday. It's your last year before you hit the double digits and become old like me."

"You don't look old. Amber looks a lot older than you." Hazel gave Amber a side-eye as she said it, and I had to stop myself from laughing. Drew's sister was feisty, but Hazel was feistier.

Ryan put his hands on Hazel's shoulders and squeezed gently. "All right, all right, enough. Everyone's here for Sophia, not to see you and Amber bicker."

"We're not bickering," Amber said. "And I wouldn't have to say anything to her if she wasn't so rude to me." She sounded more immature than the child she was speaking about.

"Saying nothing to her probably wouldn't be a good idea either," Courtney chimed in. "You have to talk to her. She's your boyfriend's daughter."

"I don't *have* to do anything. And who asked for your opinion anyway? You can give relationship advice when you sleep with more than your pillow." Amber huffed, batted her dark eyelashes, which looked weighed down by the heavy amount of mascara she'd put on them, and pulled Ryan into the kitchen. She claimed it was so she could give her mom a hand with dinner, but her cover was less than believable.

Mr. Nolan remained in his recliner like he was alone in the room with only his TV and Cheetos. Whether he chose to ignore everyone or was truly so oblivious to anything but his own interests remained to be seen.

"You call that lawyer yet?" he asked Drew, only bothering to look over at his son for a moment before the game pulled his attention away again.

Drew sat down on the couch near him, and I followed, not wanting to stand in the middle of the room without him.

"Not yet," Drew answered. "You can do it too, you know."

This time Mr. Nolan's focus was fully on his son. His scruffy salt-and-pepper jaw hardened before he spoke. "I asked you to do it."

"I've been busy." Drew offered no apology, and I figured it was intentional rather than an oversight.

Mr. Nolan laughed. "You don't know what busy is."

"Oh, I don't?"

"No. You don't. Try raising five kids and taking care of a house. Then you'll know what busy is."

"How about you try holding a job—or two for that matter— for more than a couple of months? Cody and I do most of the work on the house anyway."

Mr. Nolan sat up straighter, pointing a finger at his son. "You better watch the way you speak to me in my house."

I'd taken a seat on the couch after Drew sat down and had tried to make myself comfortable, physically and mentally, but I couldn't shake the feeling that Drew's family was so different from my own and many of the ones I'd grown up knowing.

I wondered if Drew had sensed this was the case and had caused his feelings that I was better than him. Which was still crap because his family didn't make him who he was, but suddenly, I felt like I could better understand why he might have reacted the way he had.

While the rest of the family seemed unfazed by the argument, I was still, not wanting to look at them or take out my phone to look preoccupied.

Drew hadn't mentioned his dad wanting him to call a lawyer, and I couldn't imagine what it was for. At least, judging by Drew's resistance to calling, it most likely didn't have anything to do with him. I wondered if Drew was going to say something back in defense, but he stayed quiet for a moment and settled back against the couch.

Then he muttered, "Sorry. Let's just drop it for now."

The room was pretty quiet after that except for the sound of the TV and Hazel's occasional comment. Amber was still in the kitchen, but Heather had come back in, and she and

Courtney were spread out on the floor with their wedding magazines, arguing over dresses.

Drew rubbed my thigh and gave me a smile, but it was tight and clearly forced. I knew him well enough to know he regretted asking me to come here. It was a life he'd rather keep me separate from, and here I was, taking it all in, one brash comment at a time.

"Where's Cody?" I asked him, just realizing I hadn't seen his brother yet.

The question had been directed at Drew, but Heather answered first.

"Late like always. He'll probably be here soon with some lame excuse."

I tried to reconcile that with the Cody I'd come to know—the one who'd come to visit Drew so many times, helped out whenever he could, and hadn't let any of us down since he started making deliveries for us. I decided I knew a much different version of Cody. Just like the Drew I was sitting next to who was currently fuming but unwilling to speak was not the guy I'd come to know.

Mr. Nolan glanced at Drew a few times with only his eyes, like acknowledging him with his whole body somehow showed feelings he was probably trying to conceal. Concern maybe? Regret at how he'd spoken to his son?

I didn't think Drew even noticed his father glance in his direction, and I wondered if he'd even care had he seen him.

"Why'd you come tonight if you're gonna be miserable?" his dad asked him, this time turning off the TV and standing to stretch. But he didn't wait for Drew to answer before he started heading to the kitchen. "Dinner's probably 'bout ready. Pam? How much longer?" he called.

"You can sit," she said. "It'll be out soon."

Sorry, Drew mouthed as he put an arm around me. Then he said quietly, "We can go if you want."

"It's fine," I assured him. "But if you want to leave, I definitely understand."

"I'm used to it. Not even worth arguing with him when he gets like this. He does this when he's stressed. He's been asking me to call this lawyer for weeks. Sometimes I legitimately forget, and sometimes I intentionally avoid it."

It wasn't my business, but since he'd brought it up, I asked, "What's it about?"

"Some sort of medical malpractice thing. It's a bunch of horseshit, which is why I want no part of it. He's probably worried the lawyer will think it's bullshit, so he thinks having me call and acting all concerned will help his case."

I nodded but didn't say anything.

Thankfully, Cody burst through the door a few seconds later. He rubbed both dogs' heads when they ran to him and then tossed his jacket on the railing.

"Sorry I'm late. Greg didn't get there till quarter after, and I had to stop for gas."

Drew's sisters raised their eyebrows at me, and Courtney gave him a skeptical, "Uh-huh."

"'Sup, Soph?" Cody said. He leaned over the coffee table to give me a hug, and I rose to greet him. Despite having such a less-than-stellar role model, the Nolan boys seemed to have turned out pretty decent.

A few minutes later, Drew's mom called us all in to find a seat at the table in the small dining room. I scooted around to the center, where Hazel had written a place card with my name on it. Everyone had an assigned spot, and I had a feeling that my place in the middle hadn't been chosen at random.

Once we were all crowded around the table, the family dynamic picked up a bit, especially now that Cody was home. He and Ryan exchanged thoughts on one of the Nolans' new neighbors, who Cody insisted were running some sort of human-trafficking business.

"What else could it be?" he asked. "No one ever sleeps there. Every day at three thirty, a bunch of cars pull up and all these teenagers go into the house. The cars drive away, and then at eight fifteen, all the cars come back, the kids get in, and they drive off. Eight fifteen on the dot. I could set my watch by it."

"You don't own a watch," Drew pointed out.

"Whatever. It's an expression, dummy."

Cody elbowed his brother and then returned his fork to his plate again so he could shovel some more mashed potatoes into his mouth.

"Are the teenagers girls or boys?" I asked. "Or a mixture of both?"

"Both."

"They're not running a brothel," Amber said.

"I said a human-trafficking business, not a brothel. There's a difference."

Mr. Nolan looked deeper in thought than I'd seen him all night. "Why're you just sharin' this little theory of yours now?"

Cody shrugged. "I don't know. Thought Ryan might think it was interesting."

"Well, you wanna know what I think?" Mr. Nolan pointed his fork at his son as he spoke. "I think I'm gonna take a little walk over there tomorrow and see what's goin' on. If they don't want the cops coming to check things out, then they better think of a way to keep me quiet."

It took Mrs. Nolan a minute to draw a conclusion about what her husband meant, but once she put the fucked-up pieces together, she said, "No way, Drew. You will not threaten to call the police on our neighbors."

"They're not our neighbors. You heard Cody. They don't even stay there. Human-trafficking ring or not, they're up to some shady shit, and I'm gonna find out what."

She let out a sigh, sounding defeated without much of a fight. "Can we talk about something else?"

"Fine," Mr. Nolan grunted out. "What would you prefer?"

"Andrew promised earlier that we could talk about the wedding at some point," Drew's mom said. She sounded excited, which made me feel like shit.

"Yeah, can we please?" Courtney asked.

"You know we don't have much money, so I thought my gift to you two could be that I can do the flower arrangements," Drew's mom told him.

Drew moved some peas around on his plate. "No, you don't have to do that."

I assumed that Drew was trying to dissuade her just because he didn't want to have to discuss floral choices right now. Had it been a real wedding, I wondered if Mrs. Nolan would even have come through with the flowers she'd promised.

"Yes, I insist. It's the least I can do."

"No, it's really fine. Sophia's . . . allergic to flowers."

I guessed Mrs. Nolan's expression mirrored my own: one of complete surprise. "Really? That's a shame. Which ones?" She directed her question at me, which meant I'd have to answer.

"Um, all of them actually."

Mrs. Nolan looked like she was trying to make sense of my response, like she was trying to solve a Rubik's cube and couldn't figure out how to get even one side to be all the same color.

"Hmm, I've never heard of that."

"Yeah. It's rare" was all I had to offer.

Drew's mom seemed disappointed, but she didn't vocalize it. "Well, it's the thought that counts, right?"

Drew and I nodded in appreciation and went back to our food.

"Let's discuss the bridesmaids' dresses, then," Amber said. "Everyone needs those."

"Did you pick your maid of honor yet?" Courtney added.

"Oh, no. Not yet. It'll probably be my friend Taylor, but I haven't formally asked her yet."

Heather put her beer bottle down after taking a sip. I wasn't sure if she was even old enough to drink, but my guess was the Nolans didn't exactly abide by society's norms anyway.

"Does she look good in warmer colors or cooler?" she asked.

"Both. She's gorgeous."

"Perfect," Cody said. "She'll look great on my arm, then."

Drew shot a look of warning at him because he should know better than to contribute to the conversation about a fake wedding.

"What? I'll be best man, I'm sure. So me and Taylor'll be like a couple for the night."

"Who do you think I'm gonna walk with?" Amber asked.

Drew placed his palms on the table, like he was preparing to stand in the event that we had to exit suddenly.

"Okay, I can't do this anymore," he said. "I'm sorry,

everyone—Mom, especially—but Sophia and I aren't getting married."

"Oh God, what happened?" his mom asked, a hand on her heart like Drew might have just broken it.

"Nothing happened. We were never engaged. I just said that because I didn't want to come back here to recover." He sighed loudly as he looked at his plate. Then he brought his eyes up to meet his mother's. "I'm sorry."

Everything went silent. Forks stopped picking up food, knives ceased their cutting, and for a few seconds, I couldn't even hear anyone breathe.

I'd pictured this moment, and in my version, I wasn't here to witness it. Drew would just tell me about it after the fact and how it was tough for his mom at first, but she was fine after she'd accepted it. But now I wasn't so sure.

She'd closed her eyes, and I wondered if she'd done that to stop herself from crying.

When she opened them, she said, "Okay." She breathed deeply again, pulling in as much oxygen as she possibly could. "So you're not getting married?"

"No," Drew answered softly. "Are you gonna be okay? I'm sure one day I'll get married. I just don't know when that'll be. But whenever it happens, you can do the flowers. I promise."

"Really?"

"Really," he assured her.

"Good," Mr. Nolan said. "Now that that's settled, we can go back to how I'm gonna blackmail the human traffickers."

I'd never been so thankful for an old bastard in my whole life.

Chapter Twenty-One

DREW

"I'm glad we're doing this," Sophia said as we made our way from the car to the small Italian restaurant that was close to campus.

I'd never been to Salvadore's before, but Sophia had heard good things, and I was more than happy to go wherever she wanted.

I'd finally been freed from my cast the previous week, only having to wear a post-op brace. My physical therapist had also given me the all-clear to start using a cane as long as I wouldn't be doing too much walking. I was still stiff and sore, though, made all the worse by the atrophied muscles in my leg, but I was getting stronger every day. My doctor also had high hopes that my nerves wouldn't have permanent damage, even though pins and needles still raced up and down my thigh from time to time.

Despite having more mobility, I hadn't ventured outside the house very often. It was daunting in some ways to be out on my own, and everyone had limited time to take me on field trips. I didn't want to be a burden by asking them to take me for a walk like I was a family pet or some shit. But when, on a whim, I'd asked Sophia to go out to dinner with me, she'd beamed as she'd said yes, and I realized that I was maybe a dumbass. I mean, I knew I was, but I had thought I was getting better. Apparently not.

It hadn't even occurred to me that people might *want* to hang out with me—that they weren't doing it as some sort of penance but because they enjoyed my company. Especially Sophia.

I pulled open the door to Salvadore's and held it for her. She cast me a small grin that told me she appreciated the gesture. Since I'd called and made a reservation, the hostess sat us almost immediately, which was a relief because I didn't want to test my leg's endurance. It was already starting to throb a bit. She directed us to a booth, and we slid in across from each other.

"Any idea what's good?" I asked as I opened my menu.

She did the same as she replied, "Everything, from what I've heard."

"That narrows it down."

"It's good to have options." Her tone was overly light, and I got the sneaking suspicion that she was talking about more than the food.

I narrowed my eyes at her as I tried to figure out what she wasn't saying. She kept her focus on the menu, but I could tell she was intentionally avoiding making eye contact with me. I put down my menu and folded my arms on top of it as I stared at her.

It didn't take her long to crack. "What?"

"What yourself."

She sighed, putting her menu down as well. "I don't know what that even means."

I leveled an unimpressed look at her. "Start talking, Mason, or I'm going to fake a leg spasm and start flopping around on the floor."

"Your threats don't scare me."

"No, but it sounded like *options* do."

The look she gave me was not a nice one, but she followed it up with a groan and said, "Fine. This is a date, right?"

"Yes," I replied, my tone unsure since she was confusing the fuck out of me. Didn't she *want* it to be a date? The possibility that she didn't made my stomach hurt.

"What kind of date?"

"I was unaware there were different kinds."

"Like a casual date or a . . . *date* date?"

I rubbed a hand down my face because this conversation was frustrating. Why was everything between us always so damn complicated?

"I thought it was a *date* date. Like hey, wouldn't it be nice to feed my girlfriend before I took her home and feasted on her body kind of date."

She grimaced. "First of all, don't ever use the word feasted like that again. Second, I'm being stupid. Let's just drop it." She moved to pick up her menu again, but I shot a hand out to cover hers.

The server chose that moment to come over, but I didn't want our conversation interrupted. It felt important, despite the fact that I wasn't sure what it was even about.

"Can we have another minute?" I asked, cutting her off as she opened her mouth to greet us.

"Uh, sure," she said uncertainly as she backed away.

"She's never coming back," Sophia muttered, sounding forlorn.

"Please talk to me. What's going on?"

"It's dumb. We've said I love you. I've met your family as your girlfriend. My brain is just—" She waved a hand around her temple instead of finishing her sentence. When I didn't attempt to fill the silence that followed, she seemed to deflate a little. "We didn't talk about being exclusive."

"We also didn't talk about living together, but that didn't stop us."

"So we are?"

"Living together?"

"No, you dope. Exclusive."

I smirked because I knew what she'd meant, but since she seemed hell-bent on making this as difficult as possible, I figured I'd return the favor. I took her hand in mine and pulled it closer so I could lean forward and kiss her knuckles.

"Sophia Mason," I began, much more loudly than was warranted. "Will you do me the honor of being my exclusive girlfriend?"

"You're so embarrassing," she whispered harshly.

"Oh, my love, how you wound me," I bellowed.

"Shut up."

"What's that, darling? I can't hear you over my heartbreak."

She yanked her hand from mine. "Okay, you made your point. I'm an idiot."

I grinned as I regarded her fondly. "Not an idiot, just... come on, Soph. Deep down, you knew the answer to this, right?"

"Yes."

"Okay, then." I picked up my menu and started to read it again, when she spoke.

"But sometimes it's nice to get verbal confirmation."

Moving my menu to the side so I could see her fully, I smiled. "Then consider this my confirmation that I have absolutely no interest in seeing anyone else ever. And the thought of sharing you with anyone else makes me homicidal, so I hope you're on the same page."

"I am."

"Good."

We shared a smile before returning to the task at hand. I sensed movement out of the corner of my eye and looked up to find the server hovering a few feet from our table.

"Oh, sorry. I had to talk some sense into my girlfriend here. Who I'm exclusive with, by the way."

"Okay." The server's voice was full of trepidation, as if she was being forced to wait on John Wayne Gacy in full clown costume. "Would you like to hear the specials?"

"We'd love to," Sophia said.

The server, whose name was Hannah, went through her spiel and then left to get our drinks.

"The lasagna sounds good," I said.

"Hmm, I was looking at the chicken parm."

"Also a solid choice."

"Oh my God," Sophia said a moment later.

"What? You see something even better?"

"No. Something much, much worse."

I looked up at her words and followed her gaze to a table that was about twenty feet away. And sitting at it, giggling like smitten fools, were Brody and Aamee.

"Why is my life like this?" Sophia asked, but it didn't

sound like she wanted a response, so I kept quiet.

"Did you know they were dating?"

She looked at me like I'd asked if she wanted to shave her eyebrows after dinner.

"No. Did you?"

"No way." And truth be told, I was a little salty about it. Brody was supposed to be my boy. I turned so I could gawk at them some more, but this time, Brody saw me in return.

His face lit up like a big, dumb puppy.

He said something to Aamee before he waved at us, his movement and expression animated.

Aamee slowly turned her head, looking wholly disinterested in our presence except for the slight smirk on her lips. She nodded her head in our direction before turning away.

"She should be in the Catty Girl Olympics," I remarked, unable to keep the awe out of my voice. Because I knew what was coming. With that simple look, she'd likely caused Sophia's blood to boil hotter than hell. And despite the fact it would put a damper on our evening, I couldn't help but give credit where it was due.

Sophia gave me a withering look before hiding her face behind her menu.

"Maybe he's just using her for sex and will leave her heartbroken and alone," I offered, trying to make Sophia feel better.

"Great. She won't have it in for me at all after that."

"I thought you guys called a truce. Is she still making things difficult at the house?"

"No. She's been fine in that regard. I mean, she still makes snide comments, but we both do that. I'm not sure our relationship has any other setting besides bitchy." Sophia finally looked up at me. "It's actually kind of freeing, being able to talk to someone without worrying about their feelings. We just say whatever and know not to take it personally. But fucking my brother—that's a whole different story. It's like she's trying to breach my inner circle or something."

I couldn't help myself. "I actually think it's Brody who'd be breaching—"

"You guys ready to order?" Hannah interrupted.

"Bless you," Sophia said to her, I guess because she interrupted my comment.

Hannah looked confused again, the poor thing. She wrinkled her nose as if she were wondering if she'd sneezed.

"We're ready," I said, hoping to move this interaction along.

We ordered, and Hannah skedaddled.

"Let's not even talk about them," Sophia said resolutely.

"Deal."

And that worked pretty well until Brody and Aamee appeared at our table when we were about halfway through dinner.

"Hey, guys. If I'd have known you were coming here, I'd have suggested we double," Brody said, his smile wide.

"That sounds . . . nightmarish," Sophia replied without sparing a glance at them while she continued eating her dinner.

"I know. That's what would've made it awesome," Brody replied, sounding like he genuinely meant it.

He was such a weird dude.

"I think we need to work on your definition of awesome," Aamee said to him as she let a hand drift down his button-down-clad chest.

"Come on. What could be better than spending an evening

listening to my two favorite girls sniping at each other?" He slid an arm around Aamee and pulled her close.

Sophia instantly began choking on her chicken parm.

"Oh no, she's choking," Aamee said without any inflection in her voice.

I wondered if she might actually be a psychopath.

"Ooh, want me to slap you on the back?" she asked hopefully.

"Any part of your body that touches mine won't be returned to you," Sophia threatened in between sips of water.

"That's probably a good thing, since touching you would likely leave me riddled with disease."

Brody looked over at me. "Isn't this great? We could've been watching this the whole night."

Sophia scowled at him. "Don't you have anything else to do?"

Aamee's eyebrows rose in what seemed to be glee. "Now that you mention it—"

"Well, it was great seeing you guys," I interrupted out of fear of what would happen if Aamee said anything about Brody doing *her*.

Aamee looked satisfied, even though she didn't get to finish her sentence, probably because she knew our minds had gone there even without the words.

"Okay, I'll see you guys later. Don't wait up," Brody said as he waggled his eyebrows.

Sophia pushed her plate away. "I'm not hungry anymore."

Brody laughed as he led Aamee away.

Sophia turned to watch them go and then swung her head back to face me. "He was kidding, right? About the 'favorite girl' thing?"

It was on the tip of my tongue to say yes because I doubted Sophia would top his list, but I held it in for the sake of self-preservation.

"Probably," I said.

This seemed to make her feel better, because she pulled her plate closer and resumed eating again.

"If Aamee ends up becoming my sister-in-law and I have to flee the country and start a new life somewhere else, will you come with me?"

So maybe not feeling better, then. But at least she was asking me a question that had an easy answer.

"In a heartbeat."

SOPHIA

I tried to slough off the unfortunate interaction with my brother and my nemesis, or at least look like I had, but I wasn't completely successful. Which sucked since it was ruining my first real date with Drew.

I looked across the table at him, taking in his handsome face, the way his dark hair kept falling into his eyes since he hadn't been able to get regular haircuts, the scruff that outlined his square jaw, his chocolate-colored eyes that were so kind and sincere.

He really was damn good-looking.

Too bad I couldn't enjoy any of that because my brother was probably off somewhere at that exact moment fucking the Blair Witch.

"You want dessert?" Drew asked as he looked over the small menu Hannah had dropped off when she'd collected our dinner plates.

"Hmm, maybe. Anything look good?"

"All of it."

"So we're still looking at an abundance of options."

Drew shot me a toothy grin. "Wanna share a gigantic warm cookie topped with ice cream?"

"What if I want it all for myself?"

Drew rolled his eyes before looking up at Hannah, who'd reappeared at our table. "We'll share the cookie."

"Good choice," she said as she took the menu from Drew. "Coffee?"

"I'm good," I said.

"Me too."

Hannah gave us a rehearsed smile before leaving.

"I think she hates us," I said.

Drew nodded. "Can't really blame her. We've been extra bizarre tonight."

"Really?" So much of my life had been stranger than hell for the past half year that this night had almost felt tame in comparison.

"Not weird for us but for normal people." Drew reached over and grabbed my hand so he could pull it toward him and peck a kiss on my knuckles, maybe in an attempt to soften the blow of how fucked up we were.

"Hmm, that makes sense I guess."

"Holy shit, it's true."

Drew and I both jerked at the loud voice coming from beside our table.

I swung my head toward the noise and saw a guy from Alpha Epsilon Mu. I didn't remember his name but vaguely knew him from Greek events.

"Um, what?" I asked, eloquent as ever.

"I thought it was just a rumor, but it's true. You're totally fucking your brother."

Hannah, the poor soul, chose that moment to appear with our dessert. "H-Here's your…uh…your cookie." She practically threw it at us before scurrying away.

"He's not my brother," I yelled after her but to no avail. She didn't acknowledge my words in any way. But everyone else in the restaurant did as they turned to gawk at us. "I hope you enjoyed your meal," I told Drew. "Because we can never come back."

"Wouldn't it be better if I *didn't* enjoy my meal?" Drew reasoned. "Then I wouldn't miss it."

"I'm honestly not sure what I see in you." I looked up at the interloper who was standing by our table talking into his phone, likely Snapchatting the entire ordeal. "He's not my brother," I repeated lamely.

"Yeah, sure," the guy said dubiously, never taking attention away from his phone. "Can you guys even believe this?"

Fed up, I snatched the phone out of his hand.

"Hey!" he yelled.

I looked at the demonic device to see that he was in fact on Snapchat.

I began recording a Snap. "Hello to the probably six followers this guy has. Sophia Mason here with a special announcement. I am not now, nor have I ever, dated my brother, Brody. I have been dating a cute guy named Drew." I turned the phone around to capture Drew in the frame. "Say hi, Drew."

"Hi," Drew said with a smile like he wasn't currently stuck in the seventh circle of hell. Always such a good sport, my Drew.

"I get that you all thought he was Brody. But he's not. So let's all move on."

There was obviously more to this story, and I was sure people would start wondering about all that had gone down last semester, but I had no interest in addressing any of that over some douchebag's Snapchat. It wasn't anyone's business, not to mention that coming completely clean could have horrible repercussions if the school found out.

But I couldn't say nothing at all, or Drew and I would be dealing with this nonsense every time we went anywhere. And I wasn't going to hold back on my feelings for him in public, because I'd been there, done that, got the broken heart to prove it. Hiding what he was to me wasn't something I was willing to do. So we'd have to navigate this balance of acknowledging the truth without completely exposing the lie.

I handed the guy his phone back and then opened my purse and withdrew a card.

"Sorry for ruining your moment. Here's a coupon for Nite Bites. Tell your friends." I then picked up my spoon and began eating the enormous cookie in front of me, effectively dismissing the annoying frat boy. He seemed to get the hint, because he left without a fuss.

"You're kind of a badass," Drew said when we were alone.

"Yeah? You into that sort of thing?" I teased. I felt... lighter. It was as if the lie from the fall had been weighing me down, and I hadn't even realized it until it was gone.

"You have no idea."

"Mmm, you should show me."

Drew's eyes widened a bit before he shot his hand up in the air. "Hannah!" he yelled across the restaurant.

I saw the poor girl's shoulders droop like she couldn't

believe the lot she'd drawn in life.

"We need a box!" Drew called.

Hannah didn't reply, and I was too busy laughing hysterically to see if she moved to do what he'd asked.

When I'd calmed down enough to speak, I said, "I think we need to commemorate this evening." I pulled my phone from my purse. "Publicly," I added.

I didn't want some dudebro's Snap to be what defined our relationship. I wanted to own it.

The intent way Drew held my gaze showed me he understood what I was implying. "Sounds good to me."

I smiled at him and then turned to watch Hannah approach us cautiously with a box and our check in hand.

"Would you take a picture of us?" I asked her.

She hesitated for a second, probably contemplating how the simple gesture of taking our picture could backfire on her. But she reached out and took my phone.

"Sure."

"Thanks," I said.

Drew and I both leaned over the table until our heads were side by side. I hoped the position didn't put a strain on Drew's leg, but a quick glance in his direction showed a wide smile. Quickly, I faced Hannah so she could take the picture.

"Okay, I took a few," she told us, handing the phone back to me. "You guys are a really cute couple," she added before walking away.

"Thanks, Hannah," I called. "We need to leave her a good tip."

"Absolutely." Drew reached into his pocket to withdraw his wallet as I looked through the pictures and chose the best one.

Uploading it to Instagram, I typed out a caption.

Dinner with Drew (who is NOT my brother).
Always an adventure <3

I showed it to Drew, who nodded. "Looks good to me."

Gazing back at the photo again, seeing how happy we were together, I couldn't help but agree.

"Yup. Looks good to me too."

Chapter Twenty-Two

DREW

"So business is good?" Carter asked me as he lounged on the other end of the couch from me, sipping a beer he'd snagged from the fridge when he'd first come in.

"Yeah. Really good." I shot him a grin. "You looking for a job?"

He laughed. "No way, man. Between football and school, I'm maxed out."

"There's no football in the spring," I argued.

"There's *always* football," he replied. "Well, until there's not. But I'll worry about that when the time comes." His face grew a little sad, and I felt for the guy.

I didn't think Carter had any plans for the future that didn't involve football. Luckily for him, since he'd redshirted his freshman year, he still had a full year of eligibility left. But I imagined he still felt like time was ticking down on him.

"I saw you and Sophia made it Instagram official," he said, giving me a teasing smirk.

That made me laugh. "Yeah, I guess we did. She wanted

people to stop thinking she was dating her brother."

"They still think that. But now they also think you have multiple personality disorder."

"Maybe Brody and I should take a picture together. Really blow their minds."

"Bro, that needs to happen."

"I'll see what I can do."

Carter opened his mouth to reply, but his words were cut off by Sophia storming into the apartment.

We both whipped our heads around to stare at her, and I furrowed my brow in confusion.

She was struggling to get through the door, the strap of her bag catching on the doorknob, but her arms were laden down with books, so she was having trouble detangling it.

"You know what?" she said irritably. "Just stay there."

She let the bag slip off her arm, the weight of it jerking hard on the knob before the bag crashed to the floor. She didn't move to pick it up but instead soldiered through the door and dropped her books on the kitchen table. Once her arms were empty, she stood up straight and took a few deep breaths.

"Uh, you want me to get the door, princess?" Carter asked, motioning toward the still-wide-open door.

Her head turned slowly, and she shot him a dark look.

Carter held his hands out in front of him. "Guess not. It's cool. I'm all for an open-door policy."

When she went back to breathing instead of answering, I decided to venture a question.

"Bad day?"

"A bad day that's threatening to turn into a bad semester," she replied, her voice low and deceptively serene as she continued her yogi impression.

"What happened?"

"Dr. Gilmer. That's what happened."

"The Gil-meister?" Carter asked, his voice fond. "What's he up to?"

Sophia glared at him again. "He's up to failing me, that's what! Stupid fucking sociology class with its stupid hundred pages of reading a week. What's up with him? Hasn't he heard his class is supposed to be an easy A?"

"I'm confused," I said. "Weren't you really good at psychology?"

"Dude, they're totally different sciences," Carter said, sounding affronted.

"Really?"

Carter nodded like he couldn't believe how stupid I was.

Sophia sank down into one of the chairs and put her head on the table. At least I thought she did. I couldn't see her over the low wall that separated the kitchen from the living room with her head down like that. She could've fallen on the floor for all I knew.

"So I'm guessing the class *isn't* going to be an easy A?" I asked.

"Nope. Not for me at least," she said, her voice sounding muffled. I assumed it was because her face was buried in her arms. "He returned a paper to us today. I got a D on it. A D!"

It wouldn't have surprised me to learn that Sophia had never earned anything lower than a B throughout her entire time in college. High school, even. There was no doubt the girl was a hard worker who took pride in her grades. Earning a D on a paper and being in danger of failing the class had to be a hard blow for her.

"I hate that man," she added irately.

"I can't believe you don't like the Gilmer-ator," Carter said. "He's one of the best teachers I've ever had."

Sophia lifted her head and looked over at us. "I only took the class because I needed to satisfy my stupid liberal arts credit, and one of my sisters said sociology was the way to go. She said her professor only covered like six chapters the entire semester. But it seems I got the one guy in that department who takes his job seriously. Not only do we have readings out of the textbook every week, but the guy had the university press bind him another book of articles we also have to read. The thing is another two hundred and fifty pages. And he also sends us stuff to read online. And assigns papers. And projects. And requires us to attend events around campus. I mean, who the hell does this guy think he is, the Gandhi of Lazarus University? Fuck."

"The readings are pretty interesting, though," Carter replied. "And the stuff he wants you to go to is usually pretty fun."

Sophia looked at Carter like he'd just ripped off his own head and asked her to wear it as a hat.

"Let me get this straight. You, the guy I had to read almost every chapter of his psychology textbook to, thought Gilmer's articles were interesting?"

"Well ... yeah."

"What dimension have I crawled into?"

"What? Sociology is all about people, and I'm a people person."

"Psychology is also about people."

"No, it isn't. It's about brains and feelings and other dumb stuff."

Sophia gave him a wry look. "Freud would be thrilled by your succinct definition of his vocation."

"Freud was a perv."

Sophia closed her eyes tightly, and I wondered if she was trying to wish him away. When she finally reopened them, she asked, "What grade did you get in his class?"

Carter's smile turned megawatt. "A-plus, baby. Best grade I've gotten in college so far."

I cast a meaningful look over at Sophia.

She didn't face me, but she must've seen me in her periphery. "Don't say it."

"I think—"

"Don't. Say it."

Carter looked confused. "Is this some kind of weird couple-speak thing?"

"No," Sophia gritted out.

"Then what were you going to say?" he asked me.

Sophia's shoulders drooped in resignation as I smiled at Carter. "Do you have any interest in being a tutor?"

Carter's wide eyes and bright smile were all the answer I needed.

SOPHIA

"Okay, so explain the conflict theory to me," Carter said.

I sighed. We'd been at this for over an hour, and while I had to admit Carter was actually a damn good tutor, I was tired of reviewing this stuff. "It's Marx's theory that society is in a constant state of conflict because they have to fight over limited resources."

"Perfect. And how is order maintained?"

"Those who have the resources have the power, and they

use that power to dominate the lower classes."

"Good. Now, what's the—"

"Please." I held out a hand as I let my head fall onto the table. "Have mercy."

"God, you're so dramatic. Fine, I gotta meet Toby for dinner anyway."

That brought my head up. "Toby? You guys are still hanging out?"

"Yeah, why wouldn't we be?"

I shrugged. "No reason."

"You have to have a reason or else you wouldn't have asked it like that."

"Like what?"

"Like I was intentionally trying to contract syphilis."

My face scrunched up. "Gross." When he didn't move to say any more, I sighed. "Fine. I'm just surprised, I guess. I wouldn't think the two of you would have much in common."

"Because you and I are twins?" he said sarcastically.

"We have a very similar social circle," I replied, perhaps a tad bit snappily, but he deserved it for being obtuse on purpose.

"He's cool. And I'm into a lot of things, so it's not hard to find things to talk about. Besides, he's way into sports, so we always have that."

"Okay, I can see that. Maybe it's because you look like such opposites. Like David and Goliath."

Carter made an unhappy face. "They were enemies. We're more like the guys from that book. What was it?" He snapped his fingers. "*Of Mice and Men*. George and Lenny!"

It was my turn to give him a doubtful look. "Didn't George shoot Lenny in the head?"

He thought for a second before saying, "Yeah, I think so.

Toby's anti-gun, though, so we shouldn't have that problem."

I appraised Carter for a second. "What's it like to live in your brain?"

"Wouldn't you like to know?"

"Yeah, that's why I'm asking."

Carter ignored my inquiry as he went over to the couch to do some kind of complicated bro handshake with Drew.

"I'll talk to ya later," Carter said.

"Sounds good," Drew answered.

Carter turned back to me as he put on his coat. "When do you want to study next?"

"Do I gotta?" I whined.

"Not if you don't mind failing sociology."

I harrumphed. "How about Thursday at four?"

"Sounds like a plan." He gave us both a wave before pulling open the front door.

"Carter?" I yelled after him, causing him to abruptly stop and look back at me. "Thank you. You're a really good tutor."

He flashed me a smile. "I learned from the best."

And with that, he was gone, slamming the door behind him.

"You have more homework to do?" Drew asked.

"A little, but I'm not in the mood to do it right now."

"What are you in the mood for?"

I gave him a sly look. "Wanna fool around?"

A slow smile spread across his face. "Like I'd ever say no to that question. Any idea what time your brother's coming back?"

"I'll text him," I said, grabbing my phone and firing off a quick message.

The reply came almost instantly, and it made me groan.

"He wants to know why I want to know. Why is he always such a pain in the ass?" My fingers flew over the keyboard as I asked him that very question.

"Because he's . . . Brody," Drew replied. "Tell him he better let us know, or he's going to run the risk of needing to bleach his eyes."

I snorted a laugh. Another message from Brody came through, and I threw my hands up in victory.

"He said he'll be late. He's going to the movies with Aamee."

"Wow. The prospect of sex must really mellow you out if you're happy he's spending time with Aamee."

I got up and moved to where Drew was sitting, sinking down toward his lap but careful to keep my weight off his legs.

"Sex with you could make me happy about anything."

"Such a sweet talker," he replied, his voice husky.

"I can do more with my mouth than just talk." My words were reminiscent of what he'd said to me when we first got back together.

"Oh yeah? Prove it."

I was happy to oblige.

Chapter Twenty-Three

DREW

Falling asleep next to Sophia was something I hadn't realized I'd missed until I got to do it again. But it had nothing on waking up next to her.

Maybe I subconsciously thought she might realize how much better she could do and leave in the middle of the night. I'd wake up the next morning to an empty spot where Sophia used to be, and I'd be right back where I was when I'd made the dumbest decision of my life. And I'd made some really dumb decisions, so that was really saying something.

So every time I woke up with Sophia next to me, I said a silent *thank you* to God. I wasn't exactly religious, but I figured it couldn't hurt to show my appreciation. Especially since Brody had made us thank him daily for allowing us to share his bed. If I was willing to thank that jackass, I figured I should give God some love too.

Pulling Sophia closer to me, I tried to gauge whether she was awake. I didn't want to disturb her if she was sound asleep, but I'd be lying if I said I hoped I couldn't rouse her. I was

211

always up for another round if she was.

Brushing her hair away from her ear, I kissed her softly. I tried to keep my hips still, but when she let out a quiet moan, I couldn't hold back.

We didn't even bother changing positions or removing unnecessary articles of clothing, both of us suddenly rushing to get to the main event. Moving quickly and without a steady rhythm, I wondered how long I could make this last, especially when every time I tried to slow down, Sophia whispered for me to go harder, faster.

The urgency only made the experience hotter, and we both tried to remain as quiet as possible, as we always did. A few seconds later, Sophia muffled her moan with a pillow, and I knew it wouldn't be long now that it didn't have to be.

I groaned. "So close…"

Until a loud knock on the door interrupted me. I froze. Brody knew better than to come in, but if he was knocking in the morning, he probably had a damn good reason. At least he'd better.

When we didn't say anything right away, he knocked again and then yelled, "Come get your phone, Soph. Someone keeps calling."

I didn't even realize her phone wasn't in the bedroom, and I guessed neither did she.

"Just shut it off," she called back.

"Oh, wow, why didn't I think of that? Oh wait, I did. But I have no idea where it is."

I thought the sound of Brody's voice would've killed my erection, but I was so fucking close when he'd knocked, it didn't matter.

"Ugh," Sophia groaned. "Hang on." She got up, grabbed

some sweatpants, and headed to the door. She returned a few moments later with her phone. "It was on the counter, dummy," she yelled to Brody and then closed the door and climbed back into bed.

"Where were we?" I said, crawling on top of her.

"Shit, it's my dad. He texted and called like a million times. I hope nothing's wrong."

I was hovering above her now, just waiting for an invitation. "I'm sure it's fine. If it were serious, he would've called Brody too."

"Yeah, I know," she conceded. "Let me just check the voicemail. Sorry."

Sighing loudly, I waited for her to finish so I could, well, finish.

Brody's interruption hadn't done shit to make me any less turned on, but if there was one voice that could make me go from rock hard to completely uninterested, it was Mr. Mason's. Especially when I overheard his message in her voicemail.

"I know you're with Drew. You'd better call me."

SOPHIA

When I'd posted the picture of Drew and me at dinner, I'd done it so I could announce to the world that we were together. I just hadn't thought it through that the "world" included my parents. Goddamn social media fucking me over again.

I wasn't in any hurry to call my dad, so I did my best to avoid him for most of the morning, cooking breakfast for Drew and me and even Brody. I'd shut off my phone a few hours ago, but I knew I couldn't stay off the grid forever—a fact Drew had pointed out more than once.

"Just rip off the Band-Aid," Drew said when he came into the bedroom after taking a shower.

"If by 'Band-Aid' you mean your towel, I'm all about it."

Drew tilted his head to the side and sighed. The rise and fall of his chest mirrored my emotions. Right when things seemed so right, they had to go so wrong again.

"I know. I'll go call him."

Drew didn't respond as I rose from the bed and headed back out to the living room.

Brody had left to do some deliveries, so I could at least have some relative privacy. Turning on my phone, I lay back on the couch, pulling the blanket up to my neck like I was a child, hoping the fabric would protect me from whatever might be lurking nearby. Only in my case, what I was scared of wasn't actually in the room with me, which only made me more of a wimp.

My dad picked up on less than one whole ring. "Soph?"

"Hi."

There was a pause on the other end of the line before my dad breathed deeply and released all his air.

"Don't ever do that again. I thought you might be dead or something."

"I'm not."

"I know that now. But you're away at school, and your phone started going straight to voicemail. We were imagining all these horrible scenarios. Your mom called some of the sorority girls to see—"

"Oh my God. Dad, I'm an adult. Don't treat me like I'm a child you lost in a department store." I heard my voice get louder, more defensive than the casual responses I'd given a moment ago.

"First of all, don't raise your voice at me."

Gone was the concern I'd heard a moment ago. As soon as he'd realized he didn't need to file a missing person's report, he was back to wanting to kill me.

"Second of all, you may be an adult in the eyes of the law, but you're still my daughter. And I shouldn't have to remind you that I pay your college tuition as well as the dues for that sorority you're a part of, even though you're evidently not living with them."

"Kind of like how you pay for Brody's school and the apartment he doesn't live in." It wasn't a question, and I knew even my dad wouldn't be able to think of an adequate rebuttal.

"Well, apparently you and Drew are living in that apartment, so at least it's getting some use," he said sarcastically.

"Who told you that?" My voice had gotten noticeably quieter, and I waited to hear who the traitor was. Though I should've known.

"Your mom found out from someone at the sorority after the president you tried to run against last semester was tight-lipped about it."

Nice job, Aamee.

But still, I couldn't let the comment pass uncorrected. "I did run against her. And I won."

"And for some reason you'd rather play house with some guy than accept a leadership role. I thought I raised you better than that."

And there it was—the reason my dad cared so much. What I did or didn't do reflected on him. Who I was with said something about who *he* was. Until now I hadn't realized how important it was that I seem unaffected by my dad's opinions. I was an adult. And I wasn't making any poor decisions or behaving in a self-destructive way.

Plenty of college kids were failing out of school or drinking themselves stupid. Brody had basically done those same things—worse, even—and my dad hadn't treated him like he was a toddler.

"Brody's in another country. I'm on a different part of campus. Don't you think that's a bit of a double standard?"

"This isn't about Brody. It's about you."

"No. It's not. This is about Drew. Or more specifically, it's about *you* and what people might think about me loving someone you don't think is good enough for me."

"He's not."

"You know nothing about him."

"I know enough."

"No. You don't." My heart was racing now, and I was standing, pacing around the living room because I couldn't bear to sit still. "All you know is how to pay for what you want. Well, guess what? Your money's no good here. Drew and I are together whether you like it or not."

I could hear the frustration in my dad's sigh, and I was thankful we weren't having this conversation in person. I'd found courage on the end of a phone that I knew I would've lacked if my dad had been standing in front of me.

When he didn't say anything right away, I continued. "I'm doing well in school. I've *always* done well in school, even in classes that don't come easily to me." *I'd even managed to make sociology my bitch with Carter's help.* "I earned a presidency that I allowed someone else to keep because it was more important to her than it was to me. I'm a good person and a hard worker, and I love someone who loves me back and supports my decisions more than you ever have. So you can either accept that or choose to push me away."

I didn't know where the words had come from or how I'd found the boldness to say them, but they flowed from me easily, and I didn't regret any one of them. "If you don't want to pay my tuition any longer, then don't. I'll figure it out with or without you. I'll take out loans and get a job. I'll do whatever it takes. But what I won't do is sit back silently while you dictate how I live my life."

I could hear him breathing on the other end of the phone, but other than that, he was quiet. For the first time ever, I'd managed to silence him.

Before he thought of what to say back, I told him, "I'm hanging up now. I love you."

"Love you too." There was no mistaking the frustration in his voice, but I knew he'd reply because even when he was angry, he still loved me. And he sure as hell wasn't going to be the one who didn't say it.

As I hung up, I thought briefly that I'd won this round. I'd gone blow for blow with him and had come out on top.

Too bad the game of life wasn't actually a game.

Chapter Twenty-Four

SOPHIA

"I think it's important that we do the car wash," Farrah argued. "We'd be the only sorority not there."

Farrah had just moved into the sorority house at the beginning of the new term, and since I'd been spending all my free time at Brody's, I didn't know her very well, even though we'd pledged the same year.

There'd been a fraction of a second freshman year where I thought we might become friends, but then I'd overheard her tell another sister that *Mean Girls* was overrated, and I'd decided I didn't need that type of negativity in my life.

Jenna, a new pledge from the fall, scoffed. "It's completely sexist. I can't believe the school even still allows it."

I leaned toward Gina. "How did Aamee let this girl in?" I figured our sorority president would've sniffed this chick out on the first night of pledging and sent her packing.

Gina shrugged. "The feminism is new. She was totally shallow in the fall."

"Interesting."

And it was. I was all for a little boat rocking, especially from someone Aamee had probably expected to be one of her stooges, only to have the girl flip the script. It also took the focus off me, since I'd done more than my fair share of boat rocking last semester. I was more than happy to hand off the torch to someone else who'd willingly make Aamee's life more difficult.

"I don't remember voting for her," I said.

"She didn't look like that when she pledged," Gina said.

"What'd she look like?"

"Like an Aamee clone."

"Ah, so blond and vapid, then."

Gina snorted inelegantly, which caused Aamee to shoot us a nasty glare. I looked away and refocused on Jenna, who now sported short black hair, and tried to envision her as a blond-haired, blue-eyed witch. I couldn't see it.

Jenna and Farrah continued to bicker while everyone else looked bored.

Finally, Aamee stood up. "Yeah, okay, I've heard both sides. We're doing the car wash."

Jenna stood abruptly and opened her mouth, and I found myself scooting up in my seat in expectation of the fireworks that would commence when this girl tried to argue with Aamee. But sadly, one of Jenna's friends grabbed her arm and pulled her back into her seat.

Bummer.

"Anyone have any other concerns to bring up?" Aamee asked. When no one spoke, she said, "Okay, meeting adjourned."

Everyone filed out quickly, and I'd nearly made my escape when I heard, "Sophia, can I see you a minute?"

I whipped my head around to see Aamee looking at me expectantly.

"Do I gotta?" I whined.

Gina laughed as Aamee's lips thinned. When everyone had left, I plodded over to where Aamee was standing and pasted on the fakest smile I could summon.

"You wanted to see me?"

"Well, no, I never really *wanted* to see you—"

I somehow managed to smile even wider. "Great. I'll head out, then." I didn't make it more than a step before I felt her hand grip my arm.

"Wait, I do need to talk to you," she said hurriedly, dropping my arm once it was clear I wasn't actually going to go anywhere.

I sighed deeply. "What about?"

Aamee fidgeted with a pen she held in her hand. She looked . . . nervous. I'd only seen her look this way once before, when I'd been about to unseat her as our president. I wasn't sure what was causing her to feel that way now, but I couldn't wait to find out so I could harness its power and use it at will.

"I'm dating your brother," she finally said.

I cringed. "Don't remind me."

She looked on the cusp of bitching me out but seemed to bite back her words. Another first. Opening and closing her mouth a few times in rapid succession, it became clear that she was floundering. It was a bit like watching a rabid raccoon who'd had all its claws and teeth removed.

This version of Aamee made me nervous. Because for all I joked about disliking her, we'd actually come to a bit of a truce since last semester. Our hatred had become more for show than anything else, which was still fun, but it left me without the all-consuming need to watch her burn on a stake.

The longer she remained silent, the more my concern grew. Christ, what if something had happened between her and Brody? Granted, he was a simpleton, but he wouldn't have cheated on her or anything, right?

"Aamee, spill it. You're freaking me out."

"It's just … I … Fuck it, I really like your brother, okay? But he's worried that getting serious with me would ruin his relationship with you. So I wanted to … clear the air."

I wasn't sure I'd ever been more confused in my life, and I wasn't sure where to start trying to make sense of things. Brody thought we had a relationship? Though I guess that wasn't fair. We had grown closer since starting the business. But he was worried about ruining it? He'd never cared how his actions impacted me before. Could it be possible that my Tin Man actually found his heart?

"I'm not sure what to say" was all I could think to say.

Aamee must've taken my words for a refusal to help her, because she looked as if she was going to start crying.

Jesus Christ, what's happening to everyone?

"If you cry, I'm leaving," I blurted out without thinking about how insensitive I was being, because who could think about trivial things like that when the Ice Queen was about to collapse in tears?

Thankfully, that seemed to piss her off. She squared her shoulders and stepped a bit closer to me. "Listen, I'm trying to be nice about this."

"I know, I know," I said, putting my hands up in a placating gesture. "I'm surprised is all. I didn't think either of you would ever care what I thought about you dating."

"*I* don't care."

"Noted. But Brody does?"

"Apparently." The word came out like she couldn't believe it herself.

"Huh" was as eloquent a response as I could muster. "So what do you want from me?"

Aamee sent me an exasperated look. "I want you to tell Brody it's okay to date me."

"Aren't you already dating?" I asked, because the time we'd seen them at the restaurant was seared into my brain, as most trauma was.

"Yes, but he won't take it to the next level."

I felt my face rumple in confusion. "What's the next level?" Was this their relationship or Mario Kart?

Aamee looked ready to rip my head from my body. "Exclusive boyfriend-girlfriend level. He won't commit to me until you say it's okay."

"That feels . . . all kinds of weird."

"Sophia, come *on*. I thought we were friends."

"You did?" My tone reflected my genuine surprise, but if the glare Aamee gave me was anything to go by, she thought I was being intentionally difficult. "I don't know what you want me to say. Brody's never cared what anyone in my family thinks about his choices. It's surreal that he cares now, especially that he cares what *I* think."

"I understand why it would be difficult for you to grasp why anyone would care about your opinion—"

"Hey," I interrupted, but she continued as if I hadn't spoken.

"But he does. I know we had our issues last semester, but I thought we resolved all that."

"We did." If by resolved, she meant we had one

conversation and then pretended it had never happened.

"And I've had your back on a lot of things, whether you've noticed or not. You think everyone here was okay with the fact you lied to all of us for months? You think there was no gossip to quash or drama to intervene on?"

I had thought that, yes. "Not to be bitchy, but dealing with those things helped you since you're interested in my brother and he was part of the gossip."

"Regardless of my reasons, it helped you all the same. I'm just asking for a little of that in return."

I sighed. "How is this my life?" I muttered.

The truth was, other than a genuine fear that I'd one day be related to Aamee, I had no reason to get in the way of their relationship. It had nothing to do with me, and if there was one thing I'd learned over the past six months, it was to stay in my lane as much as possible.

"*Your* life? How is this *my* life? I have to ask a guy's little sister if she'll let her brother be my boyfriend. It'd be humiliating if I cared more about what you thought of me."

I couldn't help but smile at that. "You really know how to butter a girl up."

Aamee rolled her eyes, but she also looked a little desperate—like she was actually concerned I'd ruin her chances with Brody. I grimaced a little at that thought. It was more than a little shocking someone even *wanted* a chance with Brody.

"You know what you're getting into, right?"

"Yes." Her tone was calm but emphatic.

I shrugged. "Then he's all yours."

"Really?" she nearly squealed.

"Really."

She threw her arms around me and clung, and I briefly worried that she'd been body-snatched.

"Thank you," she said.

"Remember how appreciative you were when you and Brody are living in a trailer by the river, selling repurposed tires."

She pulled away from me and ran her hands down her pink Gucci sweater. She looked a tad embarrassed by her effusive display, but her words were snarky as ever.

"Please. Like either of our parents would ever let us live in a trailer."

"Touché."

Though I wasn't so sure. My parents had to be reaching their limit with Brody, especially since they thought he was still gallivanting around Europe. He took their calls just often enough to keep them from panicking, but he was going to have to come clean to them sooner or later.

"Well, I'm going to head out," I said.

"Okay. You'll talk to Brody, right?"

I sighed heavily as if she'd sentenced me to the guillotine. "Yeah."

"Great. You're the best. Well, except for when you're being the worst."

"Can't just quit while you're ahead, can you?"

"Not really."

Shaking my head, I said, "Goodbye, Aamee."

"Bye."

I walked out of the room, casting a look over my shoulder while Aamee was still in sight.

She was smiling down at her phone, quite possibly looking happier than I'd ever seen her. I guess the saying was true: there really was someone for everyone.

DREW

I'm not sure how there ended up being so many people in Brody's apartment. They'd slowly trickled in. Brody had come home first, having finished his Costco run for supplies. Soon after, Carter and Toby showed up randomly with a bag of groceries and asked to use our kitchen. I didn't even ask them what for, opting instead to gesture them inside and leave them to it.

Toby must've texted Aniyah, because she swung by about an hour later, and Xander, who seemed to have a habit of showing up wherever Aniyah had, knocked on our door about ten minutes after that.

Aniyah rolled her eyes when she saw him, but I was also fairly convinced she'd been the one to text him where she was. It was a complicated game those two played.

I looked around at my friends and found myself supremely content with them all over my space. Well, *Brody's* space technically, but whatever. The apartment had felt like home for a while, and I'd decided to embrace it. The only thing that dampened the feeling was the fact that Sophia's dad knew I was living here and could potentially show up at any moment.

When she'd told Brody and me about her conversation with her dad, we'd all been a little tense about what he might do next. Would he show up here to throw me out and discover Brody was back? Would he go a step further and have the police evict me? Sophia doubted he'd go that far, but the worry remained.

"Why don't you have an app for this?"

I looked over at Xander, thankful he'd pulled me from my thoughts.

"An app for what?"

"Your business. The website's good, but it's not super accessible for college kids. You'd get a lot more traffic with an app."

"I'm sure you're right. There's just one problem. None of us know how to make an app."

"Speak for yourself," he said with a smirk.

"Yeah?"

"For sure. I've been doing shit like this since I was a kid."

"If you're good with computers, why aren't you getting a programming degree?" I asked him.

He pulled his laptop out of his messenger bag and began typing away. "I already have one."

I furrowed my brow in confusion. "Wait, what?"

"I already have a degree in that. But I thought a degree in business would also be beneficial so I could keep my options open."

"But . . . how old are you?"

I knew he was old enough to drink, but I hadn't thought he was much beyond that.

"Twenty-one." He continued to type as he spoke, his beanie pulled low on his forehead.

"How the hell old were you when you got the first degree?"

"Nineteen."

"Did you take a shit ton of credits your first year or something?" I was utterly perplexed how any of this was possible. "And a bunch your senior year of high school? How does that work?"

Xander sighed, clearly irritated by my constant questioning, and looked over at me.

"I started college when I was sixteen."

"Bullshit," I blurted out before I could censor myself.

"Nope," he said, not even bothering to look up from his computer.

"Shit," I said on an exhale as I relaxed back against the couch we were sitting on. "I mean, I knew you were smart, but not, like, *genius* smart."

"Yeah, well, don't spread it around. It'd ruin my street cred."

"What street cred?" Aniyah said from behind us, startling the shit out of me. "Why would you ever think you had any street cred?"

"Christ," I muttered, one hand gripping my chest.

"She should wear a bell," Xander said as his fingers flew over his keyboard.

"Like a cat?" Aniyah asked, her voice sounding overly sweet as she draped herself over the back of the couch so her head was between us. It had to be a trick. "Or a dog perhaps?"

"You said it, not me."

"Xander?" she asked.

"Yes?"

"Have you ever been throttled by a woman before?"

"No. But I'm pretty sure I could get into it. Erotic asphyxiation shit, right? I didn't know you were so kinky."

She took a deep breath. "Do you have any redeeming qualities?"

"Yup. I can make kick-ass apps."

"Can you make an app that doubles as a girlfriend? Because I'm pretty sure that's the only way you're ever going to get one."

His lips twitched. "I'll keep it in mind."

"God, would you two just bang already?" Carter yelled from the kitchen.

They both startled, Aniyah pulling her head from between us as she straightened.

"What the hell are you talking about?" she asked, her voice affronted.

"I'm talking about all that"—Carter waved his hand around—"hate-flirting you're doing. Just have sex and move on."

"We are *not* flirting," Aniyah argued.

"I'm kind of flirting," Xander quipped, his attention still on his laptop, as if he had very little interest in the goings-on around him.

But I noticed his hands weren't flying across the keyboard as deftly as before, giving him away. Xander was definitely interested in the conversation.

"You're . . . what?" Aniyah nearly shrieked as she tilted her head to regard Xander.

He shrugged. "Flirting, fighting—the basic principles are the same."

"Oh God," she gasped. "You really haven't ever had a girlfriend, have you?"

Xander snorted. "Why? Offering to be my first?"

"Gross."

"Who's being whose first what?" Brody asked as he came into the room after being holed up in the bedroom for the past twenty minutes.

"Aniyah is going to be Xander's first girlfriend," Carter supplied as he carried a pot over to the sink and dumped it out.

I hoped there was a strainer there.

Brody's eyes grew large as he regarded Xander. "Whoa. Dude. I figured you didn't get a lot of action, but shit."

Xander finally looked up from his laptop. "I've had girlfriends before."

"Non-inflatable ones?" Brody asked.

Xander gave Brody a dry look, but Toby interrupted before he could reply.

"Guys, dinner is ready."

The four of us in the living room all looked at one another, confusion clear on all our faces.

"That's what you were doing in there?" I asked. "Making us dinner?"

"Yeah," Toby answered. "What did you think we were doing?"

"Honestly, the possibilities were endless."

We wandered into the kitchen and beheld the food as if it were an atomic bomb.

"I'm so confused," Aniyah whispered. "Grateful. But confused."

"Carter said he wanted to learn how to cook," Toby explained.

"And Toby offered to teach me," Carter added, beaming at Toby.

"That's so nice," Xander said. "When's the wedding?"

"Fuck off," Carter replied, the words flippant and lacking any heat. "Dig in."

We didn't need to be told twice. Toby and Carter had made a whole chicken with roasted potatoes, asparagus, and a salad. Everything smelled delicious. We all filled plates and settled around the living room since the kitchen table didn't have enough seats for all of us.

"This is really good," I said between bites.

"Thanks," Carter said. "I know it's simple, but I had to start somewhere."

"I haven't had a home-cooked meal in forever," Xander

said. "Simple or not, this is amazing."

There wasn't much conversation as we ate, all of us too absorbed with our food. We were almost all on our second helping when Sophia came home.

"Who cooked?" she asked.

"Toby and Carter," Brody answered.

Sophia looked at the two of them quizzically for a moment before moving into the kitchen and fixing herself a plate.

"Thank God I came home when I did, or you assholes would've eaten everything." She looked around for a seat, so I scooted back and patted my good leg.

"You sure?" she asked.

"Absolutely."

She smiled as she walked over and gently lowered herself onto my lap, careful to keep her weight off my bad leg.

I kissed the back of her neck, and she turned to give me a quick peck on the lips before she began eating.

"All the couples in this room are nauseating," Brody complained.

"There's literally only one couple here," Aniyah said.

Brody scoffed. "Yeah, whatever."

"Speaking of couples," Sophia said. "I had an interesting conversation today."

Brody smiled wide. "I heard. Thanks for giving your blessing."

"Yeah, well, just don't expect me to pay her a dowry for you or anything."

Brody laughed at that, and I leaned into Sophia so I could whisper into her ear.

"Do I even want to know?"

"You definitely do," she muttered back. "I'll tell you later."

I sat back, content. The fact that there was a "later" between us was still somewhat novel. So much so that I didn't even have it in me to be disgruntled at having to wait to hear the Brody drama.

Instead, I found myself relaxing into the evening, surrounded by great friends and an amazing girlfriend.

I wasn't sure life could get much better than this.

Chapter Twenty-Five

SOPHIA

"Carter, wait up," I called when I saw him across the parking lot. I had a half hour before my next class, and I was pretty sure he had at least that.

Carter stopped, his thumbs hooked around the straps of his backpack when he turned around.

"You don't have class now, right?" I asked. "You wanna grab something to eat? I'm starving and in desperate need of caffeine."

"Which question do you want me to answer first?"

It took me a moment to realize I'd asked more than one. "Are you hungry?"

"That wasn't even one of the first two questions."

"Stop," I teased. "Since when did you start paying such close attention to detail?"

"Not sure."

Once I caught up to him, we began walking side by side. "What are you in the mood for?"

"I don't know. A sandwich or something sounds good."

"We can go to JoJo's."

He looked at his watch.

"I think they open at eleven," I said. "It's ten of now."

JoJo's had only been open a few weeks, but their food and service didn't show it. Their menu had everything from mozzarella sticks to salmon, and all of it was good. We walked the few blocks to the small cafe, which was already getting crowded, and got in line to place our order.

After finding seats at the counter facing the window, I took off my jacket and hung it on the back of my chair. We had a few bites of our food and talked about my sociology class for a few minutes before I remembered something I knew Carter would find hysterical.

"Oh my God! I almost forgot. Did you see what Toby posted today?" I was hoping Carter hadn't—mainly because I wanted to be the one to show him—so I was already taking out my phone. I found the picture I was looking for and thrust it in Carter's face, excited to see his reaction.

Immediately, his expression changed from casual to something that could only be described as *What the fuck is that?*

"What the fuck is that?" Carter asked after almost nearly spitting out his soda. He took the phone from me and studied the picture closely.

"That," I said, barely able to contain my smile, "is Toby's most recent selfie. Shirtless. In a public restroom."

"I see that. Why?" Carter looked like he'd seen a ghost. Which I guess he kind of had if he stared too long at Toby's pale body.

"Read the post. Apparently he's planning to start bulking, so he wanted to share a before picture."

"Huh," Carter said, still studying the picture. "He said he's getting 'hashtag swole for summer.'" Carter's voice was monotone, but somehow he still managed to sound confused.

"I know." I nearly snorted as I popped a fry into my mouth. "Can you imagine a muscular Toby?"

"I'm not sure. I've never seen him without a shirt on, so I'm still taking it all in."

Probably thinking it was ketchup, Carter dipped his burger in the cup of cheese he'd gotten with his fries, but he didn't seem to notice the difference. He just chewed slowly as he stared at my phone.

"He doesn't have a bad body, necessarily. Just lean," Carter said. "But he's got some definition in his abs. And his biceps and shoulders look like a swimmer's. I think he actually looks pretty good now, but good for him if he wants to get bigger."

Laughing quietly, I said, "Better be careful complimenting half-naked men in public like that. You already kissed a guy in the middle of campus last semester. You wouldn't want people to get the wrong idea about you."

Carter chuckled, clicked the screen off, and handed my phone back to me.

"Oh, I think you got an email, by the way," he said a few seconds later. "A notification popped up when I was trying to shield my eyes from Toby's white skin."

"Thanks."

I opened my school email, hoping it was my marketing management professor emailing me about a possible internship opportunity for next year. I'd emailed her a few questions about it a couple of days ago but hadn't heard back yet.

But when I opened my email, the only new email I saw was from *Nickson, Elizabeth*. I had no idea who Elizabeth Nickson was, but I quickly found out.

According to the email, she was the assistant to the dean of student affairs, and she was emailing to schedule a meeting with me as soon as possible.

"Look at this," I said to Carter.

He took the phone reluctantly. "It's not another picture of Toby, is it?"

"No. The office of student affairs wants to discuss possible student misconduct."

I watched as Carter's eyebrows pressed together in confusion. "Whose?" he asked, pulling his attention away from the email to look at me.

I was quiet for a moment, still hoping all of this could somehow be a mistake.

"Mine."

X_O

I fidgeted with the notebook I'd brought, clicking the pen over and over again until even I was annoyed by me.

The receptionist looked up a few times from whatever she was doing at her desk, but she never even asked me politely to stop. She actually looked like she felt a little sorry for me. She must've known I didn't do ... whatever it was they thought I did.

I'd spent the last twenty-four or so hours running through every possible explanation for why I was sitting here. Maybe they'd tried to email someone else with the last name Mason and had a first name that began with an *S*, and they'd just selected the first name that popped up in the address field without realizing.

But a reminder that the office knew exactly who Sophia Mason was, as if they'd been expecting my call, proved my theory incorrect.

Which left me with another possibility: There was another Sophia Mason at Lazarus University, and *that* Sophia had done something wrong. I'd go in, and they'd realize I wasn't who they'd been trying to reach, and we'd all have a good laugh before they contacted the other Sophia.

I tried to be discreet when I wiped my clammy hands on my black pants. I didn't want to look nervous, because nervous meant guilty, and I wasn't guilty of anything.

This must be what it feels like to await a jury's decision when you're falsely accused of murder. Okay, maybe that's a little extreme. But this feels pretty bad. I should've taken the Xanax Brody tried to give me.

Another possibility, which I hadn't ruled out yet, was that they wanted to interview me about another student's misconduct and not my own. Sure, the email made it *seem* like I had been the one they'd wanted to discuss, but the wording had been ambiguous in places. Or maybe I'd just read it in a way that would allow for ambiguity.

"Ms. Mason?"

Tearing my attention from the piece of navy nail polish I'd just picked off, I jerked my head up toward the receptionist's voice.

"Yes?"

"You can go in. Dr. Martin will see you now."

I stood from the antique floral couch slowly, collecting my belongings before I turned toward the dark wooden door. Taking a deep breath, I suddenly had no interest in finding out what was on the other side of it.

From the moment I'd read the email, I'd been dying to know what Dr. Martin wanted to discuss. But now that the moment had arrived, I wanted no part of it. I fantasized about what it would feel like to turn around, sprint for the stairs, and never return. Then I composed myself, walked over to the door, and knocked.

A stern voice replied, "Come in."

Despite the invitation, I entered cautiously, closing the door as soon as I was fully inside.

"Sit," she said, gesturing to the beige cloth chair on the opposite side of her desk.

She'd been standing, but she sat before I did, causing me to follow suit quickly to not look rude.

Carolyn Martin was a waif of a woman. Petite and slender with brown hair that was beginning to gray, she looked more like someone's grandmother than a person responsible for disciplining misguided students. Thin wrinkles framed her thin lips, and they deepened when she spoke.

"Do you know why you're here, Sophia?"

I shook my head before I answered verbally. "No, I don't. I mean, the email said you wanted to discuss some sort of misconduct with me, but I have no idea what it could be regarding."

Dr. Martin placed her hands on her large desk and folded them with a type of seriousness that was rarely directed at me.

"There have been some allegations, Sophia."

"Allegations? Of what?"

She lifted the paper she had in front of her and gave it a cursory glance before deciding not to disclose what was on it.

"We'll get to the specifics in a moment. But for now, I was hoping you could just tell me about the business you have with your brother and your boyfriend, I believe."

When I didn't answer promptly, she continued.

"You have a business, correct? Some sort of delivery service or something of that nature?" She looked back at the paper, moving her finger down the page. "It's here somewhere."

"Nite Bites," I provided quietly. Maybe if I were forthcoming, she'd go easier on me. I knew other students had odd jobs or little businesses they'd started up to make some extra cash, but now that I thought of it, none of them required driving around campus to people's residences.

My heart was suddenly beating so quickly, I couldn't tell if it was beating at all. What allegations were made, and who were they actually made against? I was the one who was getting questioned by the university, but Drew and Brody might have to face an interrogation on a grander scale if a girl was accusing them of something . . .

"I'm sorry, but can you please tell me what the accusations are? Are we in any kind of legal trouble? Will the authorities be involved in any way?"

Dr. Martin seemed to sympathize with my concern, because she settled against the back of her chair. "Can I offer you a bottle of water or something?"

"Yes, actually. That would be great. If you don't mind."

She reached under her desk, and I heard what I assumed was a refrigerator opening. A few seconds later, she handed me a bottle of cold water, which I opened immediately.

When I was done taking a drink, I said, "Thank you."

Nodding, she replied, "Let's get back on track, shall we?" Dr. Martin had been kind enough to offer me a drink, but she wasn't going to let her small gesture of compassion detract from the severity of the situation. "To answer your question,

I doubt the authorities will be involved. There *are* some illegal activities listed here, but I don't think they're anything serious enough that the police will want to get involved."

"Okay," I said slowly. "That's good news, I guess. So should we have gotten a permit or something? Is there some sort of campus policy we've broken?"

"I'll make this as simple as possible, Sophia. While there is the general issue with running a business on campus, the problem is greater than that. A few students have cited that your business has been involved in some activities that the university definitely does not condone. And while the students have requested that their identities remain confidential, I spoke with these students myself, and their stories seem to have some merit to them.

"For starters, they reported that you delivered alcohol to minors, which is not only an issue on campus but could potentially have legal implications."

"I didn't realize... I never made the deliveries myself. And all of our customers have an account and need to provide personal information. To my knowledge, I don't think Drew or Brody would've bought alcohol for anyone under the legal drinking age."

"But you don't know that for sure," Dr. Martin pointed out. "And while the person ordering the beer or liquor may have been twenty-one, I highly doubt every person in the house was."

I had no defense for that because there wasn't one.

So she continued. "You mentioned that the students provide personal information, correct?"

I nodded but remained quiet.

"I'm not sure what program you're using to secure

that content, but some students reported that their school accounts were *hacked*," she said, using air quotes. "I'm not sure if that term is entirely accurate here, but for lack of a better one, we'll go with that for now."

I understood that none of us knew much of anything about cybersecurity, but we'd used a financial application that was well-known and reliable.

"I don't understand how that would be our fault exactly. People enter personal information at their own risk anywhere."

Dr. Martin didn't look up from the paper, but she raised her hand. "You will have a chance to speak out in defense of yourself and your business, but right now is not that time. And I do hope, Sophia"—now she was looking up at me—"that many of these aren't true, because if they are, you'll find it a difficult feat to convince the panel of your peers that you should remain a Lazarus student. This university has a reputation to uphold and, quite frankly, looking at who your parents are, so do you."

"Can you tell me what the rest of the accusations are?" I tried to keep my voice steady, but I was sure Dr. Martin could hear me shaking. And there was no doubt she saw the tears forming in the corners of my eyes.

"Of course. It says here that Nite Bites was distributing drugs. Prescription for sure, but illegal drugs I'm actually not certain of."

I wanted so badly to yell out that the prescription drugs she was referencing were actually prescribed to the person we were delivering them to. We'd just gone to the drugstore for them. And as for the illegal drugs, I just prayed to God Brody wouldn't have been so stupid. I didn't think Drew would've been.

"A customer also mentioned that a nursing student

administered an IV as treatment for a hangover?"

Since she'd said that one as a question, I replied. "That's completely false."

"Uh-huh," she said absent-mindedly. "The rest of these are fairly innocuous, considering the others I mentioned. A delivery that never came and no refund was offered. Mr. Nolan or Mr. Mason—I'm not sure which, or possibly both—were especially 'flirty' with some of the female customers. Some other complaints regarding customer service and things of that nature." She raised her eyes from the document. "You'll receive a copy of all of it before the hearing. As I mentioned, you'll appear before a panel of your peers in one week's time. We'll email you once an exact time and day has been confirmed."

Breathing deeply, Dr. Martin locked her eyes on mine, and she looked like she felt a little bad for me. She gave me a tight smile that barely turned up the corners of her mouth. "I'd like to believe that the majority of this isn't true, at least not to the extent that it's listed here. But unfortunately, my opinion doesn't matter. The students decide what will or will not happen to you, and these students take that responsibility extremely seriously. Oftentimes, they're law students or kids involved in the political world. They don't take allegations like this lightly, and they won't let bias play into their decision."

She'd said all of it so quickly, I was still processing most of it when she added, "Do you understand?"

I choked out a "Yes."

Dr. Martin gave me a terse nod, no longer maintaining eye contact with me, which I was thankful for because the tears that had threatened to fall were beginning to touch my cheeks.

"My assistant will provide you with a copy of all this on your way out."

"Okay." I'm not sure how I got the word past the lump in my throat, but I was glad I did. Then I stood, composed myself as well as I could, uttered a "Thank you," and left Dr. Martin's office.

After getting the folder of documents from the assistant, I grabbed a few tissues from her desk. I'd definitely be needing them for my walk home.

Once I exited the building and stepped into the cool wintery air, I dug into my purse for my phone so I could call the only person I knew might be able to help. It only took one ring for him to pick up.

"Dad," I said. "I have a problem."

Chapter Twenty-Six

SOPHIA

"Here? He's coming here? Now?" Brody was pacing in front of where I sat on the couch, my head in my hands.

"Yes, Brody. I'm sorry that my potentially getting kicked out of school is threatening your AWOL status, but I needed to call him."

"No, no, I get it. And it's fine. Totally fine."

From the panic-stricken look on his face, it was clearly not fine.

"You don't have to stay," I told him. "I didn't tell him you were home. As long as you're not here when Dad shows up, he'll assume you're still in Europe."

Brody stopped pacing and looked at me. I'm not sure what he was hoping to see, but he was calmer when he spoke again.

"No, we're in this together. I'm not going to run out on you."

My eyes began to sting as a lump rose in my throat. Even though he wasn't a student at Lazarus so we therefore *weren't* in this together in a disciplinary sense, I appreciated the show of solidarity.

Drew, who'd been sitting silently beside me, put his hand over my thigh. "Do you want me to leave?" he asked.

"Do you want to leave?"

"No."

I smiled at that. "Then I want you to stay." My dad knew we were living here together anyway, and despite the fact that the conversation might be easier without Drew there, I wanted him near me whenever he could be.

The three of us sat around in dejected silence until a knock came at the door.

"Oh fuck," Brody whispered, freezing in place.

Drew looked like he was going to vomit.

"I'll get it," I said drolly as I got up and headed for the door. I pulled it open and stood back. "Hey, Dad."

"Hi, Soph."

His voice was soft and his eyes were kind. He stopped to kiss my cheek as he walked into the apartment. Having him here made me feel like everything would be okay. No matter how badly my father and I disagreed, he'd always been there for me when I truly needed him, and I knew it would be no different this time. Since he was still dressed impeccably in a sharp gray suit, I knew he'd dropped everything to come to me.

My eyes prickled again. Even though he drove me batshit crazy, I needed to appreciate this man more.

After closing the door, I turned to see Drew standing and walking toward my father with his hand outstretched.

"Good to see you, Mr. Mason."

My dad hesitated for a fraction of a second before seeming to sigh into the gesture of returning the handshake.

"Drew. Good to see you up and about."

"Thank you, sir."

My dad moved slightly to the side so he could see my brother, who was hovering behind the couch as if it were a turret protecting him from enemy fire.

"Brody." My dad's voice held no inflection: neither surprise nor anger.

"Dad."

"Finally ready to stop hiding from us?"

"I wasn't hiding," Brody replied indignantly, crossing his arms over his chest like a stubborn child. "I was . . . vacationing."

Dad scoffed. "Is that what they're calling dodging responsibility nowadays? Not that it even makes sense, given the fact you've been home for months."

We all stilled.

"You knew?" Brody asked, not even bothering to hide the surprise in his voice.

My dad pushed his hands into his pockets as he scoffed. "Come on, Brody. You do know how credit cards work, don't you? Anytime you use it, it tracks where the charge came from."

I slowly panned to my brother, who had somehow just proved himself dumber than I'd already thought. "You've been using your credit card?"

Brody looked exasperated with me. "What did you think I used to start the business? You think the supplies just magically appeared here?"

I gritted my teeth. "I thought you used the money you'd earned from your job."

Brody shot me a dry look. "Sophia, I was delivering pizzas, not trading stocks on Wall Street. How would I have ever made enough doing that to get us up and running?"

Okay, well, when he put it like that, it seemed stupid not to have wondered.

"I'm not sure. I guess I assumed you'd used your savings."

"I'd already put a dent in that when I went to Europe," Brody muttered. "I didn't want to totally decimate the account. And people say she's the smart one."

"Compared to you, I'm a genius."

"Compared to me, a Golden Retriever is a genius!"

"I . . ." I wasn't really sure how to argue with that, so I changed tactics and turned toward my dad. "How come you never said anything?"

"Why bother? He clearly wasn't ready to talk to us, and we knew he was safe, so we figured we'd let it lie until he grew up and came to us."

"Wanting to explore other countries doesn't mean I'm not a grown-up," Brody argued.

"You're right, Brody." My dad's voice couldn't have dripped with more sarcasm if he'd tried. "Hiring a stranger to go to classes for you while you took off to parts unknown without telling anyone in your family is the mark of a truly mature man. My mistake."

Brody opened his mouth to argue, but Dad lifted a hand, silencing him. "I know it's hard to not make everything about you, Brody, but I'm not here to discuss you and your life." He turned toward me. "Sophia, let me see the documents they gave you."

It took me a moment to move. I couldn't help but be shocked by the fact that my dad—who'd never in his life missed an opportunity to make a situation about my brother—was actually shutting him down and putting my needs first.

When I noticed everyone staring at me oddly, I realized I'd been standing frozen for too long. I quickly scooped the papers off the coffee table and handed them to him.

I'd gone over the major points when I'd called him, but my dad was a thorough businessman, and he gave all his attention to the copies of the accusations the dean had collected against me.

The rest of us stood around quietly, allowing him to concentrate.

Finally, he looked up at us. "Walk me through the business, showing me everything you have accompanying it. Website, terms of service, pamphlets, everything."

Brody, Drew, and I shared a look before flying into action. Drew grabbed the laptop while Brody opened the app, and I went into the bedroom to pull out the box that served as our filing system. My dad looked more than a little overwhelmed by everything, but he removed his suit jacket and settled in as we took turns explaining the business from the beginning.

As Brody was explaining how we took and filled orders, there was another knock on the door.

Now who could that be?

I got up to answer it, pulled it open, and my jaw fell when I saw Aamee.

"Brody called and told me what happened. I brought reinforcements." She gestured over her shoulder at the mob that was collected behind her.

Gina and Emma were there, along with Carter, Toby, Aniyah, and Xander.

There was no stopping the tears this time. I threw open the door so they could enter, unable to speak due to how moved I was.

Aamee stopped in front of me, rolled her eyes, and pulled me into a hug.

And while I was sure afterward I would deny it upon threat of torture, I sank into her and clung.

DREW

I sat on the couch surveying all the people who'd shown up to help Sophia, and I was immensely grateful for every one of them. While I'd been doing my best to appear calm, I was a riot of nerves on the inside.

What the hell would we do if Sophia got kicked out of school because she'd been helping Brody and me? How would I ever live with that guilt? How would she live with what we'd gotten her into? Why did everything always become such a mess?

"Sophia," her dad said, pulling my attention to where he was leafing through papers on the kitchen table that had been moved into the living room so we could spread out more. "Is your name on any of these documents?"

"No," she replied from her spot beside me on the couch.

"Then how did the dean even connect you to it?" he asked.

"I'm not sure. I was promoting it, but I marketed it as being run exclusively by Brody and Drew."

"That's a point you have to keep driving home to the panel. There doesn't seem to be any hard evidence that you were involved in the business beyond promoting it. And college kids promote things all the time. There shouldn't be a penalty for you doing so."

"But when I talked to the dean, I didn't deny my involvement," Sophia said, her voice small and defeated.

I slid my hand over her thigh and gave it a squeeze to remind her I was here for her. I hoped it was enough, and when she put her hand over mine and threaded our fingers together, I thought maybe it was.

"Doesn't matter," her dad replied as he continued to riffle through papers. "You can explain that away by saying you were concerned for your brother and boyfriend and didn't want to point the finger at only them."

Her dad managed to not sound repulsed when he called me Sophia's boyfriend, and I gave him points for the steady delivery.

"But I *don't* want to pin it all on them," Sophia argued.

Mr. Mason opened his mouth to reply, but I beat him to it.

"Sophia, you need to do what you need to do. This is your education we're talking about here. You are absolutely to save yourself in whatever way you can." My tone brooked no room for argument, and I hoped Sophia, for once, didn't give me one.

She looked ready to, but then Brody added, "Seriously, Soph. The school can't do anything to Drew or me. Being a martyr won't help anyone."

Sophia still looked like she wanted to argue but took a deep breath and turned her attention back to whatever was on her phone.

Her lack of argument and Mr. Mason's point made me feel hopeful. I remembered how Brody and I had tried to convince her to take some credit for her part in the business. Thank God she hadn't listened to us.

"What did you guys find out about the people who emailed with a grievance?" Mr. Mason asked the room.

He'd asked us if we had a record of people who'd complained, and Brody had shown him the folder where we'd saved all of them. They were all small things: people bitching that their delivery was ten minutes late, an item hadn't made its way into the box, we hadn't offered them a refund for merchandise they'd already used. Typical shit.

But Mr. Mason hadn't wanted to leave any stone unturned and sent us all to social media to stalk the people who'd emailed about the business in case we found someone who had a reason to target Sophia.

So far, we hadn't found anyone with an ax to grind.

I turned my attention back to the Instagram account of some girl who'd whined that the soda we'd delivered wasn't diet, even though she hadn't ordered diet and had only complained after drinking what we'd given her.

Carter came over and plopped down on my other side, his phone in his hand. "This sucks."

"Tell me about it," I muttered.

"People are such shitheads sometimes. Here you guys are, just trying to provide a service to lazy students, and someone has to go and wreck it."

I exhaled loudly and turned to him to respond, but an image on his phone caught my attention. "Hey, I know that guy."

Sophia leaned over me so she could look at Carter's phone.

"He's a frat guy from Alpha Epsilon Mu," she said. "Same frat as the guy who saw us out at Salvadore's. How do you know him?"

"I'm not sure," I murmured. "Brody!"

"Yeah?" Brody responded as he walked over to me.

"Is this guy familiar to you?"

Brody looked at the picture on the phone and thought for a second before snapping his fingers. "Yeah, that's the guy who asked me to run that errand for him the night I had the idea for the business."

"What did he complain about?" Aniyah asked.

Sophia grabbed her laptop and read through the emails.

"He said the delivery guy was rude. We apologized and offered him fifteen dollars off his next purchase, but he never responded."

"Weird," Aniyah said.

"What's his name?" Xander asked.

"Rob Cantrell."

"Okay, give me a second," Xander said, his hands flying wildly over his keyboard.

"Do we want to know what you're doing?" I asked.

"Nope."

We all waited with bated breath—even Mr. Mason—while Xander did who knows what on his laptop.

"Well, I'll be damned," he said after a few minutes.

"What?" Sophia asked.

Xander spun the computer around. "Looks like our boy Rob and his frat minions are looking to undercut your business."

We all moved in to look at the computer. There were email messages as well as a mock-up of a website that looked very similar to ours.

"What do the emails say?" Toby asked.

"Basically that they feel they gave you guys the idea for the business, so they have a right to it."

"That's bullshit. How could they claim it was their idea?" Brody asked, anger clear in his voice. "And what does that even matter? It's not like you can patent an idea like this."

"They're dumb frat bros," Xander said as if it were obvious, and hell, maybe it was. "They see you guys making money and think they can do the same thing. But they have to get you out of the way first."

"But that makes no sense," Sophia argued. "Why would

they put the business on the dean's radar if they intended to do the same thing? They're making it even harder on themselves."

"Not necessarily," Toby said. "If they get the panel to rule on your case, then they know the consequences, and they also know exactly how far they can push with their own business without getting into trouble. Your case will provide a blueprint of what not to do."

"Those smarmy assholes," Brody seethed.

"So what do we do? We can't exactly turn all this over to the dean," Gina said. "Not with the way Hacker Boy went about getting it at least."

"What frat did you say it was?" Aamee asked.

"Alpha Epsilon Mu. Why?"

Aamee looked thoughtful for a second. "I have some calls to make. I'll talk to you guys later." She pressed a quick kiss to Brody's cheek before bustling out of the apartment.

"She's dating you?" Mr. Mason asked Brody.

"Yeah," Brody replied on a lovestruck sigh.

His dad grunted. "Maybe there's hope for you yet."

With the look Aamee had on her face, maybe there was hope for us all.

Chapter Twenty-Seven

SOPHIA

From the time I'd stepped into the small room, I'd instantly regretted my decision to wear a long-sleeve, light-green dress.

I'd never been much of a sweater. Even when I worked out, I'd leave the gym with little more than a damp sheen on my skin. Drew told me it was more of a glow, but I sure as hell wasn't glowing now.

Sitting in front of these seven people who were assigned to decide my academic fate gave me a sense of doom that had my underarms drenched. For the last fifteen minutes, as they'd verbally itemized all my supposed wrongdoings while I sat across from them, I'd done my best to seem unfazed by all the allegations.

Maybe if I seemed confident in my innocence, they'd be confident too.

But my goddamn body had betrayed me, and I was sweating like . . . well, like someone who could get kicked out of college at any moment.

My dad had prepped me thoroughly—walked me through

all the accusations and what my responses to them should be. And before I'd come here, I'd felt pretty good.

But the longer I listened to the jury of my collegiate peers cite each of Nite Bite's transgressions, the more I felt like I was sitting opposite an academic firing squad who was deciding whether they would show me some mercy with a quick shot to the head or they should let me suffer a little while I bled out from a wound over time.

Either way, I was dead.

"Can we open a window?" I asked, already standing as I prepared to offer to do it myself, even though the windows were behind the members of the panel. The sunlight streaming in had made me feel like there was a literal spotlight on me in addition to the figurative one. "I feel warm. Is anyone else warm?"

"I'm not," said one of the girls as she looked to the others, possibly to gauge their thoughts.

"I think we're fine," another said. "But you can crack one if you'd like."

I thanked them, and as I walked to the other side of the room to pull open a window, I wondered how guilty it made me look that I was letting in thirty-degree air.

I remembered hearing about how our founding fathers had prepared to write the Declaration of Independence in the Philadelphia summer heat with the doors and windows to the room locked so no one could hear what they were saying in there. I don't think I'd ever fully appreciated their sacrifices until now.

Once I'd returned to my seat, they delivered a few last words before addressing me.

"Would you like to speak about any of these matters?"

one girl—I think her name was Mindy—asked.

"I would, yes. Thank you."

A student who had introduced himself as Nelson Jones, a senior prelaw student, said, "The floor is yours, then."

Clearly taking his role on the panel seriously, he was dressed in a suit and tie, which was more formal than most of the other people in attendance. He'd been fairly quiet for most of the meeting, appearing almost disinterested at times as he stared at anything other than me.

But now his dark eyes focused on mine. They weren't warm, but they weren't exactly intimidating either. I imagined they were the kind of eyes that would one day command the attention of a courtroom.

"Thank you." I removed the paperwork from the folder I'd brought. My dad had gone over every detail of every paper with me. I knew this inside and out. I just hoped it would make a difference. "I have some documents here if you wouldn't mind taking a look."

Nelson held out his hand so I could place the documents in it.

He laid them down in front of him, spreading them out so all of them were visible and also probably so the other panel members could see.

"What are we looking at here?" he asked.

"They're all the documents associated with the business, including a printout of the website home page."

"I see that," Nelson said. "But why are we looking at them? How does this benefit you?"

"It benefits me because my name isn't on any paperwork as an owner or co-owner or owning any piece of the business in any way."

"You live with Mr. Mason and Mr. Nolan. Is that correct?"

"Yes, but that doesn't mean I'm a partner in their business."

A girl toward the end of the table with dark, flawless skin and an eye for fashion spoke up next.

"You're part of Zeta Eta Chi, right?" She glanced up from her notes long enough to see me nod. "So why weren't you staying at the sorority house?"

"Drew was in a bad motorcycle accident a few months ago, and he needed help recovering."

"I'm sorry to hear that," she replied. "How's he doing now?"

"Better," I said with a sigh, and she gave me a tight-lipped smile. "Thank you."

"So you moved in to help him . . . " She gestured toward me to continue.

"Right. Yeah. That's pretty much it. My brother was supposed to be in Europe, and Drew needed a place to stay. But when we got there, Brody was in the apartment. I didn't expect Brody to be much help with Drew, but he surprised me. He did things for him when I was at school and even got a job delivering pizzas so he could help Drew with money. Anyway, I guess you didn't need to hear all that, but the pizza job is how the idea for Nite Bites came about. Brody took Drew on some deliveries so he could get out of the apartment, and one night they came up with the idea to deliver other items too. I wasn't even there for the inception of the idea. I heard about it from them when I came home and found them making the website."

"I heard *you* created that website," someone else pointed out.

I wondered just how she'd heard that exactly, but it didn't do me any good to ask.

"I did. The design of it, anyway. Brody and Drew—the owners—" I clarified, "created the site, but I did the general design and layout as well as most of the information."

"It says here you also promoted the company by distributing business cards and running the social media accounts," Mindy said.

My dad and I had discussed this very topic, so I was prepared to justify my role.

I nodded. "That's correct."

"So you'd consider yourself an independent contractor, then?"

"No, I'm not an independent contractor."

"How many websites have you designed for businesses before you made the site for Nite Bites?"

"None," I answered slowly. I couldn't make sense of their line of questioning. What did it matter if I'd done work for other businesses before this one? The only business ethics in question were those concerning Nite Bites.

"Did you get paid for any of the work you did for Nite Bites?" Nelson asked me.

"No, I didn't. They offered to compensate me, but I told them to use whatever money they would've paid me to get their business up and running."

A few other panel members noted something on their yellow legal pads.

I wondered if this was an "innocent until proven guilty" situation or if my fate had been all but decided before I'd walked through the door. They had all the statements and had, I assumed, spoken to the people directly. They must've felt there was a reason I should be sitting here, even if I didn't understand what that reason was exactly.

"I'm not an employee of the company, if that's what you're wondering," I added.

"Hmm," Nelson said.

"I told them to keep the money because I was trying to be nice and not take money from my boyfriend and brother. I was happy to help them."

Okay, maybe *happy* had been a bit of an exaggeration, but ultimately I'd been glad I'd done it, even if I hadn't been thrilled at first.

It was the first time I'd seen either one of those two clowns this excited about something and the first time I'd seen my brother put this much effort into anything that could be classified as work. The fuck if I'd let a bunch of jealous frat boys not only get me kicked out of school but cause Drew and Brody's love child to go under.

They were great dads, and I wasn't going to let their baby die.

Though...it suddenly occurred to me that even if Rob and his buddies wanted a "blueprint," as Toby had called it, so they wouldn't make the same mistakes, getting me in trouble did nothing to take down Nite Bites. It could survive—and even thrive—without my role in it because the truth of it was, I didn't actually have one.

"So you were just being friendly," Mindy said. "Volunteering your free time to make websites and post on social media and pass out business cards, among other things, I'm sure."

"Exactly. Yes, that was exactly what I was doing. They had other friends helping too. They're likable guys. People wanted to see them succeed."

"What people? Other students?"

Not that any of the others would be in trouble for helping pack boxes or double-check orders, but this chick was out of her fucking mind if she thought I was going to name names. Especially when the person who'd made the app was also the person who'd burned down the school library. Well, *almost* burned it down.

"Look," I said, "there isn't much else I can say other than I was trying to be a good girlfriend and a good sister by helping Drew and Brody. I don't make a profit from their business, and I don't deserve to be punished for its success."

I steadied my nerves, managing to keep my voice calm when my mind was anything but.

"I understand that you can't have students distributing alcohol to minors or pushing pills on campus," I added, "but I did neither of those things nor any of the other ones that you mentioned. And neither did Brody or Drew. If they had, we all know more than just the school would be involved here."

A few eyebrows raised, and several students on the panel exchanged glances as I spoke.

I wished I were focused and perceptive enough to read their body language, but I was so caught up in my own words, I didn't have a chance to decipher the silent glances being exchanged in front of me.

The room was quiet for a minute or so before Nelson's voice cracked the silence. "Okay. Well, we have a lot to discuss. If you'll excuse us for a bit, we'll call you when we've reached a decision."

"Of course," I said before standing and gathering my things. "Do you have a time frame for your decision? How long do these things usually take?"

"Sometimes a few minutes, sometimes a few hours,"

Nelson said. "Feel free to go home and come back when we contact you."

"I think I'd rather wait outside."

He nodded. "Okay, then. We'll let you know when we've come to a decision."

"Thank you," I said, and I headed back out and walked the fifteen feet or so to the lobby that held a few wooden chairs.

The floor was a freshly waxed tile that made the area feel more cavernous. Had there been any noise, it certainly would've echoed. But since it was a weekend morning, the building was probably empty except for the people on the panel.

I found it difficult to sit, so I wandered the halls, trying to memorize the names of the alumni on the various plaques that adorned the walls. It gave my brain something to focus on besides my own fate. I'd been in this building countless times to attend classes over the course of the past two and a half years, but until now, I'd never bothered to notice much of anything inside it.

Now my senses took in everything: the draft when I walked close to the old, skinny windows, the difference in color from where one hallway had been repainted while the other remained a dull ivory that I figured used to be white, the classroom that had held one of my first courses at Lazarus.

I wondered if I was extra perceptive out of boredom or because I was scared this might be the last time I'd get to walk these halls.

But maybe we could appeal the decision if it didn't go my way. Maybe my dad would hire a lawyer to fight back. Or maybe I could just be an adult and accept the consequences no matter how unfair they seemed.

I could only hope the university would let me leave without any disciplinary action staining my otherwise spotless record, considering I would need to apply to another school to finish out my degree, which would, now that I thought about it, take me another two years. I was sure my junior year's credits wouldn't be accepted toward my graduation requirements.

I was practically drowning in my own thoughts when the sound of voices caused me to come up for air. Male voices I didn't recognize and . . . Was that Aamee? It sounded like they were arguing with her, which wasn't surprising considering Aamee's pleasant personality.

I followed the voices, turning corners until I came face-to-face with Aamee and two guys I didn't recognize. At least at first. But a closer examination proved otherwise.

They definitely looked familiar and not in a good way. One was that guy from the restaurant, and the other I thought I recognized as the asshole Brody had pointed out as the one whose delivery had sparked his and Drew's idea for Nite Bites.

"What are *you* doing here?" I crossed my arms and felt my jaw go rigid when I spoke.

I wondered why Aamee was with them, and the best idea I could come up with was that they'd wanted to come watch my fall from grace and Aamee had tried to stop them. But how would she have known they were coming here? "And why are you with them?" I asked Aamee, not able to drop the accusatory tone I'd used when I'd addressed the boys.

"I brought them here. They're gonna tell the panel the truth about how this was all a ploy to embarrass you and take down Nite Bites. What room are they in?"

Apparently Aamee thought that had been a sufficient explanation because she didn't elaborate further.

"What? That makes no sense. They're the reason I'm here. Why would they do that?" I refused to ask the guys anything else because they never answered my first question, and they didn't exactly have a reputation for being truthful anyway.

Aamee stared at me for a moment before I noticed the hint of a smirk on her face. "Honey, I've got dirt on everyone."

DREW

"How much longer do you think it'll be?" Brody asked for like the twentieth time since Xander had pulled into the parking lot.

"I feel like she's gotta be done soon," I said. "Did you hear back from Aamee yet?"

He'd texted her about a half hour after we'd seen her walk into the building with the two frat guys. If I thought I could've jumped out of the van and kicked the shit out of them without reinjuring myself, they would've never made it inside the entrance.

Of course, that would've defeated the purpose for why Aamee had brought them to begin with, but it was fun to fantasize about.

"Nah, not yet."

Cody grabbed the handle of the van door to slide it open. "I'm going in."

"You're *not* going in," I told him. "You don't go to school here."

"That's exactly why it should be me who goes. No one knows who I am."

"Yeah, but the last thing we need is for someone to accuse you of trespassing or something. The only reason the building is even open today is because of this meeting. You'll look shady."

He let go of the handle and sank back against the worn burgundy seat.

"You're right," Cody said. "It's better to stay in a nearly empty parking lot in this unmarked white van for a few more hours, peeping out the curtains like a bunch of amateur criminals."

Xander laughed from his spot on the floor between the two front seats. "Who you callin' amateur?"

"That's it. I'm gonna walk to get something to eat," Toby said. "I'm starving."

"We just had lunch three hours ago," Aniyah told him.

"I need to eat every few hours to keep up my energy. I have the metabolism of an Olympian."

Aniyah practically snorted. "Too bad you don't have the body of one."

Glaring harshly at her, Toby said sternly, "I'm trying to put on some muscle. That requires a strict diet of complex carbs and protein."

Aniyah rolled her eyes, but I could tell she was only teasing Toby because . . . well, because he was so easy to tease. He'd recently taken to tracking his food intake with the rigidity of someone training for a Strongman competition.

"Here," Carter said, reaching into the backpack he'd brought. He pulled out two Styrofoam containers and handed one to Toby. "Grilled chicken salad with almonds, oil, and vinegar."

"Did you put salt and pepper on it?" Toby asked.

"Of course." Carter dug through his bag some more for a few forks and handed one to Toby. "Anyone want some?" he asked, holding out the other forks. "I don't need all this."

"And I don't need salmonella," I said. "I'll pass."

Everyone else declined his offer too.

Carter shook his head and then dug into his meal, like he was both offended by our reluctance to eat it and glad he'd get to eat all of it.

"Suit yourselves," he said, "but it was in a cooler."

"Yeah, still not chancing it," Brody said. "There's no bathroom nearby, and no telling how much longer we'll be here."

A few seconds passed before Xander called out, "Here they come!"

We hadn't told Sophia we were going to come over and wait for her, and though the gesture seemed considerate at the time we'd thought of it, I wondered now if it had been a good idea. If the verdict hadn't gone her way, she probably wouldn't want to see any of us, let alone all of us at once. She hadn't even wanted a ride to the meeting, opting instead to walk so she had time to think on her way.

"Can you see her expression?" I asked because I was sitting on the opposite side of the van from the building.

"No, I can't tell if either of them looks like they're in a good mood," Xander answered.

"Well, Aamee's like the Mona Lisa," I told him. "Her smile and her scowl look virtually the same."

"Watch it, asshole," Brody warned, making both of us laugh before returning to the reason we were all there. "They're going to Aamee's car now. They said something to the guys, and now the pricks are walking away."

Xander turned the key in the ignition, and the van started up with a low growl and a shake. He took off with a screech.

"Are you gonna run them over?" I asked, panicked.

"No. Should I?" Xander answered. "I was just gonna drive over to Aamee's car."

A few seconds later, we were next to Aamee and Sophia, who were getting ready to get into Aamee's car.

They jumped, startled when Xander pulled up next to them and slammed on the brakes.

Cody opened the door and jumped out before the vehicle had even come to a complete stop. I did the same, minus the jumping part.

"What happened?" we all asked like we'd spent the last few hours rehearsing the question in unison.

"Jesus Christ!" Sophia said. "I thought I was about to get kidnapped. My nerves are shot today. Are you *trying* to give me a heart attack?"

"We're the ones about to have heart attacks," Brody said. "I texted Aamee like an hour ago and didn't hear back. How'd it go? Did they kick you out? Are you suspended? What happened? Did it help that the guys showed up and admitted what they did?"

Sophia leaned against Aamee's car for a moment until Aamee reminded her that the vehicle was worth more than her life and she better not fuck up the finish.

I pulled Sophia into a hug and kissed her forehead. "What happened?" I asked softly.

Chapter Twenty-Eight

SOPHIA

It was finally over. All the fear and the headaches and the justifications for my actions. It felt good just for all of it to be done—to be with my friends, my boyfriend, and my brother. They'd shown up when I needed them the most, and I didn't want to leave them in suspense any longer.

"It's okay," I said. "I'm still enrolled in school, and you guys can still run the business. I'm not sure how much the guys' admission actually helped, because the panel still chose to deliberate for a while. But ultimately, they decided I shouldn't be disciplined."

Everyone looked relieved, most of all Brody, which surprised me. He came over and put an arm around my shoulders, pulling me from Drew as he squeezed my body into his.

"Thank God" was all he said, and I heard it for what it was.

Out of all the shit he'd done to fuck things up in his own life, he'd never meant to fuck up mine. And he'd probably never have forgiven himself for it if he had.

"Let's go celebrate," he added.

I snuggled back into Drew. "Can we just celebrate at home?" I asked. "I'm kinda wiped out."

"Of course," Brody said. "House party!"

I cocked my head at him, raising an eyebrow. "Brody."

"Fine. We'll just order Marco's and drink some beer."

Smiling at my friends, I said, "That sounds perfect."

A few minutes later we were back at Brody's apartment, climbing the steps as we filled the stairway with laughter and pure relief. We could spend the night drinking and reminiscing about all the crazy shit that'd happened over the last semester and a half until we all got so tired we passed out wherever we lay.

We all waited at the top of the stairs behind Brody as he fished his keys out of his pocket and slid the one for his apartment into the door. This was going to be a great night.

Or maybe it was going to be weird as hell.

Brody practically jumped when he pushed the door open.

"Veronica?" he said, sounding like he'd seen some sort of apparition he wasn't sure was real.

Brody hadn't actually entered the apartment, so all of us craned our necks and squeezed around him to see the person he'd spoken to.

A beautiful, dark-haired woman sat elegantly on the couch, her back resting delicately on the throw pillow. The way she crossed and uncrossed her legs as she glared at my brother reminded me of Sharon Stone in *Basic Instinct*.

I hoped this woman wasn't a psychopath.

"Brody," she replied softly but with a sternness that highlighted just how intimidating she seemed.

I noticed she had an accent, but since she'd only spoken

one word, I couldn't place the origin.

Brody stared, unresponsive, his mouth open. "How did you...? What are you doing here?" he finally managed to choke out.

Her pink lip quirked at his question. "You seem surprised I got in. Have you forgotten so much about me already?" Veronica's words sounded unnatural, even though she spoke in perfect English. Then her features hardened. "You left without even a goodbye."

"Brody, who is this?" Aamee asked.

I could hear the insecurity in her voice, and for the first time, I felt a little sorry for her. Clearly he and this woman had a history. We just didn't know what that history was.

"Veronica," he answered absently.

"We know her name, you dingbat," I said. "Who *is* she? How do you know her?"

Brody didn't answer, so Veronica spoke for him.

"I'm his wife."

ALSO IN

The Love Game

SERIES

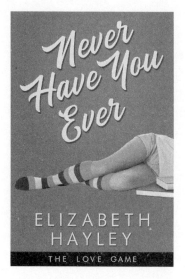

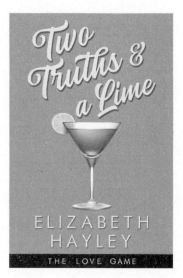

CONTINUE READING

The Love Game

SERIES

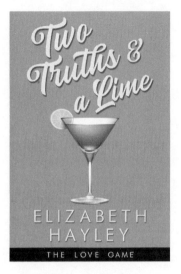

Drew Nolan and Sophia Mason have weathered many storms together over the course of their relationship, but things are looking up. Sophia is finishing up her degree and has landed an internship at a hotshot marketing firm, and Drew is managing an exciting new business venture. The couple even has the Masons' support, which is either a blessing or a sign of the apocalypse.

But if they've learned anything from their escapades, it's that good things don't remain untested. And that's exactly what happens when someone's actions threaten to destroy both Sophia's dream career and everything Drew's trying to build.

Sophia and Drew's relationship sprang from a lie, detoured around heartache, and almost crashed and burned, but the toughest test of all lies ahead. Can they unravel the many silly yarns they've spun to make love last? Because at this stage in the game, there is only one truth that matters: a future together.

Also by

ELIZABETH HAYLEY

The Love Game:
Never Have You Ever
Truth or Dare You
Two Truths & a Lime

Love Lessons:
Pieces of Perfect
Picking Up the Pieces
Perfectly Ever After

♥

Sex Snob
(A Love Lessons Novel)

Misadventures:
Misadventures with My Roommate
Misadventures with a Country Boy
Misadventures in a Threesome
Misadventures with a Twin
Misadventures with a Sexpert

Other Titles:
The One-Night Stand

Acknowledgments

First and foremost we have to thank Meredith Wild for always believing in our writing and inviting us to be part of the Waterhouse Team. We're thankful that you thought of us for a rom-com series and that you trust in our humor.

To our swolemate, Scott, thanks for making the editing process smooth and for always trusting us to get a story where it needs to be. You're always there to provide insight when we need it, and you've helped make our books the best they could be.

To Robyn, thank you for answering our million and one questions and for stepping in and taking control of things when we were floundering. We're sorry we're such disasters sometimes.

To the rest of the Waterhouse Press team, you simply kick ass. Thank you for everything you do to help us be as successful as we can. You're an amazing group of people, and we're lucky to have the honor of working with you.

To our Padded Roomers, you all are such a tremendous group of people. It's tough to find people as crazy as we are, and we've truly found our tribe with you. Thank you for everything you've done for us, such as posting teasers, sharing links, reading ARCs, writing reviews, and making us

laugh. We don't deserve you, but we're damn glad to have you.

To our readers, there's no way to accurately thank you for taking a chance on us and for your support. Thank you for letting us share our stories with you.

To Google, thank you for providing the means for us to research things including, but not limited to, fraternities, sororities, marketing degrees, alcoholic drinks, dean responsibilities, business class topics, college codes of conduct, Gen Z lingo, and popular clothing trends.

To our sons for inspiring the last names of our main characters. Our lack of originality strikes again.

To Elizabeth's daughter for being a spitfire and inspiring the way in which she wrote Sophia's character.

To our husbands, we know it's not easy. Thanks for hanging in there. We honestly don't deserve you.

To each other, for pushing one another forward when we stall. The ride hasn't been easy, but it's sure as hell been a lot of fun. On to the next.

About

ELIZABETH HAYLEY

Elizabeth Hayley is actually "Elizabeth" and "Hayley," two friends who love reading romance novels to obsessive levels. This mutual love prompted them to put their English degrees to good use by penning their own. The product is *Pieces of Perfect*, their debut novel. They learned a ton about one another through the process, like how they clearly share a brain and have a persistent need to text each other constantly (much to their husbands' chagrin).

They live with their husbands and kids in a Philadelphia suburb. Thankfully, their children are still too young to read their books.

Visit them at AuthorElizabethHayley.com